THE CUCKOO'S CHILD

a novel

MARGARET THOMPSON

BRINDLE
& GLASS

Brindle & Glass Publishing Ltd.
brindleandglass.com

LIBRARY AND ARCHIVES CANADA CATALOGUING IN PUBLICATION
Thompson, Margaret, 1940 November 5–, author
The cuckoo's child / Margaret Thompson.

Issued in print and electronic formats.
ISBN 978-1-927366-29-5

I. Title.

PS8589.H5228C83 2014   C813'.54   C2013-906017-0

Editor: Lea Fowler
Proofreader: Heather Sangster, Strong Finish
Design: Pete Kohut
Cover images: Antique bird illustration: nicoolay, istockphoto.com
Flower texture: zorazhuang, istockphoto.com
Author photo: Alan Thompson

Brindle & Glass is pleased to acknowledge the financial support for its publishing
program from the Government of Canada through the Canada Book Fund, Canada
Council for the Arts, and the Province of British Columbia through the British
Columbia Arts Council and the Book Publishing Tax Credit.

1 2 3 4 5 18 17 16 15 14

PRINTED IN CANADA

ONE

Every night watchman must find a way to fill the darkness, Stephen, and I am no exception. The monitors beside your bed spell out their hidden story in green light: blips and digits and spiked lines that tell everything and nothing, certainly not what it feels like to be dying. I, too, have a tale to tell. It has been a long time in the making, so many sinkholes and rockfalls fouling the way that any sort of happy ending seemed illusory at best. And just when there could be better times to share, you are slipping away, out of my reach.

The room is very quiet. I think you're sleeping, but perhaps you're even further away than that. I can't tell. Your face is closed off, almost stern, and quite calm. If I lay my head beside yours on the pillow, like this, will you hear how much I want to talk to you, want to listen to your voice telling me that everything is unfolding as it should? Will I pick up your whisper, like I used to do when we went camping years ago, that breathy, insistent "Sis, Sis, you awake?" in the smelly blackness of the tent, and know that you're my brother still, in the only sense that matters, and nothing can take that away, no matter what.

It's a relief to rest my head. It's too heavy, too full. I'm tired of sitting up as if I'm in command of myself, being calm. Soothing. Worrying about Holly and the kids. Mum and Dad. (Did you notice that? That little hesitation? The familiar even now feels awkward, ever so slightly false.) Neil saw—of course—how much I needed to be left to myself and you for a while. He's persuaded them to go for a meal and a few hours' much-needed sleep in their own beds.

"Do you good," he said to them, "have a breath of air and a bite," and when they hesitated, "You've got room for a hamburger, haven't you, Jason?" he asked our nephew.

The boy's nodding head gave the others permission, and they glanced at one another and stirred on the uncomfortable chairs round the bed where you lie, being remote.

"Livvy'll be here, won't you?" Neil said and got them all to their feet, shuffling through the door with apologetic glances as if they felt crass to long for escape, talk, food, all the things that would reaffirm their hold on life while you were so intent on letting it go.

Neil understands how exhausting a wait can be. Both of us, past masters at the art. This one, at least, will end soon. I think I knew it would, right from the start, when I first found out I could be no use to you. Did you realize, Stephen, just what you set in motion for me with that discovery? Will I have enough time to lay it all out, make it plain for you, before you cut the waiting short and go?

Where to start?

Maybe here? On a cold night at Thanksgiving, memorable for most because of a freakish rainstorm that congealed instantly on every power line, every traffic signal, every roof, every branch and twig until they tottered under the weight of ice, I discovered I had no idea who I was.

That sounds so melodramatic! Yet it was true, and no words could possibly convey the panic as the bedrock of my life fell away beneath my feet and I gazed on everything familiar as a stranger.

I wanted to look in the mirror to see if I had changed as much as I felt I must have, but of course, the revelation changed nothing about me at all. Friends would still have expected a response if they called me Livvy and invited me to lunch. Neil would not have stared at me, bewildered, and wondered where the person he thought usually dished up the spaghetti or dented the pillow next to his had gone. My students, too, despite their almost feral capacity for sensing weakness, like dogs smelling fear, would have noticed nothing worth paying attention to, just the old bag stewing over something, no big deal. Rita and Molly at the post office would have gone on stuffing mail addressed to Mrs. Olivia Alvarsson into our mailbox with every expectation that I would turn up with the appropriate key and remove it.

My question had been simple enough. All it needed was an equally simple answer, yet Dad would not meet my gaze and shifted from side to side as if his chair had suddenly become uncomfortably warm. He cleared his throat, ran a finger over his moustache as if to assure himself it was still there, looking just like Dr. Crippen, another meek little man hiding secrets.

Rage flooded my head, red hot. How like him to squirm and temporize! I wanted to pin him down, nail him, stop his wriggling, in spite of the pleading in Mum's eyes and the concern in yours. So I persisted and forced an answer.

"Ah, well, mmm," he ventured. "You *could* say that. In a manner of speaking."

And as I stared at him, dumbfounded, the lights dimmed and surged twice, then went out altogether. And while Dad seized the chance of escape and delay, fetching propane lamps and candles and a tiny camping stove from the basement, I sat, extinguished, plunged into a darkness as absolute and chilly as any experienced that night under the remorseless accumulation of ice.

But knowing what I know now, Stephen, and haven't had the chance to discuss with you, maybe the beginning lies much further back. Maybe the dream isn't just a dream but a fragment of the start of things, just a glimpse of one of the bottom layers of the palimpsest. *In a manner of speaking.* For as long as I can remember, it has insinuated itself into my sleep, sometimes uncoiling like a film, which almost has a storyline, but more often like a collage, disjointed images drifting past.

I hover above a moonlit path. In the strange blue light that leaches away all colour, the path wavers across a garden. To my left, tall flowers with huge round faces, open as clocks, and wiry vines, covered with motionless butterflies. To the right, plants are lower and line up neatly. There is a feathery row and a mounded grave for a long, long man.

I know all this without knowing, just as I follow the path without walking, drifting like smoke toward the garden's end. A no man's land. Then, trees. I swim through the moonlight until a piercing cry squeezes my heart into my throat. Again it sounds—"Help! Help!"—somewhere above my head, and a luminous bird wearing a crown and a bridal veil watches me intently from the branch of a tree with smooth ghostly bark. Then it swells and shivers and vanishes.

A single white feather drifts to the ground, but it is in my hand too, like a wand.

I have no sense of destination, but I know that I am approaching the place. The way is steep now; tree roots snake across it like veins on the backs of old hands and jolt me off course.

And there it is: a tiny house against the sky. No walls. A lake below. No sound, except for lonely night noises. There I wait, for this is a waiting place. When it comes, this anticipated thing, it will be at once foreseen and unlikely. A rescue, perhaps. Or a portent. I wait for the wonderful to appear, anchored there in the possibility, but it fails me, always. I wake disappointed, every time.

But one day, I know, the waiting must come to an end.

TWO

Now that was a red herring. If I'm that easy to distract, how will I ever make sense of everything? I can just hear Neil. "I thought this was a story," he's muttering. "Why don't you just plunge in?"

That would be rich coming from him, though. Neil is an artist, after all, quite used to false starts. If I close my eyes, I can see the hut at the bottom of our garden. It's just an old storage shed, really, but a bit of plumbing and carpentry and it turned into a studio. He spends a lot of time in there alone, working. Making image after image. Realistic yet not. Beautiful but disturbing.

Over the years Neil has moulded his studio to his own requirements, much as an animal will press its bedding to its own comfortable shape and construct its private place with its own unmistakable scent. Neil has much of Badger about him, such an old bachelor fug, such a rumbling reclusiveness at times—and Lord knows, that's easy enough to explain—that our marriage seems incongruous even to us at times and down-right unlikely to our friends. Yet it has the ease of a favourite old sweater with just enough rasp to the wool that you don't forget you're wearing it. Whatever else, it's not boring. Neil is too honest.

I can remember my first encounter with his directness. I was still a student at the University of British Columbia, working hard at a BSC. Remember how baffled Mum and Dad were about that? They wanted me to get a nice job in a bank or an insurance firm—something safe—and anonymous too, now that I come to think about it. I wanted to be a biologist. I wanted to be Rachel Carson. I wanted to be Charles Darwin. What I became, of course, is a high school teacher, but the glow of that passion has never quite faded.

Neil, on the other hand, was already an artist. Another student, a nice, dull fellow in my genetics class, introduced us in a casual encounter on Robson Street, just outside the old law courts.

"Livvy," he said, "meet Neil Alvarsson. He's an artist," tossing the word like a live grenade into my Peter Pan–collared life. First impression of this explosive device? It was housed in a rangy body that stooped a little, as if it were trying to accommodate itself to a world just slightly too small. A long, narrow head, crowned with straight blond hair, and very pale blue eyes that bored fiercely into everything, like a hungry eagle. His grip as we shook hands was dry and abrupt. I could feel the bumps of his finger joints. The nail on the index finger of his right hand was coated in yellow paint. He was wearing black—black turtleneck sweater, black jeans ragged at the hem where they scuffed the ground, a black jacket long since divorced from the rest of the suit. He had no socks.

He was everything unorthodox my conventional soul longed for.

Here's a confession.

I was in those days given to sudden passions for men glimpsed in stores, on the other side of movie theatres, going in the opposite direction on buses. So strong were these sometimes that I would abandon all maidenly modesty, break off what I was doing, and go in pursuit. I would scour the vague general area where I had seen them, in the hope of running into them again and triggering a flash of recognition that might lead, well, somewhere. This was only on my more desperate days, you understand, when I was oppressed by my failure to measure up to the success of all those contemporaries sporting tiny diamonds on the third fingers of their left hands. I felt the pressure of advancing years eroding my chances in the marriage market that seemed, if the magazines and Mum were anything to go by, to be the only goal I should be pursuing. Don't forget, I was twenty-one, and feminism had not yet become militant.

I ran Neil to earth, though. I shucked off the friend who had introduced us with a shameless lie about suddenly remembering another appointment, not caring whether he believed me or not. I left him staring after me, reproachfully. I can't remember even his first name now.

Neil had ducked into a small hole-in-the-wall café on Granville Street. I don't think it's there any more. I saw his light hair floating in a disembodied way in front of the coffee machine and went in. All it took was to angle myself behind him at the counter and pretend to be studying the specials written up on the chalkboard over the hatch as he turned away with his cup of coffee.

"Hello again," he said. "Following me?"

This was uncomfortable. The best course seemed to be to choke back the overemphatic denial that was springing to my lips and smile enigmatically instead.

"Want to share a table?"

Mutely, I nodded. My stomach was trembling. When I drew out the chair opposite his, I wrenched the table out of position with hideous sound effects, forcing him to snatch up his cup to avoid a mess.

There was a silence. I felt compelled to fill it.

"I was just looking the place over," I lied. "They're advertising for help."

Neil looked at my cup. Most of my coffee was slopping about the saucer. He handed me a napkin from the dispenser.

"Word of advice," he said. "Don't ever go for a job as a waitress."

Neil always was good at advice, you know. Handing it out, at least. Perhaps it's the result of shaking himself free of convention, of standing outside looking in for so long. Perhaps it's the discipline of the artist, always observing the familiar from a different vantage point. Both qualities overpowered me, but it was the oblique implication of his remark that impressed me most at the time. I don't take anything at face value, he was saying, you will never put one over on me.

So when, a few months later, he asked me to sit for a small portrait, I was filled with trepidation. Didn't tell you about that, did I? I was flattered, of course, but there was a nervous thrill attached. Perhaps I already recognized him as uncompromisingly honest and certain; what he might see and unflinchingly reveal scared me. He abandoned his usual abstraction—a relief, really, because I couldn't understand how he could convey anything about me in those huge, swooping shapes and wild colours—and seemed to offer a view of me that exactly coincided with my own chocolate box image of myself.

He is a formidable draughtsman. It was the kind of portrait Mum would sigh over, saying, "Isn't it wonderful how real it looks, you feel you could just reach out and touch that hair." He had painted me with my head turned to look out of the frame as if someone had just called my name. The background was shadowed, indeterminate, with a hint of vertical folds. I was wearing a very simple high-necked white blouse under a dark sweater—the ones you said made me look like a Lutheran bishop—and my pale face and auburn hair glowed against the sombreness. I was surprised and said so. He smiled.

"Not finished yet," he said.

When it was, he showed it to me, watching my face carefully as he did.

It was a shock. At first I couldn't make out what he had done. Then I saw that he had taken the original portrait and cut it into narrow strips vertically. These had been attached to another canvas, leaving gaps between the strips that he had filled with a wild miscellany of objects and paint. There were torn pages that I recognized as pieces of a text on DNA, bits of lace, white ankle socks, meticulously labelled diagrams of dissected frogs together with paintings of the same animals alive, feathers, butterfly wings, hair from a lurex wig braided and curled around the white bones of some small mammal, a weasel perhaps, candy wrappers, seed packets from my attempts to grow my own herbs, labels from 48s, scraps of cotton and wool, hair pins, a Barbie doll's decapitated head, a periodic table, the perfect rosy babies from old Pears soap adverts, even a tiny moss-lined bird's nest containing a few splinters of eggshell, all tumbling across the canvas, interwoven, sprawling and spilling in a tangled, intricate chaos. My fragmented self peered through it like a wary animal in a thicket of saplings. I had to say something.

"I'm not sure I like it," I said.

He snorted. "What does that matter?"

"It doesn't even look like me now," I objected.

"Are you sure? Things are not always what they *look* like."

There was a gentle scorn in his voice for my simplicity. In that moment, I believe, dawned a realization that has coloured all my observations since. I stared bleakly at the muddles and contradictions that he saw milling about behind my unremarkable face and sensed the complexities of existence, paths crossing, wheels meshing, the tumult just beneath the surface as cause and effect churn on and on, unseen.

Recalling that moment when I saw the portrait, I also

understand that I could dive at any point along the course of that river called my life and find in the depths something significant, some object, a look, a word, that makes nonsense of the scene at the surface, that calls into question everything I consider reality.

But plunging in at random won't help. Concentrate! What I really need to do is more like unravelling a sweater. I have to find the loose end and pull, gently, winding the freed yarn all the while into a neat ball. If I am to make sense of what has happened, I can only start, I think, by explaining why you are so important to me.

THREE

You never knew it, Stephen, but you were my liberator.

Hard to believe it now, with you lying there so still, so . . . detached. Who would think you could have such an effect? But then, you didn't look the part at first sight. Mum arrived home from the hospital, ferried by Dad in the pickup. Remember that old wreck? From the front window, I saw them pull into the driveway and watched as Dad clambered out and walked round to the passenger side, his boots squeaking in the snow. I waited until I saw Mum emerge, a bundle in her arms, and start to walk cautiously toward the house, Dad holding her close with a circling arm. Even as I ran to the front door and flung it wide I remember dimly noting how unusual that intimacy was. They never touched each other. Did they? They called each other "dear" and "love," and they always agreed and never, ever had a fight or shouted at each other. But they never touched either. Did you notice that too?

I was eight years old and felt very grown up. Dad had left me alone in the house for the first time while he went to fetch Mum. Things were different back then; I don't suppose he felt a moment's concern.

"You get the tea things out while I'm gone," he'd said as he left. "Mum'll want a nice cuppa when she gets home, it'll be the first she's had for a week. And you can get the Christmas cake out too. We might as well have a bit of that."

Mum kept her best china and glass in a triangular cupboard that stood in the corner of the living room. I always thought of it as a sort of prison as the door had a tiny lock and key, and the cups and saucers only got out on parole when we were on our best behaviour. Normally I would never have been allowed to touch it, but bringing a new baby home seemed like a special occasion to me, so I dragged a chair up to the cupboard and carefully liberated three of the cups, saucers, and plates.

I arranged them on a tray in a row, the handles all pointing in the same direction. I loved the feel of the china, so thin and fragile and light, and the way you could see the shadow of your hand through it. It occurred to me that putting the bottle of milk and the usual everyday sugar bowl on the tray beside this refinement would be incongruous, so I returned to my precarious ladder and took out the milk jug with the curly handle and the matching sugar bowl with its tiny lid as well. That satisfied me, so I turned my attention to the cake.

I heaved the cake out of its tin and started to cut slices with the breadknife. It was resistant, and although I tried to make the slices dainty and equal in size, they contrived to turn themselves into unwieldy, ugly lumps. By the time I had hacked off enough for three, the cake looked as if it had been attacked by a blunt chainsaw. Mum, I knew, would not be pleased. You know how she thinks her cakes are works of art. As far as I'm concerned, though, the smell is the only enjoyable part; I know you like them, Stephen, but when it comes to eating them, I'll pass.

That Christmas I hadn't even had to pretend to enjoy cake or pudding. Mum had been rushed off to hospital on Christmas Day, leaving behind a half-raw turkey and giblets simmering on the stove. Everyone felt sorry for me, abandoned in the panic, but I had enjoyed the adventure of Christmas in the neighbours' house, eating at funny times, trying things like sweet potatoes that would never have appeared on our table, and stuffing myself with chocolates and peanuts Mum would have condemned as likely to spoil my appetite. I didn't notice any such effect.

I also had my first experience of organized religion in their company, for I was deposited in their house just before they went off to Holy Trinity on Christmas morning. There I breathed in the smell of old wood and paper dust and bellowed the chorus of "O Come, All Ye Faithful" with a will. Better yet I listened to the gospel for the day and fell in love with the mesmerizing power of words.

Remember our neighbour, Mrs. Harrington? She showed me the place in the Prayer Book, and I followed as it was read by a man in a black dress with a long white shirt over the top. All day after that I heard it in my head: "In the beginning was the Word, and the Word was with God, and the Word was God." Incomprehensible but unforgettable, those capital letters audible even in memory.

You arrived very early on Boxing Day while I lay fast asleep in an unfamiliar narrow bed. Mrs. Harrington gave me the news as she put a boiled egg in front of me.

"You've got a little brother," she said. "Now isn't that a wonderful Christmas present?"

I've got to tell you, I wasn't sure. It seemed important to deflect attention from my uncertainty. Adults didn't understand one's reservations about babies.

"It's not really Christmas any more, so he can't be a present, can he?"

"Well," said Mrs. Harrington, looking amused, "it's Boxing Day. That's still Christmas. And besides," she went on, "it *is* a special day. It's St. Stephen's Day."

"Will he be called Stephen, then?"

"They could do worse," said Mrs. Harrington.

I agreed. I'd heard Mum and Dad discussing this very issue. They'd lingered on Alfred because that had been the name of both our grandfathers, apparently. Both of yours, anyway. That didn't seem a good enough reason to me. I rather fancied Perry or Frankie, but Mum firmly vetoed my suggestions.

"Good Lord, no," she'd said, "no child of mine is going to be called anything so common. A good old-fashioned name is what we want."

Dad had come to tell me about the baby and arrange to take me to the hospital during visiting hours. He looked grey and bristly.

"What's his name?" I asked.

"Alfred," said Dad.

"Oh, that's nice," said Mrs. Harrington. "Unusual nowadays." She didn't sound very convinced.

"It's St. Stephen's Day," I said. "Couldn't we call him Stephen?"

Dad looked a bit startled. "We'll see," he said at last. "Maybe that could be his middle name."

And that's how it was. That's how you came to be Alfred Stephen Porter. And you can thank me for saving you from a lifetime of Fred, or Alfie, because I always called you Stephen, and went on even when Mum scolded and insisted your name was Alfred, and somehow my obstinacy wore them down until they caught themselves calling you Stephen and I knew I'd won.

I met you for the first time that afternoon, lying in Mum's arms as she leaned against the pillows on the high bed in the maternity ward. You didn't look very promising. You were red and blotchy and your tiny feet seemed totally inadequate to bear you through life. Your head turned blindly against Mum's breast, and spasms of acute distress crumpled your face like a piece of discarded paper, forcing astonishingly loud mews from a gaping, toothless mouth. But I stuck out a finger in the general direction of one flailing hand, and your tiny fist closed instantly about it and grappled my heart to yours.

"Can I hold him?" I asked.

"Oh, no," said Mum instantly, "you wouldn't want to drop him, would you?"

"She won't," said Dad. "You'll be careful, won't you, girlie? And I'll be right here."

Reluctantly, Mum gave in. Slowly, with infinite caution, I took hold of you. You were heavier and more awkward than I expected. I looked down at you and your eyes opened, a strange, milky unseeing blue. I had to mark the significance of the occasion.

"In the Beginning was the Word," I said. "Stephen."

Mum and Dad looked at me as if seeing me for the first time. And it did seem as if that moment, and your arrival, had marked a watershed of sorts. It hit me forcefully during the rest of that day.

"You didn't need to get out the good china for me," Mum said as she sank into an armchair. "I hope you didn't stand on a chair to get them down."

You saved me the trouble of lying by starting to howl in her arms. She was too busy patting your back and jogging you up and down to worry about me approaching with a full cup, but just as she said, "Here, let me take it," your arm jerked out and caught the saucer. The cup tilted and fell on the edge of the hearth with a tiny musical ting. A triangular piece from the rim lay in the stream of tea running into the fireplace. I ducked down to pick it up, expecting recriminations. My clumsiness has always been a byword in the family.

"Trip over a fag paper, you would," Mum often said, but this time she ignored me, tickling you and chuckling indulgently. "Who's a bad boy, then? Throwing the china about already."

She looked at my stricken face. "Don't worry, pet, it was just an accident. Can't expect to keep china forever, can we? You mind how you go with those pieces, there's enough for Dad to clean up without you bleeding all over the place as well."

I was bemused by this mildness. Normally I would never have heard the last of it. I wondered what could have brought about such a mellowing. Could it be the baby? To put this theory to the test, I produced the plate of cake.

"Good Lord," said Mum. "Are you feeding the five thousand? We'll never eat that lot. Bill, you'll have to wrap the leftovers in greaseproof and put them in the tin before they all go dry."

And that was that. Before the day was over, I had been allowed to peel the potatoes with the paring knife with the wicked blade worn thin from years of sharpening on the back step, something I'd been forbidden to touch before, I had got away with not eating any Brussels sprouts for dinner, and I had got myself ready for bed completely unsupervised, ignoring my toothbrush and the soapy-tasting toothpaste and managing to smuggle a book upstairs in the process. And all because Mum had been preoccupied with you! Obviously my life had changed for the better.

FOUR

The change was overdue.

For as long as I could remember, my actions, my plans, my thoughts, even, had been hedged about with prohibition. It's odd to think that there are eight years of my childhood that you know nothing about, a whole different world you never shared, full of big things like war, bombs and terror and death falling out of the sky, and even when all that was over, there was still the rationing and the shortages and the endless skrimping and making do.

When I was very small, we lived in London, in a grimy-faced, terraced house off Tooley Street in Bermondsey. The steam trains from London Bridge rattled by, adding daily to the crust of soot on every building. Nearby, there were tumble-down warehouses, the homes of countless shabby pigeons, and dripping iron bridges, whose girders overshadowed rows of semicircular holes in the walls, like filthy caves.

Everywhere in the city of my childhood there were raw scars in the overlay of dirt. Streets looked like mouths full of broken teeth, buildings collapsed into piles of smashed brick or tumbled into vast craters, those left standing on either side cracked and bulging, propped up by huge timbers or held together by giant rivets. In places, whole streets of old tenements too badly damaged to preserve gave way gradually to towering blocks of crackerbox flats, one ugliness making room for another. For the most part, though, the rubble remained and life went on around it, so that the holes and the tottering bricks were the landscape of my childhood, no more worthy of remark than the crazed glaze of the kitchen sink, or the whitewashed walls of the outside privy with its nail for torn newspaper, or the patches of damp on the ceiling of the tiny box I called my room, or the dispirited privet hedge that divided us from the family next door.

I can understand any mother, more fastidious than most, holding the squalor at bay, encouraging a child to stay aloof, but in retrospect our retreat from the world was remarkably complete. I don't even have many memories of visits by or to relatives. There was an aunt who kept a boarding house in Southend, but we never stayed with her. A grandmother figures in my very first memory; at least I think it was a grandmother but don't know for sure. I was in my pram and it must have been raining, for the hood was up. Round the edge of the hood came a face, wrinkled as a withered apple. If it was Mum's mother, she went to live with her sister during the war and died soon after. I don't remember Dad having parents. Perhaps they were already dead.

There were occasional visitors to our house, mostly men who worked with Dad on the railway. They were loud and jolly, and I liked having them around, but Mum gave them a chilly reception. I didn't know why at the time, but one of them in particular always teased me.

"Blimey," he'd say to Dad, "where'd you get this 'un? Bit of a throwback, isn't she?"

Dad would mumble, "Lay off, Ted," looking sheepish, while Mum's lips would go thin and tight.

"Where'd you get that hair from, then?" Ted would persist, turning to me. "The milkman?"

Mum rose to the bait every time. "I'll have you know it runs in the family," she would retort. "My father had bright ginger curls when he was young."

"Is that a fact?" And Ted would roar, nudging Dad with his elbow as he did while Mum's face went bright pink with annoyance.

"Common as muck," she'd snort when he'd gone.

I was never encouraged to make friends with the neighbours' children either. There wasn't much traffic down our road apart from the occasional car or delivery van, or the rag and bone man making his slow way past, his horse sleepwalking the route, and the strange dying cry—"Ragabo, ragabo"—lingering even after they had turned the corner by the tobacconist and disappeared. Most mothers let their children play in the street, but mine didn't.

"You don't want to play with those dirty ragamuffins," said Mum firmly, "you never know what you'll catch from them."

So I would raid the recesses of Mum's wardrobe and dress up in the old high-heeled shoes and hats I found there, strangely flattened, like roadkill, and stand in front of the cheval mirror in the corner of her room pretending I was a teacher scolding a class or reading to them from a storybook. Or I would poke around in the sour earth of the tiny yard, looking for worms and sow bugs to keep in a cardboard shoe box as pets. There weren't many to find, and all too often their discovery inflicted mortal wounds on them.

When this palled, I would stand in my clean dress and neat sandals by the window of the front room, which was rarely used and as cold as a well, and watch the ragamuffins enjoy their noisy play outside. They shouted and laughed, tormented one another and roared about, kicking balls or racing up and down the street on battered bikes. How I envied them those bicycles! To be able to go so fast, so far, so quickly; to hop the kerbs and perform incredible feats of balance; to throw the machine down with unthinking nonchalance when something more interesting claimed the attention, knowing it would be there, ready to speed off again on a whim!

"You don't want a bike," said Mum. "You'd only fall off and hurt yourself, and what about the traffic? No, it's much too dangerous around here. You'd be under a lorry before you could say knife."

School brought partial liberation. Even though it had its own brand of regimentation, this was a place where parents had little influence. From the very first day when I was marched along to the local primary school, a monolithic brick building surrounded by a bare playground and a wrought iron fence high enough for a maximum security prison, I was tipped into the sea of ragamuffins to sink or swim. That first day was cautious and reserved; my memory gives me no sense of other children around me, apart from one little girl with dark hair who cried all day long, but I have never forgotten the feel of high ceilings, and the big alphabet cards around the walls, and the squeak of the slate as I drew.

Knowing what I know now about world events, I am amazed that none of that global drama and agony ever coloured my life. Think about it: my first experience of school came soon after Hiroshima, the liberation of Auschwitz and other concentration camps, the V2s, yet all I retain of that time is the round of practising my wobbly printing, listening to stories, sewing animal shapes with thick yarn with bootlace ends, and making music with miniature triangles and castanets and—wonders!—cymbals. I suppose the only hint of the war came in the occasional male teacher with an empty sleeve or rigid leg, or the sudden news that we should all bring some kind of container to school to carry home our share of the drinking chocolate supplied in a food parcel from the United States.

We tumbled up the years, unknowing. Even for me, seldom

allowed out, sent firmly to bed by seven o'clock, life was a game and an endless search. Our parents were all grimly coping with post-war austerity in a shattered city that smelled always of soot and boiled cabbage, but we chewed the delicate new leaves of the lime trees, and turned ourselves into racehorses by wearing our woolly scarves as bridles and galloping home from school, and grew like weeds, forcing our mothers to let down and out the clothes that were always bought several sizes too big so they would last. But our greatest sources of delight were the bombsites.

They were forbidden, of course, but we went anyway. Who could resist? You wouldn't have been able to, would you, Stephen?

Whenever anyone refers to something as an eyesore, I have an instant vision of the bombsite at the end of our street. It was the one I knew best, I suppose, though there was no shortage of them around my home. Being near to the docks and the main railway stations had turned the whole area into a target; every street had at least one ruinous wasteland slowly being softened by the invading weeds. Rose bay willow herb and golden rod were the first wildflower names I learned; the pink and yellow rioted over the broken masonry and piles of rubble.

Mum was able to prevent me from playing on the bombsite when I was at home, but there was nothing she could do to restrain my curiosity when I was on the way to and from school. Four times a day I passed it. The adults might shake their heads and mutter about the danger, but to the children it was fascinating.

For one thing, the bomb had smashed the house beyond repair but had not levelled it. Parts of two walls still reared into the air, splintered and blackened joists jutting out halfway up where there had once been a floor and ceiling. Tattered wallpaper clung to the filthy plaster—a faded blue like the sky on a misty morning, with the ghosts of vines and blowsy pink roses wreathed across it upstairs, and a sober cream with a thin dark red stripe almost obliterated by the trackmarks of soot-blackened water and rain below. A single door had survived the blast and stood, surrounded by broken brick, opening onto nothing. Part of a flight of narrow stairs still leaned drunkenly into the air as if groping for support. There had been a cupboard under those stairs, the air raid shelter for the owners of the house, I suppose, for the remains of a mattress, chewed by mice or rats, the stuffing oozing out, mouldered there.

That cupboard was the lure. It was a perfect meeting place for children: out of sight, unwanted by any adult, on the right scale for small people. Like the treehouse Dad made us in the poplars at the bottom of the garden, remember? We always knew we were safe from interruption up there. Mum couldn't climb the rope ladder, for a start. There were other attractions at the bombsite, of course: the old bath, lying on its side like a stranded white hippopotamus, its stubby claw feet futile in the air; the smashed sewing machine with the treadle that still creakily waved to and fro; a limitless supply of broken bricks, bright copper wire, lead piping flattened and strangely heavy, for our own construction projects. It was in the cupboard, though, squeezed into its dark corners, sitting in solemn circles on the decaying mattress, that we planned those projects and argued over possession of the things we found as we toiled over the debris just like the workers on Noddy Boffin's dust heaps.

For the place yielded up treasures too. Often we dug up single earrings, dusty beads, bent forks, matchboxes with a few broken matches inside, flowered cups without handles, candle stubs, a gas mask box with a broken strap. Things like this we stored on the little shelf in the cupboard under the stairs, knowing instinctively they wouldn't remain ours for long if the adults got wind of them.

Once, I unearthed a tiny glass bell, caked with mud but miraculously unscathed except for a chip out of the clapper, and was captivated by its tiny chiming voice as I shook it gingerly. I hid it from the others and carried it home and hid it again under my bed after I had carefully washed off the dirt and dried it on my blouse. I got in trouble for the mess on my blouse, but the reproaches rolled off me; I had something out of the ordinary, a voice left over, it seemed, from another world, and it was all mine to look after and enjoy.

Another time I took a brief detour onto the site as I was running home for lunch and found a dead cat lying beside the standing wall. It was the first dead thing I had seen, apart from the insects and worms I inadvertently killed in the garden. I can still feel the flood of sadness as I gazed at the stiff, dusty body, not so much for the fact of its death as for its loneliness, discarded and ugly in this blighted place. I felt compelled to do something for it; the only thing I could think of was to pick some of the weeds poking through the cracks and rubble and lay the pink and yellow flowers on the parched fur to cover the glazed eye and the frozen snarl. I revisited the corpse for several days, noting in a distant way its deterioration, the way it seemed to flatten and settle into the ground, and renewing the flowers every time.

One lunchtime it was gone. All that was left was a little heap of wilted willow herb. My stomach lurched. I knew all about this; hadn't we just spent the better part of a week in school learning the Easter story? Hadn't I made a model of the tomb, rather like an air raid shelter in green plasticine, with the stone rolled away from its mouth, and the grave clothes lying empty inside?

But the days of spiritual revelation and treasure trove had to end. Once again, disaster befell the site.

Mum had reluctantly allowed me to go to a birthday party

at a neighbours' house. Normally she had very little to do with the neighbours and very little good to say of them, but I must have pleaded and worn her down. Invitations didn't come my way very often, and I was desperate to go.

All of the guests attended the same school as I did, so I knew them at least by name. One of them was a girl called Pamela. Mum disapproved of her, or rather of her mother— "No better than she ought to be, that one!" she would sniff—but I thought Pamela was fun, and I liked what I saw of her mother too. She laughed a lot, and wore lipstick every day, and didn't wrap her head up in a scarf like Mum did to do the housework.

Pamela was the same. She was fun to be around, always inventive and full of energy, flinging herself into games, taunting the boys, imitating the teachers, fearless and witty. Mum said she needed a good smack—"All that sauce!"—but I relished her company at school. She was the life of that birthday party too; I can't remember whose birthday it was, or what we ate or what games we played, but I remember laughing uncontrollably till I wet my pants at something Pamela said.

That was on a Friday. On Monday morning, I found a solemn group standing round Pamela's best friend, Lillian. It was most unusual for Lillian to be the centre of anybody's attention. She was the first member I ever encountered of that subset of humans who are born middle-aged. She was a miniature version of her mother: plump, with a pale round face like an uncooked bun, a worried expression, and a tendency to lumber as she walked.

There was a faint flush on Lillian's cheekbones as she talked. Her news was awful. But it seemed to me that Lillian was enjoying her moment in the spotlight and making the most of being the only one with any information.

Pamela—lively, funny Pamela—was in hospital, barely

clinging to life. Lillian's eyes darted to each of us in turn as we huddled around her, avid for the story.

"She was playing on the site," said Lillian, "just playing about like we always do, and one of them walls, you know, the one with the wallpaper, it come crashing down all of a sudden"—here her voice faltered for a moment—"and she was underneath it."

Lillian paused and surveyed her audience before bringing out her new word, acquired from who knows what source— parent, hospital, ambulance attendant. "She was *crushed*," she breathed, and the horror of it peered out through her eyes. "I wanted to go and see her in hospital, but they wouldn't let me. They said only her mum and dad was allowed in."

Pamela died of her injuries, and the outcry about the unstable walls left standing to topple on children resulted in a crew being sent in to demolish the remaining ruins and clear the site. The treasures disappeared, and the snug hiding place. Mum discovered my glass bell and hurled it in the dustbin after she'd winkled out of me where I'd got it from.

"Whatever goes through your head? You could've cut your-self to the bone on that thing! And what about germs? I bet it's covered in germs—you'd turn septic before you know it, lockjaw even! Don't you let me catch you on any bombsite again, d'you hear me, or you'll get what for. Do you want to end up like that Pamela?"

And there she had a winner, of course. The evidence was in: things could happen to children, even popular ones like Pamela, and perhaps the world *was* as dangerous as Mum seemed to believe. Lord knows I believe her now. I don't think she had much trouble keeping me under her eye after that, but oddly her protectiveness didn't seem to come from love so much as a wish to keep tabs on me. She wanted me around, but at the same time she was indifferent, never very interested in what I did or thought, just as long as I did what I was told and stayed out of trouble.

For companionship I had to rely on Dad. He would let me help when he did things around the house, putting up shelves or painting chairs or papering over the cracks in the walls, and sometimes he would take me over the river to St. James Park and we would feed the ducks or ride on the top deck of the bus to Piccadilly Circus and look at the shops. He was the one who read to me, and taught me the letters, and listened when I had something to say. But he was often on shift work, out all night and sleeping all day, so that I had to be very quiet, creeping about, careful not to slam doors or talk loudly. I spent long hours with jigsaws I'd got for Christmas and knew by heart or reading the few books I possessed over and over again. Even then, I felt dimly this was not a natural life and spent a lot of time at the window of the front room looking out on the street, longing for action.

Change came suddenly. The decision to move to Canada seemed mercurial to me, although it was no doubt the result of months of planning and waiting. One day Dad told me we were leaving the street for good at the end of the week, and I had better say goodbye to my friends at school. That didn't concern me, but I was anxious to know where we were going.

Dad wasn't very helpful. "We're going to Canada," he said. "It's way over the sea. We'll have to go on a big boat."

"But why?" I asked.

Dad looked frazzled. "It's hard to explain," he said finally, "we're going to make a new life over there. Start again where things are better perhaps."

People at school thought I was lucky. Even the teacher seemed to envy me. She also showed me Canada on a big globe and drew her finger slowly across the wide blue bit between the two pink bits to show me the route I would be taking. The size of the blue bit, I remember, worried me. It was much, much wider than the pink bit the teacher said was England.

"Won't the boat get lost?" I asked. "How will we know where to go?"

The teacher laughed. "Don't worry," she said, "there'll be sailors on the boat who'll know the way. You won't get lost."

I was not really convinced, but the doubts and anxiety seemed to be a part of that time. I could sense them in Mum and Dad too as they finished settling their affairs and tidied the house. But finally we went, quietly leaving for the train with our suitcases, nobody apparently very interested in our going.

There is a blur of hurry and movement in my mind, of locomotives belching clouds of steam at the roofs of huge stations, of taxis and luggage and being pulled through crowds of people, of standing in long lines and finally being allowed to climb on board the biggest boat I had ever seen to take refuge in a tiny cabin where we had to walk sideways round the bunks and one another.

The voyage is a blank. All I can remember of it is standing on the deck with my parents and hundreds of strangers, watching the dock and the white rim of England slowly recede as we edged out of Southampton and round the Isle of Wight, leaving behind in the mist the only world I had ever known.

FIVE

Is that how it is for you, Stephen? The familiar skyline blurring behind you? Your hand is warm under mine; I can feel the roughness of the skin, like fine sandpaper, on the fingertips, see the blackened nail where you caught it with a careless hammer just days ago, the little nicks and scratches, half-healed, ignored, traps for the dirt you can never entirely clean off any more than Neil is ever completely free of paint. All evidence of a life, of a here and now, waiting for you, the construction sites half finished, the carpenters and roofers needing instructions, plumbers and electricians moving off to other jobs, all the frantic phone calls, orders, contracts, and blueprints piling up. They need your attention, Stephen. How's Holly going to deal with all that? With the kids? But even though you're lying right here beside me, big and solid still, you've moved off, haven't you? Still in earshot, perhaps, but your back is to us, and my voice is probably just part of the murmur from the shore behind. Only the destination counts now. I know something about arriving in new worlds, you see.

Can you picture Mum and Dad and me fetching up on Canadian shores for the first time? Arrival was like our baffling departure in reverse. Where did we land? I'm not sure. Halifax, maybe? Somewhere on the St. Lawrence? It'll be recorded in a dusty file somewhere. To my seven-year-old eyes, rivers were as vast as oceans in that strange place.

In fact, the impression of size, the change of scale that made me feel as if my mouth were perpetually hanging open, is the only thing left to me of our slow traverse of a continent. Mum fretted at my silence, convinced that I was coming down with some dreadful Canadian disease, but I had simply been quelled by insignificance in the face of unrelenting grandeur. I was used to the animal closeness of our street, hearing the neighbours arguing through the walls, narrow alleys and minute garden patches jostling hugger-mugger against noisy thoroughfares choked with traffic, and steam trains clanking and swerving across the points as they approached London Bridge. The largest open space I had ever seen was Hyde Park, and even there, the trees were ordered and deliberately set in their place. I had never seen a wild forest, not even a wood, not a spinney, not a copse.

On our train clacking west across Canada, we plunged through forests that stretched to the horizon. We would accompany rivers or lakeshores for a while, then swerve back into the trees, round bare shoulders of grey rock. Sometimes we caught glimpses of unfamiliar animals—deer, eagles, even a bear—but I can't remember any people, not even a sign of any, no houses, no smoke, no lights. I'm sure there were some, but my city eyes registered nothing but a huge emptiness. Then we left the trees behind and swam again in a sea, this time of grass and grain, racing the shadows of clouds on its rippling surface. I discovered that my experience of sky was severely limited. I watched thunderheads massing and marching on the rim of a great inverted blue bowl, and felt awe stirring inside, as it had when the cat's body disappeared. When I lay in my narrow bunk at night, listening to the locomotive wail at the darkness, the sky pressed down on me still, like a lid.

But the land began to heave, and the train took on a labouring note as it negotiated the beginning of a long incline. Prairie yielded to foothills that smelled in the sun like the stuffing Mum put in the Christmas chicken, and those in turn gave way to the mountains.

The steepest slope I'd ever climbed was probably Ludgate Hill. I couldn't take my eyes off the jagged peaks, so harsh and raw, as if they had just recently snapped off. I worried about the train managing to get over these obstacles; it crawled up and up, and round and round, but I couldn't see how it would crawl over the sharp points at the top. Never did it occur to me that we would go through the mountain, burrowing through the rock and chasing our own tail down the other side. Even Mum was impressed by this: "Fancy that," she said, "whatever will they think of next?"

More forest then but different. Every tree looked the same, dark and angular. Unwelcoming. I thought how dreadful it would be to be lost in a forest like that, unable to distinguish one tree from its neighbour, trying to find a path among those silent black trunks. In just such a forest, I knew, Hansel and Gretel had been abandoned, twice, and I suffered their terror again as the endless trees slipped past the window.

I thought we would never get off the train. I suppose I had caught some of that fatalistic rootlessness that afflicts refugees or explorers. Like Burton or Livingstone we had set ourselves adrift in the unknown; the difference, for me, was that I had no sense of destination.

It came as a shock, to step down from the train. We stood forlornly on a platform, our suitcases around us, and watched the train rock gently round a bend and out of sight.

"What is this place?" whispered Mum.

I had no idea.

I can trace our route on the map now, of course, although there are more ways to travel than one, and for some journeys there is no atlas, no compass, not even the occasional landmark.

We had come to rest in the small town of Vanderhoof, BC, where Dad hoped to find work on the railway. He did, but how he ever heard of the place I cannot imagine. You've heard the family joke, though, that Mum and Dad settled on Vanderhoof because of its position at the geographical heart of the province. It was, as Mum said with such satisfaction before we got there, so central.

Obviously, their map had neglected to show the roads, or lack of them. Equally obviously, they had ignored the scale. Some understanding of the distances involved and the population of the few villages scattered along the only highway might well have undermined their belief in the accessibility and convenience the word *central* implied to any Londoner.

There we were, transplanted Cockneys in a tiny agricultural community at the edge of the world.

Remember that first house in Vanderhoof? We were still living there when you were little. It was a tiny clapboard affair a block away from the railway that ran straight through the centre of the small huddle of dwellings and businesses. When I first saw it, the house was a faded blue and had a covered porch sagging across the front. None of the doors fitted, and there wasn't a straight wall or a square corner in the place. Dad tutted over the workmanship, and swore at the stove, a monstrous iron box squatting in the corner that had a voracious appetite for wood but refused to light when the wind came from the east, smoking sullenly instead and forcing us to fling open the doors to breathe even when snow lay on the ground and the temperature plunged to -25°C.

Learning to cope with the house, and the currency, the dearth of shops and any form of entertainment, was a lot like learning a foreign language. For a long time after our arrival, all three of us struggled with the vernacular and felt alien. It was easier for Dad, whose work soon gave him people to talk to and places to go. Even I had school, and gradually eased into the new environment, although my only real friend was Elsie Li, whose father owned the only restaurant in town, and was as much on the outside as I was. The other children were fascinated by the way I spoke—"Say 'about,'" they would demand, "say 'butter,' say 'mother,'"—and fell about laughing as I obliged with the flattened vowels and transformed consonants and glottal stops of my native dialect. And they never let me forget my gaffe when I casually asked the boy at the next desk if I could borrow his rubber to erase a mistake I'd just made in my exercise book. But that's just the stuff of childhood, and I got along well enough.

Mostly I was left alone. Mum certainly didn't encourage casual visitors, and I rarely took anyone home, so they didn't bother to cultivate my acquaintance. No free handouts of milk and cookies at my house. Since Elsie always had to go straight home and help in the café, I was driven back again on Mum for company.

She clung to me for the same reason. She rarely went out and knew nobody. The immediate neighbours were a very old couple who spent all their time roasting in front of their fire, even in summer, and drinking corrosive coffee from a blackened pot that they shared with their dog, an equally aged retriever, grey about the muzzle, with milky blue eyes. On the other side lived a single man who growled to himself as he stood out in the cold in his faded red longjohns, smashing an axe into logs and spitting a lot. There were no young women nearby and no other children. Mum didn't know where to find anything and was too timid to go looking. So I was the substitute.

When I came home from school, she had tea all ready for me—who else in that town ever had tea, do you suppose?—and interrogated me over the bread and jam and cupcakes about every detail of my day, who said what, who did what, how the teacher dressed, did I eat my lunch, what did I learn, what homework did I have. Anyone eavesdropping would have thought how concerned she was about me, how interested. They might not have noticed how often her eyes would drift, or how frequently she would interrupt me with some tale of a bird she had seen, or speculation about how many days off Dad would be getting and what they would do with them. Mid-answer, she'd ask whether I thought the colour of her dress suited her, and should she replace the curtains, and when would be the best time to clean the rug, or she'd criticize the way I chewed my food or handled my knife or scuffed my shoes.

My only escape was homework. She respected that and observed silence while I was doing it. Soon I learned to pretend I had more than I really did, and discovered that if I spread papers and writing equipment around, I could simply read a book with the same result. There was a double benefit: I had some peace to myself, and I actually learned a lot and fell in love with books too.

But you can see why I was so happy when you arrived and took the searchlight of Mum's attention away from me. She was completely wrapped up in you. Some kids might have resented that, but I adored you for setting me free. At about the same time, I encountered a teacher who was very keen on Nature Study. Mr. Blackwell was an unlikely medium, with his sagging suspenders and Coke-bottle glasses, but through him I stumbled for the first time upon the great cycles of life, its intricate patterns and subtle beat. He took us out to the river and the fields, told us the names of flowers and trees, and showed us animal tracks, wasp nests, ant colonies, spawning trout, kindling in me an abiding passion. I tell you, I would have done anything for the baby who distracted Mum so I could spend all my time with insects and amphibians, sloshing about in creeks and lying in reeds to watch the migrating waterfowl on the Nechako!

Even when you were older, I still doted on you. Elsie thought I was weird. She loathed her little brother, who spied on her and rifled through her things, then wailed for his mother when she smacked him. Most of the people I knew fought with their siblings at least some of the time. It just never occurred to me. Right from the beginning, you seemed to know I would protect you, and in return, you did your best to look out for me, showing an almost inhuman restraint, if my friends were to be believed, in passing up every opportunity to land me in trouble.

Remember when I saved you from drowning? We were larking about on the bank, against all the rules. I can still see the look on your face as your feet slid from under you. You slipped down into the river with barely a sound, just a wail, but the current snatched you away instantly. I hurled myself after you, grabbing an arm as it surfaced in front of my face, desperately clinging on and scrabbling my way to the edge, mercifully ending up by a flatter bit near the bridge, or I don't know how I'd have managed to get you out. I crawled out and hauled you from the green water, then leaned on your chest, calling your name and pressing, pressing on your rib cage until you suddenly choked and a stream of dirty water ran from your mouth. You sat up, and we clung to each other, both of us crying with relief and shock. And when we made our way home and Mum shrieked at our wet clothes and my carelessness, allowing my little brother to play by the river and letting him drown, what was I thinking of, I had no more sense than a fly, you intervened. Your teeth were chattering like castanets, but you said, "Don't be cross, Mum. She told me not to go. She always looks after me, don't you, Livvy?"

Mum was disarmed. "Well, I suppose we have to be thankful you were there," she said grudgingly, "and it's no use crying over spilt milk. Hot baths and get out of those wet clothes, the pair of you, before I have you both down with pneumonia."

That was the incident that welded us together. Our common front saw us through countless problems later with spilt paint and glue, broken windows, dried grass set ablaze with a magnifying glass, a broken arm, bent bicycle wheels, all the disasters inherent to a child's life.

That was the bond that made you my only supporter when I decided to study biology at UBC, and later when I announced my intention to marry an artist. Mum and Dad thought artists were just a shade higher than child molesters in the son-in-law stakes, but you said, "Neat-o!" and "Would he give me a painting for my room?" and somehow that seemed to reassure them.

Looking back, I can see my love for you was the main reason I was so ecstatic when Daniel was born. What more could I possibly want than another little boy, all my own, to look after?

And when I didn't, and Daniel disappeared, and I couldn't see any reason why I shouldn't follow him, it was you who held me fast and wouldn't let me go.

SIX

Still so painful, even now. The memory lives in my mind, flourishing like an ugly cactus covered with spines. No matter how I approach it, I am pierced and stabbed, the spines break off in my flesh, there to fester and work their agonizing way to my heart. But I can't ignore it, any more than the tip of one's tongue can stay away from the broken tooth, for of all things it defined me, and Neil, and shaped the way we see ourselves and each other. From the moment it happened, we became the ones whose child had vanished.

That whole week, I remember, began with loss.

At the time, we were living in Sechelt. I had a job at Elphinstone Secondary School in Gibsons teaching junior science, and Neil was happy, painting, filling the spare bedroom in our house overlooking Davis Bay with his large canvases. His paintings had just been shown in a North Vancouver gallery, and he was glowing with success. Three of the paintings had sold immediately, and the show had generated the kind of talk that leads to commissions and a following. His excitement was contagious. Our house was full of sunlight and laughter, it seemed; we had a four-year-old son we adored, friends we valued, our lives were fun, we were on our way.

But we were losing one of those friends. Jerry lived on a forty-foot sailboat moored at a marina just down the coast. We had met him several years before in the emergency room at the hospital. Neil, mud-plastered and still wearing his filthy rugby kit, was waiting for someone to see if he had broken his collarbone when a stocky young man walked in, nursing one hand in the other. I was struck immediately by his high colour. He had a round face, with bright red wind-whipped cheeks, snapping blue eyes, and black, black curly hair. He sat down near us after checking with the nurse and, after a pause, turned to us with a rueful smile.

"Been waiting long?"

Half an hour, we told him.

"Guess I deserve to wait," he said, "doing such a stupid thing."

"What happened?" asked Neil.

"Grabbed a bunch of old line and net, set a triple hook in the palm of my hand. Smart, eh?"

He held out his hand as if he were begging. It was filthy. Two of the hooks had burrowed out of sight in the middle of the palm; the third curved up, a scorpion tail ready to attack. A length of old leader trailed over his wrist.

"Need more than one hand to deal with that one," he said. "Hurts like a son of a bitch. What did you do?"

Neil looked sheepish. "Took a dive, playing rugby."

"Got a death wish, have you? Rough game, that. Not as bad as Australian football, though—now they're crazy."

"Ever seen a game of hurling?" asked Neil, warming to this topic. "Sort of a cross between rugby and field hockey—they can throw the ball and carry it or clobber it with whacking great sticks through the air. Fantastic! Irish, of course."

"Ah well, they're all mad buggers, aren't they? Oops, I hope you're not Irish, no offence. My name's Jerry Murtry, by the way. That's Irish enough, right? I live on a boat down at the government wharf. You ever want to go out fishing, I'm your man."

And that was that.

Has anyone done studies on why we take to some people

and not to others? Why some strangers immediately inspire confidence and liking, and some never get beyond our defensive barriers? It has to be an instinctive reaction to smell and body language, buried so deeply in us we don't notice the mechanism at all. All I can say is that Neil and I, discussing it afterward, both commented on the same thing; we felt immediately comfortable with this little red-faced man, as if the period between acquaintance and friendship had been skipped as a waste of time. By the time both men had been patched up, we were friends. I drove Jerry back to his boat. Before going home, we had inspected his cramped quarters aboard and arranged to meet at our house the next week.

So began months of casual, easy companionship. He would drop in for a beer, we would press him to stay for a meal, not that he ever needed persuasion, and the evenings would fly past. He returned the favour with trips to small islands inaccessible to everything but a boat, weekends of floating at anchor in small bays, watching the stars come out and the bats flick silently overhead. He would play his saxophone while Mizzen, his cat, sat on a hatch in the moonlight and lashed her tail, and the melancholy notes would linger and tremble in the soft air until they were almost beyond bearing.

Jerry's casual lifestyle was a blessing when Daniel was born. We'd had to wait a long time for a baby; I was thirty when he arrived and had almost given up hope. I took maternity leave but eventually had to go back to work—we needed the money and, besides, I liked my job. Mum tutted, of course. "What that baby needs is a full-time mummy," she said. "That's your job now." But even she had to admit it was nice to eat regularly.

I found a decent babysitter nearby, but Jerry was the saviour on the days she couldn't take Daniel because her own kids were ill, or on the weekends, or when Neil and I were both tied up or simply wanted a night out together. He was wonderful with the baby, amazingly gentle despite his fisherman's hands, holding him in the crook of his arm as he went on with mending his nets or polishing the brass fittings on his boat, talking to him man to man, as if Daniel understood every word.

When Daniel got older, it was Jerry who made him a wooden train, Jerry who showed him how to jig for herring, Jerry who constructed the big wooden hutches for the guinea pigs, George and Emily and their large family, and supplied the sawdust for their bedding.

And then, the day Daniel was four years old, Jerry announced he was leaving and trying his luck farther south.

"Why?" I asked stupidly.

"Ah, itchy feet," said Jerry, "nothing particular, just time for me to move on. Never rest too long in one place, you know—no moss on me, that's for sure!"

"But what will you do?"

"What do I ever do? I'll find something, fishing, handiman, all I need's a place for the boat. Plenty of those up and down the coast."

"But how will we keep in touch? You're not just going off and never getting in touch again, are you? Say you'll write, or phone at least."

"Well," he said, "I'm not much for writing. I'll phone, though. You won't be rid of me."

"When are you leaving?" Neil asked.

"I'll be off on Saturday."

"Ah, jeez," said Neil. "I've got a game in Stanley Park. We're all going over on Friday night. We can't even see you off."

"Probably better that way. I'm not one for goodbyes. No, you come down to see me when I get settled, how's that?"

He turned to Daniel, who was solemnly listening, folded his arms round him, and tickled him. "You'll come and see me, won't you? We'll go to Disneyland, what d'you say, eh? Is that a plan?"

And Daniel squirmed and shrieked, and we all smiled, for that did, indeed, sound like a plan, and looking forward to a visit to the United States, seeing Jerry in a new environment, was much better than dwelling on departure and goodbyes.

But we felt the loss. It was a hole in our lives, and as far as I could see, it had to be a wrench for Jerry too. Despite his cheerfulness, there was a streak of Celtic melancholy a mile deep in the man that oozed out with a few beers inside him. He was always friendly, yet he always seemed lonely. There was no woman in his life—"Tried that once," he'd told me, darkly. "Never again. Some guys are just meant to be old bachelors, I guess. I do just fine by myself." He looked wistful, though, when he said it, a little boy shut out and longing to be let in. So I worried about him going off into the blue like that, with so little purpose, but life goes on, you know, and takes turns you never expect, and suddenly those things that seem most important one minute are forgotten the next. At least, that's my experience.

We rang Jerry to say goodbye on the Friday afternoon, just before we left for the ferry, but the phone was already disconnected.

So that was that.

We were all subdued on the ferry. Daniel couldn't understand why Jerry had gone.

"Didn't he like us, Mummy?" he asked. "Won't he take me to Disneyland now?"

Neil and I looked at each other over Daniel's head. We were sitting on a locker on the ferry deck, huddled out of the wind behind a peeling bulkhead. The wind tore at our hair, lashing it into our eyes. Neil's long, bony nose looked faintly pink at the tip, the only vestige of colour in a face leached white by the chill. My own nose, I knew, would be a scarlet blob at odds with my hair. In that moment our eyes locked, I knew exactly what he was thinking. *We can say of course he likes us, of course he'll take you to Disneyland*, the little internal voice was saying, *but do I believe it? Was he a real, no-matter-what kind of friend, or just a ship passing in the night, just another person we promise to keep in touch with, come what may? Then the weeks go by, and months, and somehow we haven't managed to do anything about it, and then the first Christmas has been and gone, and you feel guilty but not guilty enough, and soon it's years and you say one day, I wonder what became of so-and-so? And there's a spasm of nostalgia, pleasantly melancholy for a minute, before you tuck the memory away again and forget a little more, and forgive yourself the forgetting.*

"It's all up to him," I reminded Neil. "He's the one who'll have to let us know where he is when he gets settled."

Neil nodded. "You'll get to Disneyland," he said to Daniel.

Friday night we spent at the Sylvia Hotel on English Bay. It was a wild night, I remember. I felt a childlike contentment listening to the wind tugging at the long strings of the creeper covering the hotel walls, rattling the windows, heaving the lights of the freighters lying at anchor in the bay up and down. We speculated about Jerry's whereabouts; surely not even he, reckless though he could be, would risk the open water in those conditions?

"He'll be tucked up in the lee of an island somewhere, never fear," said Neil. "He probably set off early because he knew there was dirty weather coming. He's not a fool."

The morning sky was a raw, cheerful blue as if a brand-new one had been installed to replace the one tattered beyond repair the night before. It was still windy, but playful now, the sort of wind that makes dead leaves hop and hats leap off heads.

"Grand day for a game," Neil said approvingly.

It gets hard, now.

Neil left Daniel and me at the aquarium and went off well before the game to meet the rest of the Gibsons team at Brockton Oval. I promised we would be there to watch. He liked to know we were there among the onlookers, cheering him on, not that he ever seemed to do anything very heroic, apart from hurling himself at opponents' legs and breaking his collarbone. I was never like some of the wives and girlfriends, avid groupies forever cutting sandwiches in the clubhouse while their menfolk sang dirty songs at the tops of their lungs in the showers. I put in an appearance and cheered when Gibsons scored, but I always carried a book in my pocket. I did that day. *Oliver Twist*. I never have finished it.

Daniel and I worked our way through the aquarium galleries, enchanted by the eerie beauty of the lives behind the glass. We watched, hypnotized, as transparent jellyfish pulsed across a tank, impelled by a stream of bubbles from a hidden aerator. Daniel found the tube worms edging out to wave their plumes, then darting back out of sight in sudden panic, hysterically funny. Neither of us much cared for the moray eel, sliding as if oiled from his hole, launching his mouthful of needle teeth at any movement, but we loved the octopus, obligingly showing us the suction cups on his tentacles in action as he glided down the glass, and marvelled at the diversity of the reef fish.

I never wanted to spend too much time with the orcas, but Daniel insisted. It made me sad, watching the black-and-white shapes swimming round and round their pool, heaving themselves up and thundering back into the water, to screams of delight from the audience. Even Daniel looked thoughtful.

"They don't have much room, do they, Mum? Couldn't they make them a bigger tank?"

"I don't think they could ever make one big enough," I said. "They had the whole ocean, once."

Daniel looked uncertainly at me, checking my mood. "Is it time to go?" he asked. "Let's go."

By the time we had walked over to Brockton Oval and made our way to the familiar navy-and-white uniforms, both teams were warming up. Neil saw us and waved, but someone passed him the ball at that moment, and he was off running. Others spread out across the field, yelling at him to pass.

The game started. Daniel soon tired of standing still and watching. From the pockets of his jacket he dragged out Tigger, his stripey black-and-brown stuffed dog, the little yellow bull-dozer, and the old Hot Wheels car minus a wheel that always accompanied him. He settled to road construction on a patch of bare earth some distance from the sideline under a small stand of trees. I sat on the grass near him and opened my book.

The sun was warm, lulling. It muted the shouts and grunts of the players, the whistle blowing intermittently, the sparrow chatter of children clambering on a picnic table nearby, the sound of Daniel revving up and crashing his vehicles among the tree roots, made them seem distant, yet infinitely comforting in their familiarity. I basked in well-being. Odd how the end of happiness can be defined so precisely, so sensually.

I was reading—the irony!—the scene in which Oliver is claimed by Nancy as her lost brother, browbeaten by the crowd that believes her, terrified by Bill Sykes and Bull's-eye, and haled off into a maze of little courts and alleys—"what could one poor child do?"

My eyes were torn from the page by a wail of fear and pain. Another child, in trouble.

Daniel had heard it too. He had paused in his game, kneeling among the roots of a cedar, and was staring at the knot of children round the picnic table, just twenty feet away or so. They were running to the far side of the table, looking down at the ground, uncertain.

"Stay there, Daniel," I said. "It looks as if someone needs help."

I scrambled to my feet and ran. The children at the table were glad to see me; they started to explain what had happened, interrupting one another, arguing over details. I ignored them, concentrating on the small girl huddled on the ground, clutching her left arm. Her face was grey, and she was moaning. No tears, just the dry-eyed keening that comes with great pain.

"Can you lift your arm?" I asked.

She looked dolefully at me and shook her head. "Try," I urged.

She leaned and tried, but instantly her face collapsed and tears sprang from her eyes.

"I can't," she gasped, "it's too heavy, it won't go, and it hurts, it hurts."

I looked at the other children. "What's her name? Do you know who her parents are?"

A boy spoke up. "That's Lisa. Her mom's over there." He pointed to the crowd on the sideline.

"Be a pal," I said, "and run over as fast as you can and tell her Lisa's hurt. I think her arm's broken."

While I waited for reinforcements, I took off my belt and put it round the little girl's body, strapping the arm close to her side for support. Her mother and other adults came pounding up. My role was over. No more than five minutes had gone by when I turned back to my book and Daniel.

No more than five minutes. The book was still lying on the grass. No Daniel.

I didn't panic. The trees he'd been playing under were huge; he would be around the other side of the massive trunks, out of sight.

I called his name as I walked to the trees. The yellow bulldozer and the shabby Hot Wheels car lay in the dirt between the roots. His small footprints were clearly visible in the earth he'd disturbed with his game.

He wasn't on the other side of the trunk, nor anywhere else in the stand of trees. I hurried back into the open space, turning wildly to check every point of the compass. Nothing.

I ran down toward the road, dashed across it to stare up and down the sea wall. There was a group of older boys playing about with bikes; I ran to them, demanding to know if they had seen a little boy, this high, fair hair, wearing jeans and . . . what *was* he wearing? They shook their heads and shrugged, riding off looking embarrassed. And I couldn't remember what Daniel was wearing, couldn't remember what I'd put out for him to wear that morning, a lifetime away. Was it his red turtleneck sweater or the little Aran Mum had made him for his birthday? Did he have sneakers on? Or boots? What colour socks?

Fear swelled inside me, drumming at my temples. It clutched at my throat, squeezing until I gasped for air, swallowing convulsively and fighting the weight in my chest that threatened to break my ribs from the inside. I heard a distant mewing and realized I was the source. I held my lips shut with a tremulous hand and ran, casting about like a dog on a weak scent, retracing my steps, looking in garbage cans and bushes, accosting everyone I met, leaving behind a trail of shaking heads and blank looks.

I raced around the pitch, pushing through the spectators, searching every group whose legs might have concealed my child from view. He will have come over to watch Neil, I reasoned, sure he will. But he hadn't. The Gibsons bunch were all on one side of the field, and I rushed up to them, shouting, "Daniel! Daniel! Have you seen him?" My friend Ella swung round as I passed. I caught the dismay on her face and heard her cry out, "Livvy! Whatever's the matter?" But I dared not stop. If I am just quick enough, I told myself, I'll catch up to him and it will be all right.

"It's Daniel! He's gone! I can't find him!" I howled over

my shoulder. Heads turned in my direction; laughter abruptly ended as I pushed past three men, jostling the arm of one so that his beer slopped over his wrist.

"Watch it!" he shouted. "Crazy chick!"

As I ran past the Gibsons coach, I heard his startled exclamation, "What the f . . . ?" followed seconds later by "Livvy! Get off the pitch! What the hell d'you think you're doing? Come off there!"

But I knew where I was going. I headed straight for the tall figure with the filthy headband round the fair hair, and without a thought for the bodies thundering toward me, the leather boots with their mud-choked cleats, the sodden ball hurtling through the air, I led a trail of anxious women through the melée to Neil. When I got there, I said, "Daniel's gone, he's disappeared," and when Neil's mouth formed the shape of incomprehension, I beat my fists on his chest, pounding him with my terror, and howled like a dog.

The game died. Immediately, there were mud-plastered players in shorts and striped jerseys scouring the park, women and children accosting joggers and walkers towed behind their anxious, straining dogs, hands shoving cups of bad coffee into my hands and patting me awkwardly. A mounted policeman rode up on a gleaming bay, a centaur with a radiophone who marshalled bigger forces. The warm smell of the horse unlocked something in my mind: Daniel has blond hair, I said, light blue eyes, a tiny scar at the corner of his mouth where he once jabbed a branch in his face, blue Oshkosh jeans, a red cotton turtleneck sweater with a blue stripe on the collar, navy padded jacket, white socks, white runners with purple stripes down the sides.

He was there, so complete in my mind I could hear his infectious giggle. Could see him folding and stroking a piece of his hair in the hypnotic way he did when he was tired, feel his small body leaning trustingly against me, his hand tucked in mine. Just as yours is now, Stephen.

In all the strain of the protracted search and investigation that followed, it seemed more and more important to cling to the images and sensations; I carried the toys he had left under the tree everywhere, just as he had; they were the most real things in a completely surreal world. Certainly the process of searching for Daniel became increasingly isolating as more and more police and volunteers were involved.

Neil's arm was always around me, his head against mine, as we talked to the detectives, repeating and repeating the story as far as we knew it, dredging for details, unconsidered snippets, a person, a car glimpsed and not seen again. We racked our brains for motive, a grudge, malice, envy, with the same disbelief you would experience on being told to look for slugs in your underwear drawer.

By the evening all ferries, major roads, and airports were under surveillance. Customs, police, and coastguards were alerted. Daniel's disappearance was the lead story on the evening news on radio and television. Neil appeared on TV looking gaunt and dishevelled, appealing for the return of his son. According to the detectives, tips were starting to come in.

There was no question of us leaving Vancouver. The wife of the captain of the Vancouver Yacht Club team put her basement at our disposal and provided us with house keys. "For as long as you need it," she said. "Don't worry about a thing." I asked Ella, who was the secretary at my school, to tell the principal what was happening and to visit the house and feed Maisie, our cat.

Two days later, after forty-eight sleepless hours in a police station growing more and more desperate, we found ourselves sitting stiffly side by side on a couch in the basement of a strange house on West 31st. I was clutching a small vial of sleeping tablets some doctor had given me, somewhere. Our hosts had gone to bed. The house made its small settling sounds. Every now and then, the furnace sprang to life with a click and a dull roar. The dim standard lamp in the corner seemed the only light in the world; we huddled in the little yellow puddle it cast, while beyond its range, the darkness pressed, absolute and empty. That was where Daniel was, alone in the dark.

"I'm scared," I whispered.

Neil's cold hand tightened on mine. "So am I," he said.

We stayed for six weeks. It was a seesaw time of hopes and disappointments. The police had hundreds of tips to follow up, but small, blond, blue-eyed boys in jeans are two a penny. You came, as soon as we phoned to tell Mum and Dad the news. I will always remember how Mum reacted: "How could you let it happen?" she asked, as if it was just some monumental carelessness on my part. We made posters and trudged the streets attaching them to hydro poles and lamp posts, store windows and café menus and laundromat bulletin boards. The police had me make an appeal to the abductor that was aired on all the channels, hoping that the weeping mother would pluck at someone's heartstrings, but by that time I was numb, too desolate to weep, too tired for any emotion but stony endurance.

Neil tried to keep us going, even managing to joke on occasion with the detectives. He was better at pretence, at keeping a stoic front. I resented him for it.

"How can you smile?" I asked. "Our son's gone. How can you ever laugh again?"

But he wouldn't rise to the bait, wouldn't get angry, wouldn't blame me for my inattention, looking after another woman's child when I should have been looking after my own. Maddeningly, he said, "Depression won't help Daniel, will it?"

I hated him for being right. But I couldn't leave it alone.

"So I'm wrong there too? I feel sad so I'm no use to anybody? I'll tell you, Neil, I'm not going to be any use, ever again, if Daniel isn't found. Smile at that!"

He tried to fold me in his arms, and I wanted to let him, but the demon in me flailed its arms and pushed him away. I pitied his downcast face, but I could not unsay the words, and the moment passed.

The day I had been dreading came too soon. The detective in charge of the investigation sat in front of us, nervously fiddling with his car keys. No results from the most extensive search and inquiry ever held in this province; hundreds of tips, all faithfully followed up, no matter how bizarre, with no progress, thousands of man hours devoted to the case without a single tangible clue unearthed. Time to scale back the inquiry. It would never be closed, he assured us, leaning forward to drive the point home; he would continue to work on it. He would stay in touch. Let us know if anything promising turned up. But for now there was nothing more to be done.

Reason tells you that if children are not found quickly, the likelihood of finding them alive diminishes with every single day. I knew that. I knew that public interest in the case, feverish and suffocating at first, would languish when there were no quick developments. But this was my child, not some pathetic little stranger. The detective's dispirited resignation and Neil's nod of acceptance tore something loose in me and quietly choked it. As if from a great distance I observed Neil shaking the man's hand and accompanying him to the door. As their voices faded, I felt a terrible loneliness and futility settle over me, pure and burning, like a weightless coat of snow.

"Let's go home," said Neil as he returned.

So we did.

SEVEN

Few of the comforts of home for you here, but you don't seem to mind. I watch the nurses bustling in and out—they must be the only people who can bustle quietly—checking monitors and drips, making notes, adjusting the flow of oxygen. Even their faces are still as they count your heartbeats through their fingertips, busying themselves, keeping you going, and all the while, you lie there oblivious.

And I know that kind of oblivion too, although there were no nurses for me then. Those months after Daniel disappeared are a blank. I was dimly aware there were people around, doing things, saying things, but they were shapes looming in a dense fog that muffled all sound. There were no connections. Despair was easier than struggling through the murk. Tell me that you haven't despaired, even now. Tell me you're letting go because it's time, not because you have no hope. I can't bear to think of you surrendering to the dark, as I did then.

I did try to pick up where I left off. I went back to work, waving aside Ella's doubts, her troubled, kindly face regarding me doubtfully across my kitchen table, still cluttered at five in the afternoon with egg-stained plates from breakfast. Maisie was sitting on her lap, gazing at her adoringly.

"Why don't you take a bit longer?" she said. "The sub's doing a good job—you don't have to worry about that. Give yourself a chance."

"What's the point of waiting? Nothing's going to change. It'll be better if I have something to do. Something that keeps me so busy I don't have time to think."

But I was wrong. However busy I had to be, I could never banish the thoughts. Lying in bed at night, watching the shadow branches of the apple tree outside the bedroom window tossing on the ceiling and listening to Neil breathe softly into his pillow, I replayed Daniel's life over and over, always coming at last to the place where the film snaps and slaps futilely in the sprockets, memory stumbles, and speculation takes control.

In those night watches my mind ranged over the land, high as an eagle, searching for the small body in mountain gorges and dense forest, looking for the flash of red at the bottom of rivers and lakes, riding the ocean currents, lodged under wharves or log booms, seeing the gleam of tiny bones in the starshine where they lay in the ferns beside a forgotten logging road.

By day I was more practical but no less obsessed. I looked at the bent heads in the science lab and thought of the boy Daniel would have been. I chewed my lunchtime sandwich and remembered his fondness for peanut butter and honey. Parents queued to see me on Parents' Night, and I wondered what the man who snatched Daniel looked like—it was always a man, in my mind—what he did, what kind of house he lived in, what his neighbours thought of him. I mixed chemicals absentmindedly and worried about Daniel's fear and sadness, if he was still alive and forced to live with someone else, his parents inexplicably failing to come for him. I would load the washing machine and turn away from it, without switching it on, overwhelmed because in all that heap of clothes there was not a single tiny sock, no miniature pants coated with mud at the knees, no T-shirts sticky with honey or pine resin.

If it sounds as if I were alone in this, that is the measure of the monstrous selfishness of grief. Neil suffered too, of course he did. Mum and Dad fluttered about intermittently, their faces pinched and solemn with woe, helpless in their inability to help. Bless your heart, Stephen, you came and went as often as you could get away from your job, silent usually, but quick to see what needed doing and getting on with it.

Did we ever thank you properly? I don't suppose so. You were the one who answered the letters and messages we found waiting for us on our return; you adjusted the brakes on my car, mended the kitchen tap, replaced the filter on the furnace, chopped two cords of firewood. Ella was a constant visitor too, dropping off batches of muffins, jars of homemade salsa, bags of cat food for Maisie when I forgot her. None of this concern registered properly with me. I was like a faulty answering machine, hearing only my own voice saying, "Livvy is not available right now," then shutting down the recording as the callers start to speak.

All I could feel was the weight. It was as much as I could do to lift a foot at each step, more than I could do at times to raise my fork to my mouth, my comb to my hair. The weight exhausted me. As soon as I came home, I went to bed. I didn't sleep, but at least I couldn't see the worry in Neil's eyes or the silent reproach of Daniel's closed bedroom door. It was exactly like being caught in quicksand; struggling and fighting do no good, so inertly I slid deeper and deeper, waiting for the bog to close over my head.

There are only two things I really remember of that time.

The first happened on a February day, grey cloud blurring the horizon where it met the darker band of sea, straight strings of rain pocking the waves and flinging themselves at the windowpanes. I was alone in the house. Neil had retreated to his studio as he did more and more. I was lying under a quilt on the couch, Maisie curled on my chest, staring me gravely in the eye as she purred.

The phone rang. Jarring. Right beside me on the coffee table. Impossible to ignore.

"Hello."

"Livvy? It's Jerry. Listen, Liv, I just heard, about Daniel, I mean. Liv, I'm so sorry. You don't get much Canadian news down here, but I just caught one of those *Most Wanted* shows, you know, unsolved crimes and stuff, and there it was. Liv, it's terrible, just terrible, I can't tell you how sorry I am. Has there been any news?"

"Not a thing."

"Oh, jeez, Liv, what can I say? How are you? Are you okay?"

It was too much effort to tell him.

"I'm okay," I said. "I'll survive."

"What about Neil? He okay?"

"About what you'd expect. Sad. Silent."

"Well, sure, sure. Stupid to ask. Liv, I feel real bad just leaving you guys to it, not getting in touch or nothing. Is there anything I can do for you? I'm supposed to be starting a job down here Monday, but I'll can it if there's something I could do, just say the word and I'm there. How about it?"

"Where are you, Jerry?"

"What? Oh, San Diego, well, not exactly San Diego itself, a little bit north. But, Liv, look, shall I come up? Just say."

"No, Jerry, there's no point. It's a waiting game now; there's nothing for you to do. Go start your job. What sort of job is it?"

"Oh, marina, fishing trips, that sort of thing. But, Liv . . . you sure I can't do anything? Posters, walking the streets? Bugging the cops?"

"I'm sure."

"Well, if you're sure, I guess that's it, then. You keep the faith now. You know he's still out there, right? And hey, Liv, give Neil my best, won't you?"

He rang off. The room was utterly quiet. How strange he seemed, how remote, with his life unfolding effortlessly far away. Just like all the others who had steeled themselves to offer their sympathies and their help, he had sounded strained, ill at ease with pain and his own guilt at being untouched and happy. I imagined his relief at putting down the phone, breaking the connection, duty done. Tragedy has much the same effect on those not directly involved as terminal illness.

You must have noticed the same thing. What would he have done, I wondered, if I had said, "Come at once!" Maisie purred and butted her head under my hand to remind me to stroke her. "You're my best buddy, aren't you, old girl?" I said.

And I realized I had not requested, and Jerry had not offered, either his address or his phone number.

The oddness of that made me tingle. I was sufficiently roused to tell Neil about it when he came up from the studio. When I'd finished the story, there was a silence. His hand stole to his face, covered his mouth. We stared at each other, and the thoughts pounded silently between us.

"We never told the police about him," Neil said finally. "Perhaps we should."

And there it was. Nothing to back it up. Just the instant flare of suspicion that can never be smothered once it is lit. Not that it came to anything. Neil contacted the police, and we told them all about Jerry and his phone call, feeling treacherous, but having to do it, because there was a chance, however remote and unthinkable. Weeks and weeks later, we heard that the California police had searched and located him at a shabby marina near the Mexican border. South of San Diego.

They found nothing to connect him with Daniel, but how hard did they look, do you suppose? One more chore, following up for some Canadian cop who doesn't even know where the guy is, hasn't got a shred of evidence of anything at all, except some vague suspicion, some possibly, maybe, perhaps. But they're hot on illegal aliens down there and made life miserable for him when they discovered he'd been working without a permit, and he sloped off to Mexico. We didn't hear from him again. Hardly surprising.

The other thing that is branded onto the surface of my brain is raw, even now. I'd never tell you this, normally. Some things you just don't talk about somehow, even though they're important and leave scars.

As each wounded day dragged into night, I had got used to submerging beneath the bedclothes, giving myself up to the narcoleptic warmth of Neil's bulk at my back. He did the same, I thought. It came as a shock, one night, to feel his arm steal possessively around me, pulling me close, insistently gathering up my weight and urging, urging, his penis hard against my buttock, his breath ragged and hot against my ear as he murmured beseechingly, "Liv, Liv, oh Liv, come on, come on, please, it's been so long . . ."

I struggled. All I could think of was escape, away from his hands pulling at my nightdress, away from his mouth roaming the side of my neck, away from his leg riding my hip, away from his force and his need, out of that bed and that room before my revulsion spewed out in the vomit that was heaving its way up. Desperation lent me strength, and Neil, God knows, is no rapist. His grip had already slackened as my feet scissored to the floor; he was just starting to say, "Okay, Liv, calm down, tell me what's wrong . . ." when I felt my flailing elbow connect smartly with his nose.

When I scrambled to my feet and turned, he was sitting up, hunched over, blood dripping between the fingers he had clamped over his face. I raced for a face cloth and ice cubes. Wordlessly, he pressed the makeshift ice pack to his nose. His eyes held mine. His voice was muffled.

"Hell of a way to make a point," he said. "What was the point, anyway?"

"I'm sorry." It sounded inadequate even as I said it.

"Well, I know *that*. Still doesn't tell me why we can't make love."

What was I going to say? I love you, but Daniel is in the way? I know sex is your way of showing love, of taking and giving comfort, but it's also about babies, about making new ones, and I can't think of that, I can't even admit the possibility of that. I blew it; I lost the child we waited so long for. How can I ever imagine replacing him? What sort of betrayal would that be, to give ourselves a substitute, a consolation prize for such unlucky losers? How could I deserve that?

"I'm sorry," I repeated. "I just can't. I just can't."

Gingerly, he removed the ice pack. His nose was scarlet and swollen. He wiped blood from his upper lip.

"Feels like hell," he said. "Must look like a freak. D'you think we could have a clean sheet?"

It was a relief to fetch one and remake the bed. When I'd finished, Neil yawned.

"I'm bushed," he said. "If you promise not to hit me, I think I'll go to sleep now."

And as I crawled back in beside him, he spoke once more in the darkness.

"One of these days, Liv, it won't seem like treachery any more."

So he understood. It was typical of his innate courtesy and consideration. But I had seen the hurt in his eyes, and I cursed myself for a fool, even as I felt relief. That night confirmed his gentle, almost imperceptible recoil. He began to spend more and more time in the studio, disappearing for hours, resurfacing looking bleary and bewildered as if he'd just woken in a strange bed with no idea how he had got there.

It was at this time, too, that his work changed significantly. He had always been a magnificent draughtsman but had a growing reputation as an abstract painter. Critics called his canvases "bold," "confrontational," "daring syntheses of colour and form."

One of the few things we did together then was to laugh at the overblown rhetoric, make a game of inventing more and more extravagant compliments that meant less and less. "Spot on!" said Neil when I came up with "incandescent vision of tonal nebulosity."

"Pitch perfect!"

One day, though, I wandered into the studio to find Neil hunched over his worktable in front of a very bright light, peering through a magnifying lens. Curious, I looked over his shoulder. With a fine brush he was painting on a tiny piece of board, no larger than the oversized stamps they always produce at Christmas. It appeared to be a forest scene; meticulously he was filling in the tiny dark tree trunks, no thicker than eyelashes. At first I could see nothing else. Then I saw a spot of red and blue, and there was a tiny boy, tow-headed, and by his side, standing, sitting, scratching, tongues lolling, eyes bright, were wolves tame as spaniels.

"Stamps?" I asked. "Are you designing stamps?"

"Sort of," he said, "but not for any country in this world."

He hesitated, then pulled out a portfolio and opened it. More miniatures, maybe six to a page, and, yes, they did look like stamps but jewelled somehow, more like the tiny illuminations in a medieval Book of Hours. Each one had a recognizable geographic context: rivers, lakes, oceans, mountains, prairie, all discernibly North American but not specific. All the scenes glowed, as if the air in those places were rarified, so that all the colours were more intense, the shadows deeper, the sun brighter. And in every one, sometimes hard to find, but there, somewhere, was the small boy. Neil was recreating the world, and Daniel roamed it, happy and safe.

But there was no place in it for me, and as Neil quietly withdrew into his fantasy, making it ever more subtle and comprehensive as he moved with his Boy from desert to jungle to Arctic waste, I slithered deeper and deeper into despair.

Daily routine became a numbing grind. Getting out of bed each morning involved a draining expenditure of willpower. Ordinary tasks like cooking and cleaning demanded more energy than I could command. As far as school work was concerned, I was an automaton, on automatic pilot in a strangely muffled world. Day after day, I trudged endlessly through a featureless wasteland, exhausted and aimless.

One end came the day I accidentally spilled a small vial of nitric acid on the top of the lab bench. It seethed venomously on the wood. I could not remember what to do with it. I stood there, Lot's wife, unable to move or think. An immense weariness overcame me, and I sank onto a stool and laid my head down on my arms. My grade 9 class found me, apparently asleep, quite unresponsive, while a small puddle of acid at my elbow smoked and gnawed at the bench top, filling the air with its stench. The sight apparently cowed even the brashest boy in the class to silence.

I floated on an uncharted sea, and events arranged themselves around me. The school board hastily granted me extended leave. The substitute teacher who had stood in for me before was summoned again. Somebody decided I should go for a while to Mum and Dad in Vanderhoof; they would look after me, and I could have a good rest, they said.

So, you materialized again to escort me north, Stephen, and on a sparkling April day, I let Neil pack me into your battered pickup.

As we turned onto the highway, I looked back. The lonely figure standing at the door, one arm raised, and Maisie twining her ginger form about his ankles, made my eyes prickle. The act of leaving felt significant in an undefinable way. There was portent in Neil's arm held in still salute, in the clanging approach to the dark hold of the ferry, in the widening gap filled with churning water as the boat pulled away from the dock at Langdale, in the seagull that for a time kept pace with us as we crossed the Sound and then, its mission completed, suddenly veered away and was gone.

That sense of a door closing, of finality, was still with me when we stopped for the night in Hope. We stayed at the Swiss Chalet motel. Remember the tiny cabins with heart-shaped holes in their front doors?

We went to the Kan Yon restaurant and ate Chinese, or rather, you did while I picked at some fried rice, and then the empty evening loomed. The thought of sitting in my cabin appalled me. So did the effort of conversation.

"Why don't you go and watch TV?" I suggested. "I fancy a bit of a walk."

Your face instantly took on an anxious doggy look.

"You sure? You'll be all right on your own? You don't know the place—perhaps I'd better come too. It'll be dark."

"No!" It came out too sharp. "No, don't be silly. How can you get lost in a town this size? I won't be long, just need a bit of air."

You were reluctant. Wary too, now that I think about it, but you gave in and opened your own front door.

"See you then," you said.

I headed out of the back entrance of the motel and found myself on a road beside a large stand of firs. A wind stirred them gently, soft black feathers in a fan; it was quiet. The few steps I had taken had shut off the noise from the highway, muted the garish lights on the main drag. Another door closing behind me.

I walked along the road. My white runners gleamed in the half-light. Soon the path angled downward, and I passed the driveways of old wooden houses half buried in bushes and trees that obviously rested on the bank of the river. I could hear the soughing of the water. The path turned and dipped again. Now it led straight to the Fraser's edge. Overhead, the narrow highway bridge made a dark bar against the sky. Headlights stuttered by its railings and tires zinged across the metal road bed.

Down where I stood, the sounds and lights were an irrel-evance. The river filled my consciousness. Its mass rolled by, even and unstoppable, its sombre green streaked occasionally by a little play of white as it encountered an obstacle on its way, the faint susurration it made a steady counterpoint to the whine of tires above.

I swear I had not thought of suicide up to that point. Not with the leaden weight of memory and guilt, not with the daily reminders of Daniel's presence in the house, not with the hal-lucinatory glimpses that teased with appalling hope only to be dashed the next instant, not even with the insomniac hours in the dead watches of the night. But at that moment, by the quiet hurrying water, it seemed the most natural, inevitable thing in the world to walk out and drop into the current and let it carry me away.

I even took the first step. Your voice stopped the second.

"Livvy, I'm getting married in June. I'll want you at the wed-ding, you know."

I wrenched myself round to face you. You continued, straining to be light and matter of fact.

"Holly's got relatives coming out of her ears—her side of the church will be stacked. I'll have to bribe everybody I know to come, just so it'll look even."

"*Holly?*" I managed and burst into tears.

You caught me in a bear hug. "She can't help her name, her mother loved Audrey Hepburn."

You were silent a moment. Then, "It's not on, Liv. There's always a chance he'll be found, always a chance, as long as we don't know for sure what happened. You can't go while there's that chance."

That night, for the first time since Daniel's disappearance, I wept uncontrollably. After a while, I stopped trying to mop up the tears and let them flow unhindered. They poured down, dripped in a steady rain from my nose and chin; my clothes were soaked; I left little puddles on the tabletop. I would have had to retreat to higher ground if exhaustion had not set in. Mice would have been swimming by, telling tales. But just as the river I had turned from the night before scoured its beds and banks, carrying all the debris away to the hidden sea, so my tears purged something in me. I woke, my face a pulpy, sodden mask, and felt lightness—not happiness, by no means, there's never any release from the daily wakening to loss—but a lessening, a more supportable burden.

As we drove north, past Spences Bridge and the herd of mountain sheep almost indistinguishable in their dun coats from the sage they browsed, past Cache Creek and the Hat Creek Ranch, past Clinton and 100 Mile House, into the rolling ocean of the Cariboo and a sparse landscape that had not yet quite forgotten winter, you told me about Holly and your plans. I was startled to learn this was nothing new; you had known her for a year or more, and the wedding day was fixed for June 24. With another pang of guilt, I realized how impervious I had been. What else had I ignored, buried head first in my own misery?

We said nothing about the river. You'd rescued me as I'd once rescued you, and nothing needed to be said. Just before you left for Prince George, though, after delivering me like a valuable parcel to Mum and Dad, you caught at my hand and spoke urgently, forcing me to look you in the eye.

"Go to the doctor and get something for depression. If he tells you to pull yourself together and it'll be all right, go somewhere else. Got it? Will you do that?"

I nodded. You turned to Dad, and I saw the first of a new, authoritative Stephen. "You see she goes," you said. "She needs treatment, not pep talks," and Dad, also looking a bit startled, nodded agreement.

And so I arrived at a watershed of sorts.

EIGHT

At first, aided and abetted by Mum and Dad, and probably the medication their doctor prescribed, I did nothing but sleep. Lucky timing—a patient ducking out of his sessions just as the doctor referred me—got me in to see a therapist in Prince George. It was only after visiting her for a few weeks that I realized how rare a bird a psychological professional of any sort was up there. I could so easily have missed out on those conversations in the tiny office she had on the fourth floor of a grey cube of a professional building downtown. I think she won my trust right from the start with her honesty.

"I can do something about your depression," she said, looking at me intently as she stuffed a green velvet cushion behind her back and settled in a corner of the couch opposite my armchair. "I can't cure your loss, though we can talk about it. Will that be helpful, do you think?"

It was. For a while those trips with Dad into Prince George to see Dr. Thorburn were the high points of each week, about the only things I could entertain Neil with when we talked on the phone. I couldn't get much mileage out of shopping with Mum at the Co-op or helping Dad pull chickweed out of the flowerbeds!

To tell the truth, I kept a lot of those sessions to myself. I may have made Neil laugh describing Dr. Thorburn's almost clichéd manner: head tilted on one side like a robin listening for a worm; her wordless pauses that compelled me to speak; her habit of answering questions with a question; the mantra phrases like "And how does that make you feel?" But she forced me to inspect myself, to pick at scabs, made questions lodge in my mind so that finding answers became a task, one that was not always pleasant or even fully accomplished. I think it was that half-baked feeling—that I hadn't really got it yet myself—that made me cautious when Neil pushed for details.

But when he asked if I was better, I could honestly say I was. I seemed to have regained the knack of getting through the days and finding some point to them. The general boredom of life at Mum and Dad's drove me to the river and bird watching again. I looked up old friends, the ones without houses full of children at least. The sight of a tricycle abandoned in a front yard, or tiny sneakers for sale in a store, even the lump of plaster that immortalized my own infant handprint, still displayed on the mantelpiece, made my eyes well. But I found myself longing for the feel of Maisie on my lap, for the smell of turpentine, the sound of the latch as Neil came in from the studio, even for the stupid jokes of the grade 9 boys.

I had instantly liked Holly when I met her, despite her aggressively rosy health and glossiness, the irrepressible chirpy smile and good humour of one whom life has barely grazed. Although she came across like an aerobics instructor on speed, there was an earthy kindness beneath the bubbles; it was easy to visualize her looking after sick and abandoned animals, as she did at the SPCA in Prince George.

She was frazzled at the time, of course, driven half distracted by all the preparations for the wedding.

"What did *you* order for vegetarian guests?" she asked me one day. I hadn't had any guests apart from you, Mum and Dad, and three friends from university, and not one of them would have been caught dead near tofu, so I wasn't much help.

Nor did I have any diplomatic suggestions when one of her bridesmaids staged a revolt against peach lace.

"It's your day, Holly, and your choice," I told her. "Tell her to put up or shut up."

I was having problems of my own, anyway.

Mum was having an identity crisis on her own account, and on behalf of Dad, as Parents of the Groom. She had compelled me to review Dad's entire wardrobe with her. Useless for him to protest that his good navy suit would do just fine, it just needed cleaning, he'd only worn it a few times.

"Look at this," she said, holding up the blameless navy pinstripe. "It'll never do, will it? We can't let Stephen down, can we?"

And when I cravenly said I supposed not, she said triumphantly, "There, Livvy agrees—you need a new suit!"

But it was her own outfit that completely demoralized Mum. She towed me into Prince George to find what she called "something special—but not too posh." She couldn't define this more specifically than "maybe a nice dress, with a jacket, perhaps," and seemed to hope that the perfect solution would rear up and there'd be a moment of mutual, relieved recognition.

She begged me to go with her.

"You always seem to know what to wear," she said. "You've got *style*."

It was news to me, but I went and steered her away from shiny polyester floral prints that made her look like an over-stuffed sofa, ran interference between her and overzealous or patronizing sales staff, and fetched and carried a bewildering array of sizes and styles between rack and fitting room.

She hated every minute. She doesn't really fit any standard size, being short and dumpy. Everything was too big, too small, too tight, too loose, too hot, too revealing. On one return trip to the fitting room, my cautious knock revealed her standing in front of the mirror in her limp and faded slip, white flesh puffing beneath the straps and tears crawling down her flushed cheeks. I could see sweat pearling on her forehead.

"They don't make clothes for people my shape," she said. "We might as well go home."

Mum and I were never exactly close, but I felt for her in that moment. I knew exactly how hopeless she felt in that claustrophobic space, unable to ignore the mirror, every imperfection heightened by the ill-fitting, ugly garments, every one of which shouted at the top of its supercilious and overpriced lungs that she'd never, in a million years, be anything special.

I gave her a quick hug.

"Maybe we're going about this all wrong," I said. "Why don't you get dressed and go and have a nice cup of coffee somewhere and I'll look around and find some possibles for you?"

It was a desperate throw—I had no idea what we'd do if I couldn't find anything—but she agreed with relief and I left her furtively easing off her shoes with a coffee in front of her.

I veered off into a fabric store and attacked the pattern books. It didn't take long to find patterns for a simple sleeveless dress and an elegant fitted jacket with a peplum. A bit more ferreting turned up a supple green fabric for the dress and a beautiful heavy shot silk that reminded me of a peacock's feathers for the jacket. Mum was enchanted.

"But who's going to make it?" she said. It was apparently a revelation that there were seamstresses who made a living that way.

"Saved the day, I hear," Dad said, and that sort of approval made the remaining days buoyant. But the family could still take me by surprise.

I was talking to Neil a couple of days before he was due to arrive and we were speculating idly about the reception.

"Will there be speeches, do you think?" I asked. I couldn't imagine Holly's logger father making a speech any more than I could see Dad getting up in front of a crowd. "I suppose the best man will make one at least. I don't even know who the best man is."

There was a little silence at the other end of the line.

"It's me. I thought for sure Stephen would have told you that!"

For a second I felt absurdly offended. Not at Neil being your choice, you understand, who better? Just at not knowing, at being no more in the know than the most distant second cousin twice removed among Holly's tribe. And the niggling, humiliatingly unworthy feeling that Neil was actually closer and more involved in the family than I was. I gave myself a shake.

"He probably thought for sure *you'd* tell me!"

Neil arrived for the ceremony, and we dressed up like mannequins and did our best to fill up the right side of the church. We gazed, somewhat bemused, at the crowded pews on the other side of the aisle. Mum, I saw, was checking the outfit Holly's mother was wearing, a strained-looking apricot sheath with a floating chiffon tunic, accompanied by a matching tulle hat like a meringue. "Could have done with a size larger," she whispered, "and that hat does nothing for her, does it?" Dad smiled vaguely and you fidgeted in the front pew.

Then the noise died and the organ played and Holly came down the aisle with her father, and you turned to watch her with such pride and longing in your face that I could have wept on the spot except that Neil winked at me and for a while he was the only person there.

What do you remember most about your wedding now, Stephen? You were probably too nervous to register the vicar's mistake just after the *Dearly Beloved* bit—perhaps you were still waiting for someone to yell, "I object!" from the back and missed him addressing you both as Michael and Tiffany. I heard Holly's mother gasp, and Holly looked at you, but it was Neil who set him straight. I wonder if you'd have been really married if nobody had corrected him?

There was one seriously bad moment. Holly's five-year-old nephew was a pageboy, dressed in a kilt and a black velvet jacket. I looked at him and saw Daniel and was nearly unseamed by the torrent of regret. But weddings are good for tears and nobody even noticed.

By the time you walked back down the aisle with Holly on your arm, your stunned look had evaporated, and I don't think you stopped smiling for the rest of the day. Your grin is there in all the wedding photos and echoed in all the faces pressing around you both. It continued through the reception at the church hall, through the lame speeches and Holly's brother having one too many Scotches and trying to do the limbo under a table, through the screeching feedback from the microphones as the band set up, through the garrulous uncles and gushing aunts, one of the cousins fainting in a corner, and the pageboy throwing up in the bushes by the front door.

For part of the time, Neil was busy with best man stuff, and knowing nobody, I could sit quietly and watch. It fascinated me to see this large family in action, to see the ones who would always be the organizers clutching arms, drawing people together, sending them on errands, jollying the shy ones, and carrying glasses and plates to the elderly. And I saw how easily you seemed to be assimilated into this throng of strangers, and how readily people talked to Neil. Even Mum was deep in conversation with a woman who could have been her sister, and Dad was standing in a knot of men with loosened ties, face flushed, drinking beer. Only I seemed disconnected and I wondered, not for the first time, why I had such a talent for isolation.

And then the dancing started, and Neil walked the length of the hall to collect me, saying, "Your turn" in my ear as we swept into a waltz and collided with Holly's Mum and Dad, and the rest of the reception folded in on us, became rhythm and warm contact, the soft slide of fabric on flesh, Neil's breath mingling with mine, and utter surrender to contentment and the climate of love.

As we drove away together afterward to return to Sechelt, Mum and Dad and many of the other guests crowded round the car, waving and smiling, banging on the trunk and tying ribbon to the aerial, as if we were the newlyweds, off at last on the honeymoon we had never been able to afford when we got married.

And the mood lingered so that when we got to Hope, we looked at each other, and without a word turned into the Swiss Chalet car park and fell, laughing, into each other's arms on a creaking, hollowed bed while the traffic whined by outside, unregarded.

NINE

Eleven years passed after Daniel disappeared.

Sounds like a fairytale, no? They always have those incanta-tory phrases, usually involving a magical number—a year and a day, seven years of bad luck, a hundred-year sleep—to invoke the power of a spell, the terms of the bargain, the respite between the curse and its fulfillment. Take your pick. There was an element of sleepwalking about them, moving through day after day, dulled by routine, but never forgetting, rasped raw by all the reminders. All it would take for the grief to rise and consume us again would be the turn of a child's head, a toy in a shop window, a lone miniature sock at the back of a drawer.

There were the deliberate reminders too: the yearly reports from Detective Mallory, still officially on the case; the faded pictures in the post office and the bus depot; the TV program on the fifth anniversary of Daniel's disappearance and the oddly familiar but utterly strange approximation of his nine-year-old face the police artist produced for the occasion. Worst were the hideous echoes—news of other abductions, or the discovery of skeletal remains, which always prompted the press to speculate and us to relive the agony of waiting for news that never comes. These are private griefs, but they have a public face. They never go away. We smile even, occasion-ally, but we carry open wounds beneath our clothes that fester and will not heal.

Eleven years passed. Neil became a celebrity. Alvarsson's Boy was a cult figure among the cognoscenti, a miniature Everyman, a symbol, as *The New York Times* had it, of "our perennial, fragile hope for a better world." He continued to produce the stamp-sized miniatures, exploring every corner of the globe, every facet of life, and moved on to larger canvases too, all with the heightened reality of the world as he thought it ought to be.

And me, Stephen? I became more of a fixture in the staff-room, one of the Old Brigade, testy about falling standards and the inadequacy of elementary schools, cynical about principals and ministers and people who called themselves educators, skeptical about the magical new band-aid of computers, happiest when left alone with the kids to get on with things in the classroom. The experienced teacher, I suppose, no different from thousands of others, with a comfortable enough home life and, as a new member of staff once remarked brightly, to a strangled silence, nobody to worry about, really, except ourselves.

Fast-forward then, to a January day in 1986.

I was sitting in the school library listening to Ed Watkins, one of the shop teachers, bickering with the vice principal about lunch duty. The staff meeting was already an hour and a half old; I had crossed through only half of the agenda. To my right, Miss Penfold's head was inclining backward to meet the bookshelves, and as she relaxed against volumes 3 to 5 of the *World Book*, her jaw slumped and the faintest of ladylike snores rattled in her throat. I caught Ella's eye and choked on a giggle.

Ed had flustered the vice-principal to his satisfaction and allowed the principal to wrench the meeting back on track. Balding—Mr. Spalding—was tentatively approaching a delicate topic. On my left, my good friend Sheila Oddy, queen of the English department, waited expectantly.

"Firstly of all," said the principal, "we have to face the fact that we are going to have cutbacks next year. Secondly of all . . ."

"God," whispered Sheila, "that makes seven times he's said that so far."

She was keeping a score with neat blocks of four vertical lines crossed through with a fifth oblique stroke. These documents had become a legendary tally of Mr. Spalding's misuse of the English language during his lengthy monologues in staff meetings. The record was twenty-seven solecisms in an hour and ten minutes. Sheila could not have said what she intended to do with this mass of data, or even what it meant. On bad days she would mutter darkly, "They want to know what's wrong with education? I could show them!" Usually, she would laugh and call it The Impotent's Revenge. She was just an English teacher, after all, and Balding Spalding had vaulted to his present position after a career in physical education with a glowing reputation for administrative ability based, it would seem, on the impeccable organization of round-robin tournaments.

I came back from a contemplation of the ceiling fan sluggishly stirring the air far above my head. Several of my colleagues were restive. Hissing Ed was in full spate again.

"Will the administration give an assurance that any cuts they have in mind will not have an adverse effect on the level of service offered at the classroom level? They keep docking the money and telling us we've got to do more with less. They expect us to do everything for these kids—we're social workers and nannies, that's what, but no extra money, oh no. Why should teachers and programs get the axe when the fat cats at the board office never feel the pinch? What the hell do we need *three* assistant superintendents for?"

"Up the workers!" whispered Sheila as Ed came to a stop, breathing audibly, his chin stuck out as if daring the principal to throw a punch.

Mr. Spalding gathered himself.

"Firstly of all, we're all in this together, all part of the team . . ."

"Oh my God," groaned Sheila and marked two more little strokes on her scorecard.

"Secondly of all, we don't have much choice in the matter. The board's running a deficit. We'll just have to tighten our belts and spread ourselves a little thinner."

I felt intensely weary. Another invasion of the available resources. How far could they stretch before they burst like the unfortunate host in *Alien*? And how much did it all matter, anyway? Like Miss Penfold, I sagged against the reference section. The room was amazingly hot. I could almost believe the tired views and empty huffing rhetoric were literally raising the temperature, fuelling strong thermals that rose visible as currents in water. I could feel my own thoughts, caught by convection, rising helplessly out of my grasp, slowly widening the gyre, until they disappeared into a shimmering haze far above to glide in expanding circles about the twirling blades.

To recapture some grip on reality, or at least consciousness, and make the distant voices speed up once more into recognizable words, I rolled my head to look at Miss Penfold, gaunt after a day in special ed. Even as I took in the faint flush on her face, and the translucent blue eyelids, there came a sudden pause in the argument and in the stillness, the top plate of Miss Penfold's notoriously ill-fitting dentures fell with a clack on the bottom teeth and she woke, fumbling at her mouth with a tiny mew of distress.

"Is there any more questions?"

"Oh God, oh God," breathed Sheila.

"Then we'll adjourn. Perhaps the timetable committee could stay for a moment to arrange our next ad hoc gathering?"

"After the union meeting." This from Ed, who was predictably keen on protocol. Huffily, the principal gathered up his files and withdrew.

With his disappearance, the room unbuttoned. People chatted, laughed, asked Sheila for the day's total—seventeen— fetched coffee and cracked open a window. The phone rang; the librarian answered it and immediately hung out of her office door, phone in hand.

"Livvy, it's for you."

My immediate thought was that it must be Neil. No parent would bother to ring the school that late. Perhaps he wanted me to collect something from the store on the way home.

But it wasn't Neil. It was you, Stephen. Do you remember that conversation, I wonder?

"Liv. Got a minute?"

"Of course." You sounded odd. Flattened, somehow. A little squeeze of fear in my chest. Then those words. Stiff. Almost self-conscious, as if they embarrassed you.

"I've had a bit of bad news today. The doctor just told me. I've got leukemia, Liv."

The word clanged about in the stuffy little office. Leukemia. Stephen.

"Liv? You there?"

"Yes. Just trying to take it in."

My mouth was dry, and the words stuck in my throat.

"It's a bit of a facer, isn't it? I don't know quite what to do with myself. What do you do with yourself when the doctor's just told you you're scuppered? I couldn't stay at the doctor's. I don't want to go home. Holly's still at work. There'll just be the kids. I can't talk to them, can't quite trust myself to sound normal. Can't stay here; it's bloody freezing."

"Where *are* you?"

"Pay phone, near the Connaught."

I could picture him, pinched and grey with cold, at the big intersection in Prince George, Woodward's car park corrugated with dirty snow ridges, and the wind howling down from

73

Connaught Hill and the underground caverns of the public library, setting the traffic lights twisting and tugging at their restraints high above the ground.

"Go home," I said. "Get warm. Let the kids babble, it'll be all right. Give me half an hour and I'll ring you back. I've got to get out of here too."

That was no less than the truth. Weakness was stealing over me. My limbs were leaden; I couldn't even feel the floor. I might well have been levitating. A head swam across my vision, a large pale face turning slowly in my direction as its mouth began to open. Perhaps it spoke, but sound was lagging badly, distorted as it struggled through some thick, strange element.

I'm underwater, I thought, *so I must be a fish. And so is Charley, and that's why his mouth keeps opening like that. He's just breathing.*

The mouth drew nearer, gulping. The lips formed a little muscular O, over and over, pushing closer to my face.

He's like a grouper, I thought remotely, *Groper the Grouper, Grouper the Groper. How appropriate*, I added to myself, as his fins brushed mine, clammy and cold, and his slab of a face and chilly eye slid closer.

From an immense distance, I heard my name—"Olivia, Olivia, Olivia"—a protracted sigh borne on a gust of stale breath.

Can fish use Listerine? I wondered but managed no more than a mumble before sinking onto the floor.

The union meeting dissolved abruptly as Ella and Sheila hovered over me, issuing directives for ice cubes and water and more air. Miss Penfold produced a tiny green glass bottle of *sal volatile* from the little tapestry drawstring bag I always thought of as her reticule and waved it under my nose. Whether it was the fumes or the ice cubes Sheila was rubbing on my wrists that revived me, I was soon sitting up and sipping water while Miss Penfold used her agenda as a fan.

Charles Roper rumbled overhead.

"You gave us a scare. I could see you were going to drop. Are you ill?"

"It was the heat," said Ed. "How many times have I told them to do something about the ventilation in this place? No wonder we get sick, tropical one minute and freezing the next, downright unhealthy, I call it. If they don't want us to walk off the job, what they need to do—"

"Yes," said Ella firmly, "but what we need to do right now is get you home, isn't it, love?"

The weakness had evaporated more or less. All I wanted to do was escape. Think what to say to you.

"I'm okay now," I insisted. "I can drive myself. Perhaps if you drove behind me, Ella? I'll be all right, really."

The faces were doubtful, but I prevailed finally and hurried to fetch my coat. Ella went with me down the hallway where the custodians were already sweeping the day's debris into long, dark lines, flotsam left by a receding tide.

"What gives?" she asked quietly. "It was that phone call, wasn't it? It wasn't anything about . . . Daniel, was it?"

"No. Oh no," I said, amazed at myself for that possibility had not occurred to me, "just almost as bad."

Not much later, I sat by the phone and steeled myself to pick it up. Much depended, I thought, as Maisie cast herself across my lap, rolling onto her back and peeping coyly at me from underneath her right foreleg, on saying the right thing. But what was the right thing? What do you say to somebody who has just been told he has a life-threatening disease?

You must have been sitting by the phone, for your voice cut off the first ring.

"Can you talk?" I asked immediately. "Are the kids around?"

"No, they're watching the box."

"Tell me, exactly what sent you to the doctor in the first place?" Cautious, feeling my way.

"Just feeling tired. All the time, for no reason, but absolutely flattened if I went running. Then I started getting these huge bruises, but I could never remember hitting myself or bumping into things. And nosebleeds! Real gushers. I haven't had nosebleeds like that since I was small. But it was chiefly the exhaustion, aching in every joint."

I could hear it in your voice, monotone, dreary, as if even inflection were too much effort.

"Okay, now what exactly have you got?"

"Oh, it's got a grand-sounding name. Acute myelogenous leukemia."

"Sounds bad enough to scare the living daylights out of anyone."

"Well, Liv, it's not good. Bloody death sentence, in fact."

"But they can treat it, right?"

"Oh yes, they can stretch things out a bit with chemo and stuff, but it'll just postpone the inevitable a few years."

"And if they did nothing?"

"Three or four months."

That hit like a punch in the stomach.

"Then it's worth a fight, isn't it?" I asked sharply. You hesitated. I could hear it.

"I'm not sure, Liv. I've only got about a twenty to thirty percent chance of long-term survival. Not very good odds. And I'd need a bone marrow transplant. I don't even know if that's possible yet. I don't know if it's worth putting Holly and the kids through all that, years of it perhaps, when I could just check out in a few months."

"Hey!" I said. "Don't you think Holly and the kids might have different thoughts about losing you the day after tomorrow? I stuck around for you, kiddo; now it's your turn. You said you'll probably need a bone marrow transplant. Well, I'm the likeliest donor—siblings are the best bet, I think—and I'm ready and willing, so there you are."

"Yeah, I know I'll go through all the treatments they can dream up. You do, don't you, if there's just a little bit of hope, but it doesn't stop the little voice inside saying, 'What's the use? You know nothing's going to work. You've had it, mate.' It's hard to ignore. There doesn't seem much to look forward to."

What do you say? You can't agree, can you?

"Perhaps you're being too long-sighted. Perhaps you have to be a bit myopic, and look at the nearer things if you want to see clearly. What I mean is, perhaps it would be better to look forward to Jason going into high school soon, rather than graduating from med school fifteen years from now. Lower your sights, you know. Fill your life with little steps rather than brooding over the big ones that might be unattainable."

"Could be."

"So your first one will be telling Holly. And don't forget to say I'm queuing to donate."

"Okay."

"Then the next one will be having the first lot of treatment. What's on the cards?"

"Chemo."

"So the first milestone could be remission after the chemo?"

"Right."

"Then that's what we set our sights on. Go for it, Tiger! Nobody ever had to prod you to stick up for yourself."

"Well, that's true, and I've got the scars to prove it."

A small joke. It felt like a victory.

"Shall I come up there?"

"No, no point. We'll keep you posted. I don't think I'll be a very gracious host for a while."

"Host be damned! We don't need entertaining! If you need

anything, you'll ask? Ring me tomorrow, okay? Any time, when you feel like it."

"Right. Thanks."

"It'll be all right, Stephen. It will. It has to be."

"Yes."

"I'll say goodbye for now, then."

"Yes. Goodbye, Liv."

"Go and hug your kids. Talk to you soon."

"Yes. Goodbye."

I held the receiver to my ear, listening to you listening to me, until I heard the clatter from your end as you hung up. The quiet of the room was punctured by the soft tick of the clock as the second hand swept the face. The fluorescent light hummed to itself. I could see myself reflected in the kitchen window, a stranger's sombre face turned outward as if weary of imprisonment. Beyond the glass, like a negative image, ghostly snowflakes drifted, trickled over the windowsill and clung, weightless as down, to the bare branches of the apple tree.

TEN

For the most part, life is undistinguished. We move through our days on fixed tracks, like the little players in a foosball game, not expecting surprises and rarely causing any, mechanically following the routine because that's what we've always done and it's easier to keep doing it than to think of something original. What percentage of our lives, I wonder, is dedicated to stodgy status quo? If we include sleep—and there's a third gone right there—eighty-five percent? Ninety? More? And I don't suppose it's any different if one is famous or a genius or a hero. A prima donna may sing in every opera house from Sao Paulo to Beijing in the course of a year, but then travel is her norm: living out of a suitcase, booking in and out of palatial hotels, fighting with conductors, worrying about her vocal cords, wearing outlandish costumes, and upstaging the tenor merely the daily trivia of her life.

In retrospect, she will probably find it very hard to differentiate between successful performances, but just let Mimi have a sneezing fit after she's died, or let an overly dramatic member of the chorus fall into the kettle drums during an aria, and the event takes on an indelible flavour all its own. Memories may just be our five percent of the extraordinary: the little foosball man twirled too hard, detaching himself from the rod, performing a graceful arc across the crowded bar, and landing slam dunk in a pint of Guinness on the far side of the room.

And if that sounds a trifle inebriated, hallucinatory, unreal, that was definitely the Flavour of the Year. Mum called that time "When Stephen Was Ill," as if it had defined limits and was succeeded by another period called "When Stephen Was Well." The capitals were appropriate, though. Our first exposure to acute illness, watching as you were caught up in the sprockets and rollers of the medical machine, reduced all our ordinary concerns to nothing. We lived and breathed Stephen. Work, shopping for groceries, marking, keeping dental appointments were simply ways of negotiating the voids between visits to the hospital, or bulletins on your progress, or detailed analysis of your doctor's latest pronouncement. We learned the disease; words like *leucocyte, platelets, anaemia, nonlymphocytic* fell nonchalantly from our lips. We discussed blood transfusions, bone marrow aspiration, chemotherapy, and WBC counts as if they were on special at Safeway.

In the end, of course, life with leukemia stopped being an extraordinary visitation in our dull lives and became the norm, a spectacularly trying one but routine nonetheless.

Even so, there are memories from When Stephen Was Ill that flare out of the darkness like the silhouettes of trees startled by lightning at midnight.

The lurch I felt, as if all my insides gasped as one, when I saw you soon after you told me you were ill. I hadn't seen you for six months, but I was completely unprepared for the change in you, your pallor, your panting at the slightest exertion, the way you'd shrunk inside your clothes.

Vanessa in tears after she had briefly visited the isolation ward, where you were suffering the ravages of nausea, wailing, "He doesn't look like my daddy any more."

Mum awkwardly folding her arms round Holly and patting her like a horse that has to be soothed, crooning, "There, there, poor girl, poor girl, he'll be all right, you'll see." That was the night we thought we'd lose you to pneumonia.

The ICU that same night, lights blazing, machines winking and bleating, rubber soles squeaking on the composition floor. How busy illness is, I thought, how noisy; you could only put up with it if you were so sick you weren't aware of anything.

The day I walked in on Holly when she was taking a pair of shears to her long blond hair. She had just cut a hank off one side and looked like Barbie making a change to Raggedy Anne.

"I worked it out," she said seriously. "It takes me about an hour a day at least to keep my hair looking decent. Too long— I've got better use for the time. Wash and wear from now on."

When I asked why she didn't just go to the hairdresser to get it cut, she looked at me as if I were stupid.

"That would be another hour wasted."

It didn't seem the moment to point out that she looked awful. Instead, I took the scissors from her and finished the job.

The best one, perhaps, is the sight of you through the glass of your isolation ward on the day they first reported you were producing normal cells again. You were sitting up, bald as an egg, a pallid Gandhi against the pillows. When you saw Neil, your face creased in a smile, the first I'd seen for weeks, and you slowly raised an arm and punched a triumphant, defiant fist in the air.

Remission. That was the new word of the moment, whispered at first as a faint hope that might be scared off if confronted too directly, but later said out loud, more confidently. It's a temporary kind of word, one you use with your fingers crossed behind your back, one that shakes its finger at you in a minatory way and says, "Now don't go getting all excited, there's no guarantee I'm going to last, I could leave any time," as if you need a reminder of the odds with cancer.

It allowed us to think of the next step, though. It was time to search for a bone marrow donor. My moment had come. I no longer had to be satisfied with occasional visits and second-hand reports, or gnash my teeth at my own impotence.

Tests, tests, and more tests. Unearthing of medical history that would have made a forensic anthropologist proud. Information overload. Serious discussion to ensure I knew what I was committing myself to. More tests.

Then, I waited.

We were all set to go up to Mum and Dad's for Thanksgiving. The whole works, it was going to be. You were back home at last, back at work even, part-time at least. You and Holly and the kids would be there for dinner, the whole family round the groaning board sort of thing. But for once there didn't seem to be anything sentimental about it, nothing contrived. Something to give thanks for, Mum said predictably, but then, what are clichés if not absolutely true, absolutely right on the mark? Which all goes to show Fate is a cardsharp, never without an ace up his sleeve.

I don't think I ever told you about the next bit, not in detail. And then there were the other revelations, so much right on top of it all, and suddenly the moment for filling you in was swept away, and there was no going back to it. All you knew was the fallout.

Just before that long weekend I got a call from the doctor's office. The test results were in, the receptionist said, and the doctor would like to discuss them with me. No, she couldn't tell me what they were, she didn't have that information, I would have to talk to the doctor. I couldn't wait, although for the first time there was a tremor of apprehension, a tiny qualm. What if the news was bad? I hadn't allowed that thought before, and it left me queasy. Ironic, looking back.

So there I am. The nurse has plucked me out of the sullen stew of streaming noses, coughs, plaster casts, swollen stomachs, and evasive teenagers chewing their nicotine-stained fingers in the waiting room and ushered me into a cubicle at the far end of the hallway. I sit facing a desk, a warning about STDs, a poster depicting a man, flayed to reveal muscles tightly wrapped as a mummy's bandages, and an illustrated letter of thanks from the kindergarten class of Sechelt Elementary. Dr. Wilson breezes in, plucking a file from the holder on the door. He welcomes me cheerfully as if I'm just another minor ailment needing a quick fix, but his face sobers with a glance at the now open folder on his desk.

"Yes, well," he begins. Abruptly, he gets up. "Hang on a minute."

He pokes his head into the hallway and hails the receptionist. I hear a mumble and one clear word—"uninterrupted."

"Just wanted to make sure we weren't disturbed," he says bracingly, replacing himself behind the bulwark of his desk. Once there, he pauses, gazing at the pages in front of him, pursing his lips. He eyes me consideringly, as if he's contemplating a risky jump from one rooftop to the next. *He's gathering himself*, I think in alarm. *It's something awful. I've got it too. He doesn't know how to say it.* A clammy sweat is beading my upper lip.

"What is it?" I blurt out. "Am I sick too?"

The doctor looks up quickly, surprised.

"No, no, nothing like that. You're in excellent health. But the tests have revealed something a little puzzling. You realize, of course, there are no perfect matches, apart from identical twins, but we can get pretty close with children of the same parents."

"I know all that," I say impatiently. "I'm the best chance."

"Well, yes, you should be."

Should be?

"But the fact is . . ."

Yes?

"The fact is . . ."

He's going to jump!

"Mmm," the doctor finishes with a rush, "the tests show that biologically—genetically—you are no match at all. There is hardly any point of comparison, certainly not nearly enough to be considered a donor."

He's just landed right on my lungs. I can't breathe.

I gape at him. The enormity of what he has just said hangs in the silence. Dr. Wilson waits, toying self-consciously with a cutaway model of a hip joint standing on his desk.

"But that's impossible," I stammer. "He's my *brother*. There has to be *some* similarity. We've got the same parents, for God's sake!"

The doctor pauses delicately. "Are you absolutely sure of that?" he asks.

"Of course I'm sure!"

"No possibility, for example, that you were adopted as an infant?"

"I can show you my birth certificate if you like. How could I have a birth certificate with my name, and my father's and mother's names, and where I was born, if I wasn't their daughter? Are you suggesting it's a forgery?"

"No, no, that would be most unlikely. And let's see, you would remember when Stephen was born?"

"I remember it vividly, going to see Mum in hospital, holding the new baby, Boxing Day, we never did get the turkey cooked. I was eight years old."

"Yes, well, the tests bear that out. Stephen is unquestionably the son of your parents. So we have a mystery, Livvy. Because those same tests prove conclusively that you cannot possibly be their biological daughter. Quite apart from anything else, the blood groups give us incontrovertible evidence that your mum and dad had nothing to do with your conception. D'you know anything about blood groups?"

"Yes," I mutter.

"Well," he continues as if I haven't spoken, "your father is type A. Your mother is AB. They could only produce children with type A, B, or AB. Stephen is A. You, on the other hand, are type O. It just doesn't fit. It's impossible."

I can't take this in. Who . . . ? And if . . . ?

"Oh my God! What about Stephen? If I can't help him, who will?"

"That is a problem, but you must let us worry about that."

"But his children are so young, and Mum and Dad are too old, surely?"

"We'll see. There are other family members in England, I understand?"

"Well, yes, I think so. But we've never had anything to do with them. I don't think my parents—" I break off, catching myself up with a humourless bark of laughter. "I don't think my *parents* have ever been in touch with them, not since we came to Canada in 1947."

The doctor looks at me kindly. "I think you will have to talk to your parents. And don't forget, whatever the story, they're still the only parents you know, despite the biology."

That was a thought I forced myself to repeat like a mantra in the hours following the detonation of the bomb. I left the clinic in a daze, surprised to find the sun still shining, for it seemed as if hours must have passed, as if everything should be different. Just like coming out of the cinema in the middle of the day, you know the feeling. Mechanically, I unlocked my car and sat behind the wheel, staring blankly through the windscreen at a filthy plastic bag dancing in an eddy of dust trapped in a corner of the building.

I scared myself on the way home. Half a mile from the house a blaring horn shocked me back to the right side of the road. How many other narrow escapes had there been? I had driven right through town, across pedestrian crossings, past school buses and loaded logging trucks, all apparently on autopilot.

Neil was making a pot of tea when I walked into the kitchen. He turned to greet me, still half absent in his studio, and froze, kettle in hand, at the sight of my face. He pushed me into a chair and leaned over me anxiously.

"Liv, what's wrong? What's happened?"

On the way home I'd been rehearsing answers to these questions, simultaneously chiding myself for letting your plight slip to the back of my crowded mind. "I've just discovered I'm Jane Doe," seemed too melodramatic and oblique; "I'm not who you think I am," too ambiguous; "My parents aren't my parents," too bald. Besides, was any of it true? Mentally, I kept tripping over my birth certificate, that worn pink sheet, fragile at the folds, with the careful copperplate writing in each column, unmistakably official, identifying me as Olivia Mary, born April 3, 1940, daughter of William and Mavis Potter. There had to be some rational explanation. Neil was waiting for an answer.

"I can't help Stephen," I said finally. "I'm not a match."

Neil's face crinkled with concern. "Oh, Liv, I'm so sorry. I know it meant a lot to you. But . . . it's the luck of the draw. There'll be someone else."

I could not accept the comfort.

"That's not all. I can't do anything for Stephen because I'm not related." I felt Neil's hands stiffen round mine. "Those tests showed that my parents didn't produce me, no, they *couldn't* have produced me. But I know they produced Stephen. So if what they say is true, Stephen's not my brother, he's *never* been my brother, or half-brother, or even stepbrother. But I have a birth certificate, don't I? You've seen it. How could I possibly have that birth certificate if I'm not my parents' daughter? It doesn't make any sense at all." Neil stared at me, still holding both my hands.

"That's really weird," he muttered finally and belatedly set the lid on the teapot. "There's got to be a mistake of some sort. The lab must have switched samples or something."

"No." I had already thought of that, but the doctor had shaken his head. There was no possibility of error; they had checked.

"Maybe the mistake is even further back, then." Neil's voice became more urgent as his idea took shape. "You were born at a pretty chaotic time, after all, war and air raids, all kinds of upheaval. Suppose you were switched with another newborn, by accident? Got sent home with the wrong parents? Who would ever be the wiser if it wasn't noticed right away?"

"Oh right," I said. "I'm really a princess! Now I can reclaim my throne! Neil, that only happens in fairy stories."

"No, it doesn't," he said stoutly. "I was just reading about a case the other day. A judge is having to decide what to do about two babies who were switched at birth because of some snafu with identity bracelets. They've lived for three years with the wrong parents, and nobody the wiser. Now one set of parents wants to change over, and the other won't agree."

"It's awfully hard to believe in something like that."

"But it's the only thing I can think of to explain how you come to have that birth certificate. Otherwise there has to be something wrong with the certificate. Do you see your dad as a forger?"

"Give me a break!"

"There you are, then. You'll just have to ask your mum. Well, your dad might be a better bet, at least he's got a grip on the real world. You'll see them this weekend."

"Yes, but Stephen will be there too and the kids. I've got to get this sorted out before I talk to Stephen. I'll have to phone tonight and hope Dad's there."

Fat chance. When I called, it was Mum's girlish treble, the flat Cockney vowels still distinct after nearly forty years away from London, that breathed in my ear. I can still hear her.

"Hello, my duck. Now don't you tell me you're not coming for Thanksgiving because I don't want to hear it. I've got a lovely bird all ready—it's a fresh one too, none of your frozen muck—and the giblets and the neck to boil up for a nice drop of stock, there's nothing like a good stock if you want a good gravy, most people over here haven't a clue about gravy, putting that brown gluey stuff all over their chips and all, I don't know how they can face it . . ."

"Mum!"

"What, dear? There's no need to shout, you know, I'm not deaf, well, not really, though . . ."

"Mum! We'll be there on Sunday. But I need a word with Dad. Is he around?"

"No dear, he popped in to Prince George overnight, something to do with his Lions or Kinsmen, I couldn't tell you, anyway he's staying overnight with a mate of his, I'm not sure when he'll be back, daft I call it, he can never sleep in a strange bed, but there you are, he would go, never mind . . ."

"Mum," I interrupted, "stop talking and just listen, will you?"

"What's the matter, love? You sound so upset. It isn't anything bad, is it? I'm just so fed up with bad news, there's never anything good, I was just saying to Dad, not two days ago, or was it yesterday? Never mind, all we seem to hear about is disasters and crimes and wars, doesn't anything good ever happen? And then there's Stephen on top of all that, but what can you do, we just have to grin and bear it, that's what I say, not that it isn't depressing, but we do seem to have more than our fair share, don't we?"

I gave up. Feeble of me, but there was nothing to be gained by telling Mum or asking her questions. You know what she's like. Any comment, no matter how mundane, prompts the same torrent, the flow instantly deflected by the smallest pebble of memory or association into a thousand smaller streams, straying farther and farther away from the source. Forcing her to concentrate on a specific topic has as much chance of success as nailing jelly to a wall or keeping dropped ball bearings together.

"It'll keep until Sunday!" I shouted. "I'll wait until I see Dad."

And Mum allowed that that was probably the best idea. "After all," she said, "you always did take your troubles to your dad, didn't you, even when you were a little girl?"

Yes. And I wonder why that was? My anger took me by surprise, but I put down the phone very gently.

ELEVEN

.

There was never anything as tedious as that journey north.
Normally, I would have enjoyed the ferry trip simply because of
the licence it offered to do absolutely nothing but enjoy the sea.
This time, I was enraged by its slowness, poking along, butt-
ing through the waves, easily outpaced by seagulls. Trudging
around Vancouver uncovered a conspiracy involving the traffic
lights, which I could swear had reproduced like fruit flies since
I last saw them, and construction crews removing the very
lanes we were occupying. Even at 3:00 PM the Trans-Canada
was choked, with more and more vehicles barging in at every
on-ramp. When does anyone work in Vancouver? Or do they all
simply commute?

The crowd had thinned by the time we reached Hope, and
the country had tilted on its axis to become vertical, infinitely
more interesting than the horizontals of the floodplain. But the
light was dying, and at the bottom of the canyon deep shadows
masked the leaping water and the stark eroded rock that reared
from it. The winding road became no more than a yellow pencil
of light boring through the darkness, briefly illuminating tiny
graveyards with wooden crosses, startled eyes, abandoned
orchards, the dead trees bare as midwinter, elderly motels, the
shabby little cottages locked tight and dark with NO VACANCY
signs flickering overhead. The tunnels were brief orange
chutes pitching us out into a darkness even more profound;

the huddles of houses and gas stations and cafés merely toys dropped by the road by a forgetful child. We stopped for the night in Cache Creek, a place that always seems to me like those flimsy Western towns built on movie lots, all fronts with nothing behind. The motel was called the Castle Inn. It had wooden battlements and a single phone in the hallway that would permit only outgoing calls. Its basement level was a labyrinth of hallways with hidden alcoves, pictures of soldiers in battledress and old Legion magazines littering the shabby coffee tables.

Neil and I ate something, somewhere. After that, we went for a walk, searching out the side streets that led away from the two highways that intersected downtown. We followed quiet streets lined with old frame houses held up by vines and creepers. Invariably these roads eventually bumped into the soft curves of the hills and stopped, forcing us to retrace our steps. Finally we found a newer road that climbed one of these hills, winding higher and higher until the houses petered out and there were only streetlights humming over yellow pools on the tarmac as they waited for developments. Up there, the noise of the constant traffic below was insignificant, the neon glare muted. There was nothing but wind and darkness, the breath of sage and savage stars an arm's-length away.

"Just one stride and we could step into space," Neil murmured.

I've lost track of the number of times he has echoed my thoughts.

"I don't think there's anything but space," I replied. "No earth yet. It's only the Second Day."

I could just make out the pale disk of his face turning toward me.

"So no people either?"

His words, ordinary enough, seemed charged with significance. The wind stirred about me and something inside was crumbling, trickling steadily down as if I were an hourglass emptying, leaving behind an empty, echoing shell. In its place, the wondrous darkness flooded in, through my eyes, my ears, my nose, my mouth, coursing among the roots of my hair, infiltrating every separate pore in my skin, seeking out capillaries and following the snaking blood vessels to my heart and lungs, surging along neural pathways and ganglia and pouring into my brain, filling it up and up until it lapped darkly at the very top of my skull and I disappeared.

"No," said my invisible mouth, "I haven't been invented yet."

That night, protected by plywood battlements, I floated once more through the garden and the wood, and, in the hollow house above the water, waited in vain for a sign.

TWELVE

The weather that next day was downright insensitive, Stephen. As we got nearer to Vanderhoof, my mood darkened, but the sky was an improbable slab of ultramarine, the poplars, by contrast, lit from within to a shivering incandescent yellow. Hey, I wanted to shout, haven't you guys heard of the pathetic fallacy?

Neil, too, was unreasonably cheerful. He kept up a stream of observations, and the flora and fauna obligingly provided him with material: crows doing rollicking barrel rolls; a coyote trotting across the road with a dead chicken in its mouth; a particularly striking stand of aspen posing for maximum effect against some black spruce.

I couldn't muster any interest or admiration. The hum of the tires echoed a drone inside my skull, maddening as the whine of a mosquito in a darkened bedroom. *What if there's no mistake? If you aren't who you thought you were, who are you? Where do you come from? What will become of you, losing yourself, bit by bit?* This infuriating litany without responses filled the miles, filled my head with its upturned inflections. It was like being trapped with a Valley Girl in full spate, and the only way to turn her off was to confront my father, but the number of kilometres on the sign posts were shrinking far too slowly.

At last, we turned left onto Highway 16. For the very first time, I welcomed the sight of Mr. P.G.'s absurd stick figure by the Tourist Information Office. Last lap. Climb up and up out of the bowl that holds Prince George and the stink of the pulp mills, past the farms with their great bales of hay stored in long lines, the newly cleared fields littered with piles of tree trunks waiting to burn, past the track where the trotting horses used to practise and now graze quietly, past the trees crowding to the edge of the road, past the mouths of logging roads, the small dark lakes, the beaver dams, the herd of goats and the Holsteins, past the sawmill and the tiny forest planted in the 1960s, then past the sign that lists all the churches in Vanderhoof, and down and down the long hill, past the Co-op and across the railway line, to the river and home.

"Damn!" I said as we pulled into my parents' driveway. Your big pickup was parked by the door. "I hoped we'd get here first. I wanted to talk to Dad before Stephen arrived."

Neil looked at me. "Take your time," he advised. "Choose your moment. It's waited for you more than forty years, it won't go away now."

But I was like the child who sees all the presents piled under the tree on Christmas morning and is then compelled to wait until after breakfast to open them. Waiting, after all the waiting, seemed unthinkable; my legs were already striding across the driveway, round the side of the house to the back door, the statements, sounding strangely like accusations, and the questions lining up, jostling, just behind my lips. I threw open the kitchen door.

Mum turned from the stove where she was attending to a large turkey. She was wearing quilted silver oven mitts and held a baster in one hand. Her glasses were steamed up. She looked as if she had been conducting some obscene medical procedure or, alternatively, welding the turkey's orifices shut.

"Oh," she said, "there you are."

Mum always had an eye for the obvious.

"Where's Neil?" she went on before I could respond.

"Here," he said, stepping over the doormat and seizing her in a bearhug, whirling her around, feet off the ground, while she squealed and held the baster out of harm's way.

"Put me down, you silly bugger!" she commanded. "I'll be getting grease all over your nice sweater."

She pretended to be cross, pounding his shoulder until he dropped her with a thump, but she was secretly pleased and giddy as a girl. Watching, I felt a familiar stir of envy. You could always tease her the same way, Stephen, but it fell flat whenever I tried it. What was it about me that made playfulness impossible? Around Mum I was still the little girl I had once been, held away, forced inward, but conscious all the time of the watchful eye, the unspoken criticism, and something else, something unnamed. Could it have been fear?

"I could do with some help with the Brussels," she said. "There's a sharp knife in the drawer."

I opened my mouth to ask where Dad was, but Jason and Vanessa erupted into the kitchen at that moment.

"Where are you going?" asked Mum.

"We're just going to play," said Vanessa.

"Stay away from that river," said Mum. "If you fall in, I'm not going to jump in to rescue you. Don't say I didn't warn you!" She burrowed in a drawer. "Here," she said, holding a knife out to me, "the sprouts are on the bottom shelf in the fridge."

"I rather wanted to talk to Dad."

"He's in the living room, watching the football with Stephen and Holly. He does like his football, though what he sees in it I don't know, there's more stopping than starting in that game, and as for those silly costumes they wear, what's the point of a game you have to wear armour for, that's what I say, and those daft towels they have flapping about in front, how could grown men make themselves look so silly? But then, your dad enjoys it, and what's the harm really, though I have to say it takes up an awful lot of time, and they run on into the regular programs far too often, that's not fair, is it?"

I got no help from Neil.

"That's for me," he said.

"Ask them all if they want something to drink," called Mum as he disappeared.

I started on the Brussels sprouts.

While I was still carving Xs in their stumps, you came into the kitchen with Neil to rummage in the fridge for beer. I can still feel the weight of your arm slung around my shoulders, hugging me close.

"Hey," you said, "how's tricks?"

"Okay, how about you?"

"As well as can be expected," you replied with a grin. "Isn't that what they say?"

"You look good," I said.

You did look quite good if you didn't look closely. Your head was furred with a bloom of pale hair and your colour was better. You had regained some weight and no longer looked as if you'd stolen the clothes of a much larger street person. But when I looked closer, I could see a puffiness about your face that was bloated rather than a healthy sleekness, and a wariness in your eyes that had never been there before, as if you were always listening for ominous sounds deep inside, inaudible to anyone else, that would herald some minute shifting, a crazing, hairline cracks that would signal imminent catastrophe.

"Can't complain," you said, and I heard the despondency behind your familiar jaunty smile, the resignation forced to masquerade as upbeat optimism for the sake of Holly and the kids. Sadness had drifted down onto your life like tiny particles of silt, and I was about to add another layer to the sediment. In the meantime, like you, I could only take refuge in banalities.

"Chin up," I said, "you're doing great."

"He certainly is," Mum chimed in, looking up from the packet of stuffing she was reading, "and when he gets that transplant he'll be right as rain, won't you, love?"

"Oh, right as rain," you echoed. You looked out of the window, where a hard grey line now edged the sparkling sky, and grinned at me ruefully. It was so hard to meet your eyes.

"I have to talk to you," I muttered, "but not now. I really need to talk to Dad first."

Your smile slipped a notch and you held my gaze for a long moment. Then you squeezed my shoulder, nodded, and turned away.

"I'll go check on the kids," you said. "Make sure they're not drowning."

"Put a coat on," Mum called after you, "we don't want you getting a chill."

I thought I might be able to corner Dad after that, but Mum found me other jobs. I could almost believe she was trying her best to sidetrack me. I polished cutlery, lifted rarely used bowls from the top shelves of cupboards, washed and dried the best glassware, whipped cream and squeezed it into ornate patterns on top of a towering chocolate cake that was standing in for dessert. Mum had long ago fallen into the habit of Thanksgiving dinner but had resisted some of the North American trimmings, like pumpkin pie.

"Can't see what all the fuss is about," she would say scornfully. "Anything that needs that amount of spice and sugar to make it edible can't be worth eating in the first place."

It was the same with yams, or sweet potatoes. "Unnatural," she'd say, "ugly things, and I've never held with sweet things on your dinner, it's just like spreading jam on your meat."

By the time I'd exhausted all her distractions, Neil had gone out to help Dad split and stack some firewood, Holly had come into the kitchen and was stirring gravy in a large pan, Mum was loudly ordering Stephen and the two kids out of the way as she heaved the turkey out of the oven, and I had been pushed into a corner by the fridge with a bottle of Schweppes and a lemon to make myself a gin and tonic. There was too much noise, too much canvassing of opinion about the relative merits of brown and white meat, too much judicious poking and exclamations of satisfaction at the turkey, steamily perfect in its brown glory on the serving dish, too many bodies in the way. I began to see the force of Neil's suggestion to choose my time; I also began to despair of ever finding it.

"Dinner's ready!" carolled Mum, and everyone trooped to the table.

The meal was an ordeal. I passed plates and dishes, ate, talked, and joked with the rest, but it was a performance, the big dinner party scene in a play from the 1950s. The illusion of acting on a stage was heightened by the darkness outside the window. The brightly lit room with the flames from the fireplace reflected in the brass ornaments, and the glass-fronted china cupboard was a highly realistic set, and beyond the fourth wall, invisible to us, sat rows and rows of pallid faces avidly eavesdropping on our lives.

I considered giving them the drama they craved. I could seize the next lull in the conversation, I thought, and toss my question into the momentary silence.

"The doctor tells me I can't be your daughter," I'd say. "How do you explain that?"

And it would roll there on the table, a little hand grenade without its pin coming to rest by the remains of the chocolate cake, while everyone gazed stupidly at this thing that would blow apart all pretence, before scrambling, too late, to defuse it with explanation and apology.

Or it might be a dud, I thought. *There'll be a perfectly*

simple explanation, and everyone will laugh at my histrion-
ics, and it will be the most awful anti-climax in the history of
theatre. I hesitated.

But it had not occurred to me that this performance we
were giving might be a puppet show. The puppet master had
other plans.

Mum was just stirring herself to ask who would like coffee
or tea when Holly blurted out a question. Her voice was
strained as if she were keeping tight rein on her desire to know
the answer, passing it off as a casual interest, no more. Her
fingers were twisting and untwisting her napkin, I noticed.

"Livvy, by the way, have you heard any results from the tests?"

I looked at Neil. He nodded faintly.

Centre stage. Spotlights full in my face. I swallowed.

"Yes," I said and stopped. The others waited.

"Well?" said Holly. How appropriate, I thought, that it's the
other outsider who's precipitating this.

I looked straight at you. Your face filled my vision as if there
were no others in the room.

"I'm so sorry, I'm no match, not even borderline. I'm so sorry,
I'm not any use to you."

Holly's hand had gone to her mouth and her big blue eyes
filled like pools.

"What will he do?" she quavered. Jason and Vanessa looked
anxiously from face to face.

"Is my daddy going to die?" Vanessa's small voice wobbled
too.

"No, stupid," said Jason firmly. "If Aunty Livvy can't give Dad
some of her marrow, I will, or you can, but you're a bit young for
that, I expect."

Vanessa subsided with this assurance and clung to Holly
instead, two pretty faces equipped for perkiness creased
instead with anxiety.

"There's a brave boy!" cried Mum approvingly. "But you won't have to do that, dear, it's obviously all a mistake. Aunty Livvy will make them do the tests again, and it'll all be all right, you'll see."

Dad nodded and looked at me beseechingly.

But you were before me. "That's already been done, I bet," you said, "hasn't it?"

It was my turn to nod.

"So that's it," you said firmly. "We'll have to go another route. But I don't understand. Didn't you say you weren't even a borderline match? How's that possible? Wouldn't that mean . . . ?"

"Yes, it would."

"But . . ."

"What are you talking about?" demanded Holly. "What *would* it mean? You can't guarantee a match, can you? Even with brothers and sisters?"

"No," said Neil gently, and I suddenly realized he had taken my hand in his, "but there are always points of similarity between siblings. If there are none, it means they aren't related at all."

"What do you mean? Livvy's Stephen's sister, isn't she?"

"That's how I feel," I said, "that's how I'll always feel, but the biology gets in the way. Stephen is Mum and Dad's son, but with my blood group I can't possibly be their daughter."

Mum had been silent for a time following all this, but now I became aware that she was rapidly coming to a boil. Her face was flushed and she was making flustered little movements with her hands, rapidly folding napkins and throwing them down again.

"That's a wicked thing to say!" she cried. "What do you mean by it? Of course you're our daughter! No doctor's got the right to say different, what can he know, silly fool, we'll get another one and you'll see, we'll make him eat his words. How dare anyone say such a thing! Fine thing when doctors tell you your own children don't belong to you! I'd like to see him tell me to my face! Who does he think he is? What does he think we are? Tell her, Bill!"

I turned to Dad, who was staring at the cake crumbs on his plate.

"How about it, Dad? Am I your daughter or not?"

He squirmed uncomfortably and would not look at me.

"Er, not exactly," he mumbled finally. "*Technically*, I suppose, you could, you'd have to say, mmm, *not*."

Rage made me cruel. I wanted to force him to say it all, to stop wriggling and come clean. The force of my intensity clamped his hands to the edge of the table and turned the knuckles white.

"So I'm adopted."

He stroked his Crippen moustache.

"Ah, well, mmm," he said cautiously. "You could say that. In a manner of speaking."

"Bill?" whispered Mum. "What are you doing? What are you saying?"

And as we all stared at him, dumbfounded, the lights dimmed and surged twice, then went out altogether.

THIRTEEN

Dad escaped to the basement with a large flashlight and exhumed propane lamps and candles, handing up the emergency box packed with supplies for just such an occasion, including a tiny camping stove. Soon there was a wan, unstable glow from candles stuck on saucers, and the lamps hissed like infuriated snakes. Neil had been commissioned to fetch in more wood, even though there was still a pile on the hearth. It would have been a cozy family scene, everyone sitting round the fire, the red glow reflected on their faces, except that the abandoned table, strewn with plates and the lopsided remains of the cake, was a reminder of what had just gone before.

Neil came in with an armful of wood.

"Easy to see what's happened," he said. "Have you looked outside?"

The children ran to the door; the rest of us merely looked inquiring.

"It's raining," he said, "but the temperature must have dropped like a stone when it got dark. It's freezing out there, literally. The weight of this ice has probably brought some lines down, or a tree."

Vanessa ran back in. "It's all shiny," she said. "Jason fell on his butt on the driveway. And the trees have gone all bendy, like this," and she demonstrated a graceful arc with her fingertips nearly brushing the floor.

"We're not going to try to drive back to Prince tonight, are we?" asked Holly anxiously.

There were murmurs of agreement, which ended with Holly bustling off with Mum to find bedding and places to put it for all the extra bodies, the two children nipping at their heels. In the sudden silence, Neil and you, Dad and I tried not to look at one another, none of us willing to poke the subject that lay quiet for now, but each knowing that someone would have to reach out a prodding foot eventually.

A log slumped in the fireplace, and a vein of resin exploded in a startling flare. You took the plunge.

"So," you said, "there's more to the story, isn't there, Dad?"

Dad checked his moustache again. *The good doctor, scuppered by radio, met by police as he docks in New York, little Ethel on his arm, wonders if his luck has finally run out.* I watched his Adam's apple jerk convulsively between the stringy tendons of his throat.

"Well. Yes, I suppose so."

There was a pause. You looked exasperated. I could have kissed you.

"Come on, Dad! You can't just leave it there! Don't you think you owe it to Livvy?"

Dad stared at his hands. Finally, he looked up, took a deep breath, and nodded.

"You've got to understand," he said, "it was wartime. Everything was different then. You just did what you thought you had to, it was such chaos, specially in the Blitz, specially at night."

For a second, the horror of those nights of bombardment peeped out in his voice.

"What I mean," he continued urgently, "things happened, and people did things, I could tell you, that they'd never dream of normally. Sometimes they were good, and sometimes they were bad, I don't know how to explain it . . ."

"Nobody was playing by the usual rules, I guess," offered Neil.

"That's it, exactly," said Dad gratefully, looking directly at us for the first time. "It wasn't that there weren't any rules, there were rules coming out of our ears—I knew all about that because I was a warden, I had to enforce the blackout and make people go to the shelters, stuff like that—but you knew anything could happen, one minute things would be like they always were, and the next, who knew? Your whole life could be blown to kingdom come in the middle of the night. And you had to be prepared to act in that sort of mess, no time to think. It does things to you, that does."

Holly slipped quietly in between you and Neil on the couch. I wanted to jolt Dad out of his preamble. I was now convinced he'd done something shameful.

"Okay," I said, "so this was a time when anything was possible. So why not just tell us what happened, and what you did."

"Yes. Well, we're talking about 1941, early on. I don't know if you remember where we lived in London, Livvy? Magdalen Road, it was, just off Tooley Street in Bermondsey. It wasn't much, but it was near London Bridge Station, so I could walk to work. Trouble was, it wasn't far from Tower Bridge and the docks neither, so we made a lovely target for all the bombers. You've no idea what that was like, night after night, huddling in the shelters, listening to the sirens and the bombs going off, bang, bang, bang, getting louder and louder as they dropped them in line, wondering if you'd catch the next one. People were brave, but they must have been affected. Half of us were barmy, probably, but everyone was the same so nobody noticed, I suppose. Nothing you could do about it, anyway."

Out of the corner of my eye I saw Mum standing in the doorway, but Dad went on, caught up now in the stream of his narrative, sustained by our attention, and she did not approach.

"Well, one day I come off shift and walked home as quick as

I could. I should tell you, we had a baby, a little girl, we called her Olivia because she was born during a war, olive branches, peace, get it? She was a lovely little thing, about a year old then, but she'd always been delicate ever since she was born, and we always worried. I didn't like to leave your mum alone too long, but I had to. Anyway, it was dark, and I knew she'd be scared.

"I thought for a moment Mum had gone out. When I opened the front door, it was pitch-dark inside. I called out, and felt for the light, and when I switched it on, I got the shock of my life.

"There was Mum, sitting in her chair by the fireplace, holding the baby on her lap, all wrapped in blankets. She looked like a blooming parcel.

"'What you doing in the dark?' I says, joking like, but I could see already it wasn't no joke. The baby didn't stir, and nor did Mum. In fact, she looked as if she'd been turned to stone. She was pale as pale, almost blue, like the milk we got in them days. Olivia's face, what I could see of it, was darker, lavender colour, not right. And when I took Mum's hand to stir her up a bit, she was cold, but not half as cold as the baby's face when I touched her cheek.

"'Mavis,' I say and shake her arm. 'What's the matter? What happened?'

"Her eyes sort of focus on me then, very slow, and she says, 'I just can't get the baby to wake up for her lunch.'

"The baby's bath's still standing on the table, towels hanging over the chair. The water's stone cold.

"'I've wrapped her up, but she doesn't get warm,' Mum says. 'Should we take her to the hospital?'

"Guy's Hospital's just down the road, but I know Olivia's beyond any help from them. I haven't a clue what's actually happened. But there's your mum, acting very strange. I didn't know what would happen if I just up and told her the baby was dead. I didn't even know if she'd had any hand in it or if it was just an accident. I couldn't leave her alone like that and go for help, and we didn't have any truck with the neighbours. Going to the hospital seemed as good an idea as any.

"I'd just got Mum's coat on her, which wasn't easy because she wouldn't put the baby down, not for a minute, when the sirens go off. That sound! It just hits you in the pit of the stomach, that awful howl, sliding up and down, up and down, till you'd like to scream. I got us bundled into the shelter in the back—I think Mum would have gone out in the streets otherwise, I don't think it registered there was an air raid—and we huddle in there for what feels like hours, not saying a word, while the bombs fall.

"Well, the All Clear sounds at last, and we crawl out. It's still dark, of course, but the sky looks red in places, and you can hear the fire engines. Nobody takes any notice of us.

"We turn left out of our street and almost run down Bermondsey Street. Mum never liked going under the railway bridges even in daylight, and I have to admit, they were stinking dirty things, always dripping filthy water and pigeon muck, and you'd think they were coming down on your head when a train went over. So we run that bit, and then slow down to get our breath when we turn into St. Thomas Street. If we hadn't, I don't think we'd ever have heard it. There was a building up nearer the hospital that had been hit and was on fire, but nobody had got there yet, probably because it was a warehouse of some kind and all locked up for the night.

"Anyway, as we pass the end of Fenning Street, I hear a cry. Well, I had enough to worry about with Mum so strange and the baby and all, but I was a warden, I couldn't just walk away from the chance that someone needed help, injured maybe, but still alive, so I stop. Mum stops too, but I don't think anything registered, she was just stopping because I did, like a robot. Then I hear it again, and that time even Mum's head turns, because it sounds like a child sobbing, hopeless enough to break your heart. We never say a word, just turn down the street. There was a seed merchant's near the corner, big old barn of a place, with steps up to a covered porch and a great solid door.

"The bomb that had done for the warehouse up the road had shaken loose some of the big facing stones over the doorway, and they'd crashed down. They're lying there, and so's a young woman. And beside her sat a toddler, crying her heart out.

"There was nothing to be done for the poor girl. One of those big stones must have hit her head, smashed it. Not even her own mother would have recognized her face. I felt for a pulse in her wrist, just in case, but nothing. She was a goner, poor thing, though her hand was still warm. I reckon she'd put the baby as far back by the door as she could when she was caught out in the air raid and tried to shield her with her own body. That way she was right underneath the stones when they fell, but they missed the kiddie. I reckoned she had to be a stranger; nobody who lived round there would have been out at that time of night with a child.

"And what were we going to do about *her*? She sits there, howling, louder than ever now that we're there. Her face is scarlet and her nose is running, and as I look, she holds up her little arms to be picked up. Before I can do anything, Mum stoops down and lays Olivia beside the dead woman and picks up the other baby. She drags a hankie from her pocket and wipes her nose and face. Then she turns and walks down the steps.

"I tell you, it was like a dream. One of those dreams where you can't move, or you open your mouth and no sounds come out when you talk. There's my wife walking away up the street with somebody else's baby, and I freeze. I can't do a thing to stop her. It's almost as if I don't *want* to stop her. There's this little voice inside my head saying, *What difference does it make? Your baby's dead, and this little girl's mother is dead, it won't matter to them. The little girl needs a home and you've got one, and maybe it will be just the thing for Mavis.* God help me, it even whispered that I couldn't afford a funeral, and this way I wouldn't have to, somebody else would find the bodies soon and deal with them and we could just go on the way we always had. And what if Mavis *had* done something, what would happen to her, to us?

"I'm not making excuses for myself. I know it was wrong. I should have stopped her right then, when she put Olivia down, made her go to the hospital and face the truth, I know I should. But can you understand? By the time I'd got myself moving and followed Mum down the road, it was too late. She was going back home and I just fell in step beside her. She said, 'It's too late for Olivia to be up. She needs to be in her bed,' and I nodded and that was that."

There was a muffled sob. We'd forgotten all about Mum. She was sitting on the floor, leaning against the doorframe, tears streaming down her face. Dad got up and crouched awkwardly beside her, murmuring comfort and rubbing her back as if she were a baby suffering indigestion.

And how did I react? I think it's true to say I didn't. I couldn't. I was completely numb. Like a butterfly in that vulnerable moment when it splits open the chrysalis and struggles soft and damp and crumpled into the world, I stayed quite still. I could feel my skin losing its exquisite sensitivity as it hardened in the air, the folds smoothing out, the colours sharp and new. Underneath the exoskeleton, blood banged along its pathways, all the systems ticked over, gurgling and replicating, air wafted in and out, neurons fired, but all unattended. In my head, there was a great calm. The fact was there, installed and taking up all the room, but all I could see was the image of that small child, who was me, crying in the dark, and holding up her arms in supplication, and the still figure, who was my mother, lying crushed and faceless by her side.

"I wonder who that poor girl was?" mused Holly.

And that, of course, was the question.

With the shock of revelation past, the others turned to ways of dealing with the discomfort. Holly went off to make tea and check on the children. You and Neil helped Mum and Dad off the floor and settled them into their chairs, made up the fire that had burned low, fetched boxes of tissues, and supplied yourselves with beer. There was an air of bustle, the normal busyness of life starting up again all round me, while I crouched in my carapace, where sound was muffled and distant, and the heat of the burning wood did not reach.

Mum's tear-stained face was beseeching. "I'm sorry," she snuffled. "I'm so sorry. My mother always told me my sins would find me out. Well, they have, but I never meant to hurt you."

Dad looked at me sheepishly, and I realized they were waiting for a response. Forgiveness? Exoneration? Was I supposed to say, Oh well, never mind, it doesn't really change anything, does it? But there was a chill coming over my heart too, and the words that would have made their anxious faces relax stuck in my throat like kipper bones. As if she could sense this, Mum spoke again, sadly.

"I'm sorry," she repeated. "I don't know what came over me. I thought it would be all right, but it never has been, has it?"

Dad broke in then. "I hoped you'd be a little more understanding," he said reproachfully. "After all, you of all people should know what it's like to lose a child. You go a bit mad, don't you?"

I stared at him in disbelief, the anger that had been swelling just under the surface erupting into a full rolling boil. I jumped to my feet.

"Somebody *took* Daniel," I shouted, "just like *you* took *me*! Is that what you'd say to my real family? Don't you think *they'd* find it hard to make excuses for what you've done? How do you think they felt when they lost my mother and me? We belonged somewhere, you know!"

As I ran from the room, I had the satisfaction of seeing their faces flatten with shock.

Outside it was very cold. It had stopped raining, and the clouds, apart from a few stray rags, had cleared. The stars were pitiless, and the moon rode high among them. Everything glittered in the strange blue light, and I could see that all the trees and shrubs, which still carried most of their leaves, were bent under the weight of the ice that had coated every surface. The air was full of noises: tinklings, like thousands of tiny wind chimes, slitherings, creakings as branches strained and sighed, followed sometimes by loud reports almost like gunshots as the branches snapped off, thudding unseen to the ground with a rush and a distant shattering of glass.

I stood there hugging myself until a fine tremor shook me uncontrollably. My mind groped about. The question lit up a billboard somewhere in the frontal lobes, relentless flashing neon, as impossible to ignore as a strip joint in an elementary school. WHO AM I? WHO AM I? WHO AM I?

I was really in danger, I felt, of disappearing. The ecstatic sensation that had swept over me on top of the hill in Cache Creek now seemed mere fantasy, idiotic and ugly when there was a real chance of having to recreate myself. I didn't completely lose touch with reality. I knew I couldn't wash out the relationship with you, that love, simply because it was founded on a lie. Nor, in fact, could I ignore my upbringing, angry though I was. I was still Neil's wife. But how, I wondered, would Neil see me now? Even with the best will in the world, thinking to yourself, it doesn't matter, it makes no difference, would it really be possible to carry on as if nothing whatsoever had happened? Wouldn't there have to be a little recoil, instinctive as the snail's horn, from contact with the unexpected and bizarre?

As for me, I felt bereft. What is a mother without her son? What is a daughter without parents? A sister without a brother? What is a person without a name? The only thing left, it seemed, was Neil, and the suffering we had shared that bound us together tighter than joy.

An arm descended on my shoulder, and I was suddenly aware that my body was shaking without any help from me and wouldn't stop.

"Come inside," said Neil, "we don't want a case of hypothermia on top of everything else."

"How about a case of mistaken identity?"

"Ah," he replied, "some people will do anything to be interesting. Just adds to your mysterious allure."

We were a quiet bunch at the breakfast table next morning. Mum moved about softly, filling cups and cutting bread, dark circles under her eyes. Dad gazed out of the window, the bristles on his chin clearly visible, a grey-and-silver stubble that lent him a down-at-heel look, as if he had fallen on hard times overnight. Even the children were subdued, and Holly soon swept them off to pack up their things ready for the trip back to Prince George. By mid-morning the roads had cleared enough to drive safely. You drew me aside just before leaving.

"Don't be too hard on them," you said. "So you can't be Wonder Woman for me this time—you bought me some good years before. And you'll always be my big sister, doesn't matter who you are, and don't forget it."

I tried to remember the first part of your instructions when I went to say goodbye to Mum. She looked at me appealingly, waiting to see what my lead would be before she spoke. I could hardly bear her need.

"It's been a shock," I said at last, then added what she wanted to hear. "But I'll get over it. It'll be all right."

Dad had disappeared. I tracked him to his workshop. He was

sitting on a stool beside a vise holding a half-constructed bird feeder. The familiar clean smell of sawdust and wood stain hung on the air. On the bench in front of him lay a small square bag with a strap, rather like an old-fashioned box camera. He pushed it toward me as I stood there waiting for him to say something.

"You should have this," he said. "I've kept it all these years. Maybe it'll tell you something."

I opened the catch. Inside was a child's Mickey Mouse gas mask. I laid the grotesque thing on the bench. On the inside of the strap that would have gone around the head, someone had written *R. Goodman* in purplish pencil. A search of the carrying case yielded two other treasures. One was a scrap of lined paper that seemed to have been torn from an address book; it read, *Sarah Murphy, 14, Morocco St., London SE1*. The other was a tiny manila envelope. It contained a few seeds with feathery plumes. The outside of the envelope, worn now to the softness of old flannel, bore a very faint inscription, written a long time ago in pencil. I could just make out *Stephanotis* and *—scot —ark*. What the first letters were, I couldn't determine. Squinting at it made it even fuzzier.

"That was round your neck when we . . . found you," said Dad. "We didn't think to leave it behind."

"Good job you didn't!"

The reply came out more energetically than I'd intended. Fact is, I'd just realized that these few objects were all I had of my other self. Valuable in themselves for that reason, but if I was going to recreate myself, they were also the strands of the thread I was going to pull on until I unravelled the whole mystery and finally looked into the face of the person holding on to the other end.

FOURTEEN

When does wish become obsession, Stephen? At what point does a faint desire, the thought that always begins, "If only . . ." turn into need? The morning after the great revelation, when Neil and I drove down the driveway through the tunnel formed by the sagging branches of the willows on either side, I was prepared to be philosophical, to accept what had happened so long ago and move on, somewhat shaken but unbowed. Above all, the morning light encouraged reason. I told myself firmly I had not changed in any way, I was still the sum of my parts as I had always been, and the awkward truth that some stranger had brought me into the world should make little difference to me or anyone else.

But I carried the shabby little case on my lap, and its pathetic contents, though mute, were eloquent.

In the weeks that followed I was drawn to them more and more. When sleep evaded me, I would sit at the kitchen table with the companionable hum of the fridge in the background and spread them out in a line, willing them to give up their secrets. I would finger the strap of the rubber mask and imagine myself as a tiny child compelled to wear it—I, who panic when I get stuck taking off a sweater, convinced I will stifle before I can tear the fabric away from my face. How would I have endured its clinging, smelly rubber embrace? Was I R. Goodman? Rosemary? Rebecca? Roberta? Ruth? I fancied Ruth. I would say the name out loud, testing its feel on my tongue, experimenting with the way my lips had to push out to say the first two syllables, utterly different from the tongue behind the teeth, wide smiling mouth of the name I had used for years. I tried writing it on scraps of paper, taking pleasure in the sinuous R, infinitely preferable to my angle-iron L, but disliking the row of circles in the surname, lying there like runty peas in a pod.

And who, I wondered, was Sarah Murphy? A friend? But if a friend, why had her name and address had to be torn from someone else's address book? The "M" tab was still attached to the scrap of paper. If the book had belonged to my mother, surely she would have brought the whole thing with her, not ruined it by tearing out a page. Was it a relative, then? The surname was different, so an aunt, perhaps? A grandmother? A married sister? The dimensions of the scrap showed that the address book had been very small, one of those that used to come with a short slim pencil to slide down the spine. It was blank on the reverse too, suggesting that the owner of the book knew very few people whose name began with M, or perhaps very few people, period.

From Sheila, whose parents still lived near London, I borrowed an old A–Z. Morocco Street was easy to find. It curved off Bermondsey Street, and there was the Leather Market and Leathermarket Street and Leather Court and Tanner Street, and I had a sudden olfactory memory of the dreadful stench of a tanning factory. But why? And then I saw it. Just a little higher up on the map. Magdalen Street. And what had my father said? They'd turned down Bermondsey Street and run under the railway bridges because Mum was scared of them, and there they were, black lines leading straight to a big square marked London Bridge, and then they'd turned right into St. Thomas Street—yes, and there was the massive block of Guy's Hospital straight ahead—but they'd been diverted into Fenning Street, that little narrow street just on the left, there, when they'd heard my cry. So my mother, if that was my mother, had been making her way to a street just a few blocks south of where Mum and Dad and Olivia lived when she was caught in the open by the air raid and died in the doorway of the warehouse. Was Sarah Murphy expecting her? I wondered. Did she worry when the sirens went off and the bombers droned overhead, and fret even more when the All Clear sounded but nobody came to the door?

It occurred to me that the A–Z might throw some light on the fragmentary "-ark" name on the little envelope. A Park, maybe? I scoured the maps, and the index, patiently running my finger down hundreds of entries in tiny print until my head reeled, but I drew a blank. Whatever it was, it wasn't in London or its immediate environs.

I looked up stephanotis in the *Shorter Oxford* and learned that the name came from a Greek feminine adjective meaning "fit for a crown or wreath" and that it was any of several tropical twining shrubs characterized by fragrant waxy white flowers. Apart from the tongue dexterity I gained by saying "tropical twining shrubs," this was unhelpful, as was the information that S. *floribunda* is also known as Madagascar jasmine. More to the point, the dictionary firmly pointed out that this was grown as a hothouse plant. Now that did introduce some interesting ideas.

The only hothouse I knew of in England was the huge glass and iron edifice at the Royal Botanical Gardens at Kew. I had seen it only in pictures, but I knew it was an engineering marvel, rivalling the Crystal Palace, and the achievement of people who did not have to worry about money, who could afford to indulge their hankering for a tropical paradise of their very own, captive under glass, kept steamily perfect with its own system of boilers and heating ducts. While the hothouse at

Kew was a giant specimen, even modest ones would be expensive to run. You would not find them in backyard gardens, and certainly not behind rows of two-up-two-downs in Bermondsey. But what about all those stately homes that peppered Britain? Wasn't that more likely? And mightn't whatever it was—ark or Park—be one of those? Perhaps I was barking up the wrong tree altogether, deducing a mountain out of a molehill, but it was a place to start looking.

Was I looking?

I was.

By the time I had squeezed this much from the three relics, I was hooked. I could tell myself as often as I liked that it didn't matter, I had to know. The frustration then was the difficulty in accessing more information from a place like Sechelt, with its nice little library and not much else. I could feel the information out there, waiting for me, but for how much longer? The people who'd been around in the war would be getting old, if they weren't dead already; how much longer would the memories I needed to tap be available to me?

Events were already ganging up on me, Stephen, but I think it was Neil who actually made my decision. The brief revival of interest in Daniel provoked by the tenth anniversary of his disappearance—the release of another of those aged photographs whose strangely alien, distant features made me weep and the usual flurry of sightings painstakingly followed up by Detective Mallory, who had finally contacted us once again with the dispiriting news that there was no news—had depressed both of us. I had been toying with waiting until the end of June and spending my summer holiday in England, but the months stretched before me, grey and interminably wet, the evergreens dripping, dripping, and I knew the delay would become unendurable.

Already I found it hard to concentrate on dissecting fetal

pigs, and I was getting a reputation for absentmindedness, forgetting to read memos, forgetting appointments with parents, not completing or returning forms, all of which earned me reproachful looks from Ella and the kind of solicitous questions from Mr. Spalding that concealed a tiny Exacto knife of criticism. *Perhaps they'll be happy to give me a sabbatical. After all, I've worked plenty long enough to earn one.* Even as I had these thoughts, I had dismissed them.

But as I was hanging around Neil's studio one day after school, doing a little desultory tidying, I drifted to the window, where I stood playing with the cord of the blind and staring out at the sea. It looked sullen and fretful, slopping about among the rocks. I couldn't remember if the tide was coming in or going out, and the sea looked as indecisive as I felt.

"You know," said Neil suddenly, "I think you should go to England and see what you can find out."

How like him to cut straight to the point. I tried to do the same.

"You wouldn't mind?"

"Why should I mind? You're obviously never going to be satisfied until you've done all you can to find out. It'll be an itch forever. Scratch it, for God's sake!"

"When should I go then?"

"Sooner the better, if that's what it takes to get you out of my light and to stop fidgeting so I can work. Seriously, why don't you take a leave of absence from school, and go during the next semester? Leave at the beginning of February?"

It sounded so easy, put that way. But.

"I can't just go off and leave you alone," I protested.

"Sure you can," said Neil. He turned away from his work to face me squarely. "There's been enough hopelessness. Maybe *this* search will be successful. Don't you think that would make me happy too, to see you find what you're looking for?"

They won't let me go just like that, I told myself, as I wrote the letter requesting a leave of absence. But they did. Mysteriously, the board granted me leave without hesitation. Possibly it had something to do with the fact that my leave was unpaid, and they could save money on a less costly substitute for a semester. Whatever the reason, I was grateful.

Ella was thrilled.

"It's just like a novel,"she enthused, "or one of those miniseries. That is so *exciting*!"

Sheila was more pragmatic.

"What will you do if you find your family and they're not quite . . . what you expect?"

"You mean will I accept the throne right away or let the usurper stay on?"

"I think I mean more on the lines of what if your father's a mass murderer, or the whole family's spent more time in jail than out? What if they're people you don't like? The kind you'd never want to have anything to do with?"

Trust Sheila to put her finger on the sore spot and keep pressing.

"Well, none of us gets to choose our family, do we? Chances are good we won't like them all, even if we are related. That's not the point, really; I just want to know who they are and where I came from, that's all. I'm missing some vital information about myself that most people have at their fingertips. I just want the same."

"They might not want to know *you*," Sheila said sternly. "Thought about that?"

"Of course I have! I'm not going to force myself on them! I won't demand they put me on their Christmas card lists, for heaven's sake. Credit me with a little sense!"

Charles Grover looked up from his newspaper at the other side of the staff room, alerted by the raised voices. I subsided. Miss Penfold clasped her hands together.

"Well, I think it's very romantic," she said, "just like the knights of the Round Table setting out on a quest, not knowing what they would find or even if they would succeed but going anyway."

I rather suspected Miss Penfold of being a secret admirer of the Pre-Raphaelites and Lord Tennyson and did not quite see myself on a charger, tilting at hostile knights in black armour who wouldn't let me cross fords for no apparent reason apart from bloodymindedness, but I held my tongue, reluctant to spoil her vision. Sheila had no such compunction.

"Oh yes," she said, "or one of those heroes, setting out on the journey full of trials with his tatty old sandals in his hand, ready to face the monster and save the world!"

The gas mask case and its trivial contents flashed across my mind, and I saw myself boarding the plane with them, heading for the unknown, a strange country, strange people, interrupting the story of their lives with the melodrama of my own. Did I have the right to do that? Was my wish to know the only right I needed to intrude and possibly throw their placid existence off course? But surely I was part of their story too. A missing part? A part they had got wrong all these years? Wouldn't they want to set the record straight too? My confidence in the enterprise was oozing away.

"I just want to know my own story," I said lamely.

Ella was her usual practical self.

"And you probably will. Just don't be disappointed if it doesn't work out. There's been a lot of water under the bridge since then."

"Yes," Sheila added, "and don't forget to change the colour of the sails when you come back!"

So in February, I left for England, the gas mask case at the bottom of my carry-on bag. Neil saw me off at Vancouver

Airport on a raw day, when the cloud ceiling pressed close to the sea and the mountains were invisible. The tops of taller buildings poked into the mist, and the air was full of droplets that clung to hair and eyelashes and ran hesitantly down chilled skin.

We stood together in that awkward space just before I walked through security and had to leave him behind. Neil's hands were jammed in the pockets of his pea jacket, his shoulders hunched about his ears. I looked at his familiar long head, the pale hair, tinged now with grey, like a scattering of wood ash, committing him to memory just as he was.

"I'd better go through," I said.

"Yes," he agreed, shifting his weight from one foot to the other. He looked like a disconsolate heron. "Sooner you go, the sooner you come back, I guess."

"I'll be back," I insisted, kissing him. "Look after yourself. Don't forget to eat."

"Right."

I had to end this inane exchange. I turned away, bumping into another woman with a fat, swinging shoulder bag. The apologies got us both past the X-ray machine and the metal detector, and when I turned for a last wave, Neil had already gone. Then I felt miserable, leaving him with so much unsaid, all the fears and regrets hovering between the clichés. I knew he wondered who would be returning; I knew he had even admitted the sneaking anxiety that I wouldn't return, that I would find something over there that would hold me as fast as Calypso hung on to Odysseus, dimming my memories of him, and his claim on me, finally erasing them.

Just to say this could not happen was not enough, nor was it honest. The one reassurance I might have given, that Daniel was a tie that could never break, was the one thing I could not say. So I said nothing, and added my silence to the list of wounds I had inflicted on my husband.

FIFTEEN

I nearly gave up before I even started, you know.

I set out with such *resolve*, so much romantic claptrap about finding The Truth, finding *myself* (as if I weren't hiding in plain sight all the time). All fuelled by intense curiosity, of course, but less noble things too. Resentment. Anger, even. Those months between Thanksgiving and leaving weren't easy, were they? No matter how often all of you told me nothing was different, I couldn't—wouldn't—believe you, not really, deep down. I felt confused, so it seemed everyone must be lying. From the nicest of motives but still faking it. And I was furious that I could do nothing for you, Stephen, and that the fact that I could do nothing had been there all along while I sailed on, seeing myself as your saviour. A cosmic joke. I could hardly bear the thought of you searching out another donor while I had to be just a spectator, as useless to you as I was to Daniel.

So I set off with a fine head of steam, but it's amazing how fast it dissipated. You never consider how hard the little ordinary things are when you've left the familiar.

First my suitcase got rerouted to Glasgow. It caught up with me the next day, but only after I'd stood by the carousel at Heathrow and watched everybody else's bags whirl round without seeing mine. There I was, in a panic before I'd even left the airport!

Then I had to find myself a semi-permanent perch. I had booked a room in a small hotel near the British Museum, thinking that a week there would give me ample opportunity to find somewhere more reasonable. Two days were enough to induce despair. My hotel room, though adequate, was expensive. And cheerless. It was on the third floor, at the front of the building, so the noise of traffic filtered up day and night. The room was very small: a bed with the most unyielding mattress I've ever encountered took up most of the floor space and crowded a desk affair that supported a tiny television, a straight chair with chrome legs, and an armless chair upholstered in Regency stripes into an uneasy line under the window. The only way to circumnavigate the room was sideways, and I banged my leg on the corner of the bed by the door until I had a permanent bruise that didn't fade for weeks.

One look at the ads and a few calls and I was consumed with anxiety about finding a place to live that wouldn't bankrupt me before I even started looking for any long-lost relatives. Almost immediately, I twigged that there was no such thing as a cheap hotel in London, even when the exterior or the surroundings suggested that the owners couldn't possibly charge much with a straight face. My options took a downward slide. I found myself scouring the Rooms for Rent ads for Kings Cross and Brixton and Lambeth, checking stations farther and farther out on the branch lines, considering the YWCA and youth hostels. At night I would roll about the bed like a billiard ball, hearing the clamour from the street, wondering why I had come at all.

It was the chambermaid who rescued me. Her head, beaming like the Cheshire Cat's, popped round the door one morning. I was slumped on the bed trying to summon the energy for the day's search.

"Oh, I'm sorry," she said, "I t'ought you'd be gone. I'll come back later."

Her cheerful black face was already retreating. I didn't want the warm Jamaican accent to follow suit.

"No, come in!" I shouted. "If you can get in with me here," I added as she edged round the door.

"We be all right long as you stay on the bed."

"Kind of defeats the object, doesn't it?"

She smiled and gestured at the litter of classified sections surrounding me.

"You want me to take these out of your way?"

"You might as well," I said, "they're not doing me much good."

"Are you looking for somet'ing special?"

"I'm looking for a room to rent that doesn't cost the earth, somewhere I don't need an armed guard if I'm out after dark."

She laughed.

"Hard to find that somewhere. Have you t'ought about places outside London? Somewhere like Wimbledon? Kingston? Try the local papers, and places where people put up adverts—laundromats, newsagents, like that. They're the ones don't cost so much, not like these," and she rattled the papers in her hand.

So it was that I set out for Wimbledon and started a search for those boards covered with plain white cards and torn scraps of paper in the corners of windows crammed with cheap sweets and toys, newspapers and plastic pens, or hanging over the worn chairs and cracked laundry baskets, vying for wall space with the detergent and bleach dispensers, the industrial-sized dryers and the boxes full of odd socks.

In the end none of these produced anything worth pursuing. I gained an indelible impression that the entire population of Wimbledon were semiliterate owners of aging cars dying to get rid of their white elephants. There was a thriving business in the exchange of baby garments and nursery furniture "like new," and a somewhat less flourishing trade, to judge by the dinginess of the cards, in gents' suits, bridesmaids' dresses (fuchsia satin, worn once), and assorted LP records (mono only).

Depression was setting in once more, when I caught sight of a tiny store a little way down a side street. It was a grocery of a kind long since mown down by the supermarket juggernauts. It resembled one I could dimly remember Mum going to before we moved to Canada. I wondered if this one had tins of broken biscuits, big drums of dusty currants, and a gleaming bacon slicer? Maybe even bags of Smith's Crisps with a twist of salt in dark blue waxed paper?

The interior was dark, and the only thing I could see through the window was a display case for Mr. Kipling's cakes and a refrigerated cabinet full of Coke and 7 Up, disappointingly modern. There was an old-fashioned counter, dim in the background.

On the inside of the door, where you couldn't avoid seeing it as you went in, was a single white card. It was written in a beautiful angular hand. It read:

For Rent
Single room in a large house in an older residential neighbourhood. Suitable for mature lady. References required. Applicants should be able to climb stairs and tolerate animals. Enquire within.

I pushed open the door. A bell jangled discreetly. The shop was overcrowded, the result of modern packaging and promotion techniques at war with the solid fixtures of an older style. I squeezed past piles of Tide and Omo. Packets of Ryvita and Jaffa Cakes mounded in front of tall dark wood shelves that wouldn't have been out of place in a library. I was breathing in the smell, which was exactly right despite the Coke cans and the thoroughly modern freezer compartments, when the owner parted the bead curtains at the back of the store and took her place behind the counter, the long strings of beads clashing behind her.

"Can I help you?"

She was a small woman, deft and contained. She looked at me, head slightly tilted, dark eyes bright and alive. Like a wren.

"I've come in to inquire about the card on the door," I replied. "I'm looking for a place to rent."

"You realize it's just a room?"

"Well, yes, that's all I really need. I just want a place to call home while I'm in England."

"That's all right then. I didn't want you to go round and then find it wouldn't suit. We don't want to disturb the ladies for nothing."

"The ladies?"

"The house belongs to three old ladies, regulars of mine, been coming here for donkey's years. Between you and me, I don't think they really wanted to rent out, but I suppose they find it hard to keep that great barn of a place going. You'd think they'd sell and move somewhere smaller, but they've lived there for years and it's hard to change when you get older, isn't it? Did you want the phone number, then?"

A short call from a public phone at the station got me the address from a gentle, refined voice after it had asked me a preliminary question.

"Do you have strong legs?"

I wondered what kind of tower this room might be in.

"I think they're in tolerably good shape."

"They would need to be," said the voice. "This is how you get here."

The house, I was delighted to learn, was a ten-minute walk from the station. But going there from the noisy main street and the busy railway lines was like entering another world. Prosperous Victorian merchants and businessmen had built these houses for their large families and small armies of servants. They would use the newfangled railway to get to their offices in the city, but could retire at night to an almost rural calm, surrounded by fields and heath and small villages. Life in the country for the landless but wealthy bourgeoisie.

The street was lined with huge old trees, limes and chestnuts, and sycamores as I learned later. The houses were all tall, three storeys at least, a fantastic miscellany of architectural styles from Gothic arched windows with stained glass to black-and-white Elizabethan half-timbering. The overall effect was confused, but a confusion that time had softened to an endearing eccentricity, backed as it was by the certainty of so much enduring red brick.

My destination was a case in point. The long driveway, much obscured by dripping laurel bushes and rhododendrons, led to a circular gravelled area outside the front door. Like its neighbours, the house was built of brick, but here the dominant influence was medieval. The windows were white stone, Perpendicular style, and the panes were leaded. The front door was a Gothic arch, at the top of a flight of worn steps. More steps led down to a basement or cellar door.

There were three floors as well as the basement. The edge of the roof, far above, sported crenellations like miniature battlements, and I could just see tiny dormers in the roof, which indicated an attic. Was the room up there?

A further eccentricity was the tower at the corner of the house. It was attached to the house proper by a colonnade at ground level, rose up foursquare, punctuated by lancet windows, and culminated in an open belfry. There was even a bell. It reminded me of the pictures I'd seen of Tuscan churches.

A large white cat sat on the top step. It stared at me with eyes green as peeled grapes.

A gargoyle head of brass hung on the door, but I opted for an ancient bell push. The house was so large, I thought, the ladies probably wouldn't hear my knocking, not even if it reverberated like the sound of doom in "The Fall of the House of Usher."

The door swung open silently, and a face peered cautiously round its edge as the cat shot inside.

"Good afternoon," I said. "I've come about the room. I phoned just a little while ago."

The face, and the hand clenched on the door, relaxed visibly. The door opened wider.

"Of course, do come in. You got here much sooner than I expected. May I take your coat?"

I decided to hang on to my coat. The air in the dim hallway was decidedly chill.

"Come through this way, my dear. We tend to stay the other side of the house mostly. Come and meet the others. Mind the umbrella stand, it always takes people by surprise."

It did. Suddenly a massive stand with receptacles like elephant legs at the bottom for umbrellas and a rack of hooks and pegs, branching out like moose antlers, at the top for hats and coats loomed out of the darkness. My guide was disappearing down a long hallway and I feared losing her altogether, but then she flung open a door and a stream of light showed the way.

"Girls, here's the young woman about the room."

There was an instant twitter of anticipation. By the time I entered the room, my guide had joined the other ladies, and the three of them stood in a line facing me, beaming nervously. One of them was holding a ginger cat firmly in her arms. Its tail was lashing furiously, and it was struggling to find purchase with its back feet and writhe out of her grip.

"Hello," I said, "you seem to have a problem there."

"Oh, my dear," said the cat's jailer, "he's being so naughty. I just can't get him to take his medicine. He's had an abcess at the back of his neck and he's supposed to take antibiotics, but do you think he'll cooperate? How are you going to get better, Orlando," she continued sternly, addressing the flailing animal, "if you don't take your medicine like a good boy?"

I suggested wrapping the cat up and offered my help.

One of the ladies hurried away and returned with a large towel. I took the cat and swaddled it so that its legs were all contained and only its head was sticking out, then tucked it under my arm, feeling like Alice with the flamingo. The cat behaved in much the same way as that uncooperative bird, but I managed to hold it reasonably still and cooed to it while it concentrated all its hostility into a furious stare and one of the ladies gently introduced the dropper into the side of its clenched mouth. Most of the medicine went down, to cries of approval, and I let the cat loose to escape.

"That was kind of you. I don't know why I didn't think of that. You'd think *three* of us could manage something between us, wouldn't you? And we haven't even introduced ourselves yet! What must you think of us?"

The lady who spoke was Evelyn Hoar—"as in frost, dear, not the other sort." The lady who had let me in was Mildred Plover, and the third, plump and girlish, was Isobel Rowntree. They were very different, physically, yet gave the impression they would all bear the same trademark if you tipped them up and looked for the stamp on the soles of their feet. All three wore light tweed skirts with deep pleats fore and aft, rather baggy in the seat, but good for many more years of wear. Their feet were shod in sturdy, sensible walking shoes, brown to go with the tweed, and polished to a high gloss. Each one wore a blouse with tiny pearl buttons up to the neck, blue for Miss Hoar, pink for Isobel, and a strange greenish fawn for Miss Plover. Lambswool cardigans in neutral shades of grey and oatmeal completed the outfit. Isobel wore a string of pearls and a turquoise ring, Miss Hoar had a gold signet ring, and Miss Plover wore no jewellery except for a small gold watch with a fine guard chain. They might have been wearing the uniform of the girls' boarding school they had undoubtedly once attended.

"Would you like some tea?" chirped Isobel. "Do say yes, we get so few visitors."

Miss Plover intervened.

"Perhaps Mrs. Alvarsson would like to see the room first," she said firmly. "We can think about tea after that."

"Oh right," said Isobel, "that's me all over, getting the cart before the horse. I'll just put the kettle on while you're upstairs, then."

"Better get your climbing boots," observed Miss Hoar.

"Now, Evelyn, it's not as bad as that," said Miss Plover. "She will tease, but she doesn't really mean it. Are you ready? Splendid!"

And she extended her bony hand, the fingers carefully together so that the hand looked like a paddle on the end of her arm, in what I came to know as an utterly characteristic *Shall we go?* gesture.

She led me out of the kitchen into the chilly hallway and made for the stairs that rose in the centre of the house. The first landing ran around the stairwell with doors opening off it on every side. Miss Plover stopped here, breathing hard.

"Isobel and I have our rooms here," she said. "Evelyn's on the next floor. She used to go climbing—got better wind."

We climbed again, and this time I caught a glimpse into one of the rooms, not a bedroom, more like a workroom, almost a laboratory. Miss Plover nodded.

"Evelyn likes to work on her specimens. She taught botany, and she's never given up on it though we retired many years ago."

She led me round a corner and opened a door at the end of a short passage. Behind it was yet another flight of stairs, with a plain whipcord on the treads this time instead of the faded Indian carpet on the main staircase.

"Not much farther," she encouraged, and indeed it was just a few more steps to another door that she opened wide. "Here we are," she said, holding out her hand like a small signboard again. I stepped past her into the room and an involuntary exclamation escaped my lips.

"Oh!"

It was the room every child wants. High up on the back of the house in a little turret overlooking the garden. A circular room with a great sweep of windows and a wide, polished window seat piled with cushions. A huge tree outside, some of its branches tapping on the side window, a copper beech with wine-dark leaves, I later discovered. A bed. A desk. An easy chair. A big wardrobe.

"The bathroom is just down the stairs," said Miss Plover. "I hope that isn't too inconvenient, I know people like to have bathrooms attached to their rooms nowadays, but this is rather an old house, you see. At least you would have it all to yourself; Evelyn's got her own, don't you know."

"I think it's wonderful," I said and meant it.

Miss Plover looked around the room.

"I used to like it," she said wistfully. "It was my room when I was a child. I just can't manage all the stairs these days."

"You've lived here all your life?"

"Yes. My father left it to me when he passed away. Isobel and Evelyn came to share it just after the war. I couldn't have kept it on without them. Do you think you would like the room?"

"I would," I said, "no question. But I'm afraid I can't give you any references quickly. I'd have to send to Canada for some; I don't know anybody over here."

"That's all right, dear, we can dispense with that. I think I'm quite a good judge of character. After all, I was a deputy head mistress for many years! So, you'll take it?"

"Yes."

"Splendid! When would you like to move in?"

I thought. I would have to pay for that night at the hotel, but did I really want to spend another sleepless night with the traffic? There was plenty of time to get back there, pack and return to Wimbledon.

"Tonight?"

It was Miss Plover's turn to look surprised, but then she smiled.

"Splendid! Let's go down and have that cup of tea, shall we?"

So the final arrangements were made around the kitchen table by the Aga, the usual living area, I gathered, because it was the warmest place in the house. I learned they were all retired teachers from the same girls' grammar school—"Gone now, such a dreadful pity, all those comprehensives"—and I told them why I was in England, setting them all twittering at the romance of it all. The ginger cat, who obviously had a short memory or no tendency to bear grudges, jumped up onto my lap and settled, and I was formally introduced to Mao, the white cat, and Fergus, Miss Hoar's ferret who lived upstairs in her workroom but was, they warned, perpetually on the run.

Isobel plied me with ginger snaps and Earl Grey tea in weightless flowered bone china, and Miss Hoar stopped barking monosyllables when she learned I taught science. I felt like the head girl invited into the staff room, but they were artlessly friendly and kind in their old-fashioned, fussy way, and I loved them on the spot. All three crowded to the door when I left and waved me off as if I were departing forever instead of returning that same evening.

It took longer than I expected, of course, but I accomplished it in a happy haze and finally closed the door of my room, after many offers of help and cocoa from the ladies, just as the Westminster chimes of the grandfather clock in the hall announced ten o'clock far below.

I leaned against the door for a while, drinking in my domain. The windows were black, and I could see myself reflected, a small figure in an island of light, suspended in air. *Childe Roland to the Dark Tower came* . . . Quickly I disposed of my few possessions, setting the gas mask case on the end of the window seat, where I would see it when I woke.

Then I got ready for bed, turned the light out, and curled into the hammock-like curve of the bed. Now the fitful moonlight cast wavering shadows from the tree into the room, and I could hear the faint scratching of the branches on the glass as they tossed in the wind. Just what young Catherine would have heard when she sat in her little closet bed at Wuthering Heights, scratching out the different versions of her name, dreaming of the person she would become, the possibilities her life held.

Tomorrow, I thought drowsily, *I will find Morocco Street.*

SIXTEEN

Strange how sleep can muddy resolution. You go to bed one night with a decision made after endless anxiety—your path clear, downright obvious—and somewhere in that dreamless night the buoyancy deflates, so that you wake up the next morning still with the same plan but with niggling apprehensions attached. You must have noticed that yourself, Stephen. Of course you have. Remember telling me one night, after weeks of misery, that you were going to beat up Larry Smedley and never let him push you around again? That was the first night you slept right through without nightmares for ages. But next morning, you weren't so sure, threw up at breakfast, and convinced Mum you were too sick for school! You were only about seven, but it's the same no matter how old you are.

I wasn't so sure of myself either as I got ready to leave the next morning. Miss Hoar inquired in her bluff way what I intended to do. I showed her the torn scrap from the address book and explained why I thought it was important to go there and find Sarah Murphy if I could. She looked doubtful, and my confidence wobbled.

"That area of London has changed a lot," she said. "Much of it has been rebuilt. You have to be prepared to find that nothing is left of the old street. Those old buildings, slums in Dickens's time I shouldn't wonder, could have been razed after the war, replaced by tower blocks and people relocated all over the place. It may not be at all straightforward, you know."

I made my way to London Bridge Station and walked down St. Thomas Street past the sprawling bulk of Guy's Hospital toward Bermondsey Street. I tried to imagine my mother hurrying down this road in the dark with me clutched in her arms, assailed by a different kind of noise, not the sound of a bustling metropolis unwinkingly pursuing life but the menacing wails and drones and explosions of a deadly war. I couldn't.

Ahead of me, there was a white enamelled plate on the wall: FENNING STREET, SE1. I turned down the narrow street and stood. The buildings stared back. I couldn't see a seed merchant in any of the likely buildings, nothing that looked like a warehouse, no covered doorways. There was nothing to tell me exactly where she had taken shelter and died, but I stood near the end of the road in the middle of the sidewalk for some time. A couple who had to separate to pass me stared curiously as they went by, then shrugged. Stranger things were to be seen on every corner, every day.

I soon found Morocco Street. From a confluence with Leathermarket Street it curved away and became Leather Court. Number 14 was an office block. There were some apartments above stores, but no houses, and all the buildings looked fairly new despite the layer of London grime each one wore.

At the end of Leather Court I found a small newsagent. It hadn't taken me long to realize that these stores were the centre of many communities in the city. Their proprietors were on familiar terms with a lot of the residents, knew where they lived, because of delivering newspapers, knew their history and all the gossip. This one looked hopeful. It was not modern. In fact, it could have survived unchanged from the turn of the century.

A young Indian woman in a sari was tidying the magazine rack. I bought a local paper and casually broached the subject of Number 14.

"Dunno," she said, ignoring my outstretched hand and slapping the change down on the counter together with a wrinkled till receipt, "there's never bin no 'ouses there, not since I've bin 'ere, anyway." Her Cockney accent was startling, and her tone implied that nothing before her occupation could possibly be of the slightest interest. But I persisted.

"Have you ever heard of anyone called Sarah Murphy living anywhere around here?"

She was concentrating on the innards of the till by then, installing a new tape. She looked as if she held the till personally responsible for running out of paper. "Nah," she said finally, "never 'eard of 'er."

I stood outside for a moment, baffled. I think it was pure shame at being so easily stopped that got me moving again. But it was aimless, and so was my decision to enter a grubby little café down the road. I bought a cup of execrable coffee, poured from two large jugs, one filled with a black liquid, one with white, which turned out to be hot milk, and resolved to drink nothing but tea thereafter. The owner shook his head when I asked about Sarah Murphy. For want of anything better to do I turned to the paper I'd bought.

I found it on page three under the headline STILL GOING STRONG! LOCAL RESIDENT HITS 100. There was a photograph of an old woman stuffed in an armchair, glowering mutinously at the camera while a younger woman twinkled over the chair back. A large cake covered with candles stood on a table beside the old lady. "Director of Southwark Lodge, Hilda Warner, congratulates the oldest resident, Mrs. Jessie Blacklock, on reaching her centenary today," read the caption. The article was predictable enough, but there was one detail that leapt out at me; for many years, including the 1940s, Mrs. Blacklock had lived on Leather Court. Wasn't there a chance this old lady might remember something of the people who lived in the neighbourhood at the same time? I could phone the Lodge.

I felt buoyed by this tenuous lead. The euphoria at a small clue took me out of the café and well down Bermondsey Street before it occurred to me that public phones were in short supply. One I found outside an off licence had been vandalized, panes of glass shattered, the phone cord dangling with frayed ends and no mouthpiece, the instructions smeared with something dark and unspeakable, and an overpowering reek of urine in the shabby claustrophobic cabin. There was no phonebook, of course. Why hadn't I asked the café owner if I could look at his? Stupid, stupid!

The mistake cost me a lot of time. I finally found somebody willing to lend me a phonebook in the bookstall at the station but only after a series of rebuffs, including one from a man behind the steaming counter at a crowded café who listened to my request, hands on hips, then leaned over a vat of bright orange baked beans and said, "It's lunchtime. I sell food. What d'yer fink this is, bleeding Directory Enquiries?" The man at the bookstall was much more polite, even cheerful, but his helpfulness led nowhere. The relevant pages had been ripped out.

But I was fired up and not about to let vandals and rudeness stand in my way. The article! If I phoned the paper, surely they would be able to tell me how to get in touch with Southwark Lodge?

One of the phones in a line outside the station actually worked. Staff at the newspaper passed me from one extension to another, but eventually I was talking to the reporter who had written the piece on Mrs. Blacklock. He was wary, reluctant to give me any information. Maddening, except that the rational part of me was saying, *Well, what do you expect? Here you are, a complete stranger ringing up out of the blue with some cock and bull story about lost relatives. How does he know I'm legit? I*

*could be some demented wacko, or somebody who can't wait for
an inheritance, or a burglar, or one of those freaks who thinks it's
her mission to end the suffering of the old.*

"Look," I said finally, "if I could find a phonebook that hasn't
been vandalized I wouldn't need to bother you. I'm not asking
for anything that's classified. Suggest someone else I can ask
and I'll leave you alone."

"No," he said, "okay, just hang on a sec . . ."

I could hear rustling, and I visualized him at his untidy desk,
rooting through the layers like a pig after truffles. A few seconds
later I had the address and phone number.

But that was the end of my luck for the day. A call to Southwark
Lodge duplicated my experience with the newspaper; transferred
from one official to another like the parcel in the kid's game, layer
after layer of my over-elaborate story torn off, it seemed to me,
until it was reduced to an impossibly bald question.

"May I talk to Mrs. Jessie Blacklock?"

The director, for I had at last penetrated to the inner sanc-
tum, sidestepped with a question of her own.

"Are you a family member?"

"No, I don't know her at all."

"We have to be very careful not to overtire her," said the
director. "She's very frail, and she's had a lot of excitement this
week. May I ask what is your purpose in visiting an old lady who
is a stranger?"

I explained. The director's voice had lost some of its caution
when she spoke again.

"Now that *is* interesting. She represents a possible short-
cut, doesn't she? I'd hate to have to go through all the Sarah
Murphys in the country! Mrs. Blacklock would probably help if
she could—she prides herself on her memory, on her good days,
that is. How accurate she is, I can't say. Not too many around to
contradict her, are there?"

"Depressingly true."

"Well, let me see. I don't see why you shouldn't come. She'd probably enjoy a visitor. Today's out of the question, she'll be off to bed soon, and what's today? Friday, mmm. I think we'd better give her the weekend to recover from all the attention she had for her birthday. Why don't you plan for Monday morning, round about ten-thirty. She'd be resting in the lounge then. Call me first, so we can be sure she's up to it. Really, this is quite exciting! I *do* hope it isn't a wild goose chase for you."

So did I. The weekend yawned ahead. I saw it as a void to be filled, somehow, with waiting for the encounter with the old lady. The possibility that she knew nothing, or did know something and wouldn't be able to remember, nagged at me. Suppose she wasn't well enough to see me on Monday? Suppose she was so exhausted by her triumphant scaling of centennial heights that she had to rest for the rest of her days? And *days* was the operative word. You couldn't have that many left when you got to a hundred. Suppose I rang up on Monday and they said, "Oh, we're sorry, she just died." What *would* I do about sifting through all the Sarah Murphys in England? Just how many of them would there be, for God's sake?

My landladies rescued me from my funk. They were in the kitchen as I went down to make myself some tea. Miss Hoar was dismantling a toaster, Isobel was knitting something pale pink, and Miss Plover was turning the pages of a magazine with her big ugly hands. They all looked at me expectantly.

"How did you get on, then?" Miss Hoar said impatiently. "We're dying to know."

I told them.

"Splendid!" said Miss Plover. "You *have* done well."

I felt unreasonably cheered, as if I had come top in a French test against all the odds.

"Going back on Monday, then?" asked Miss Hoar. "Just have

to hope the old girl doesn't kick the bucket before you get there, won't you?"

There was a flurry of reproachful remonstrances from Miss Plover and Isobel, but I was grateful for the bluntness that laid my chief concern out in the open. Exposed like that, it dwindled.

"She's made it to a hundred," I said, filling the kettle at the old brass tap, dull and rough from long use. "She's tough."

There was a metallic thud as Miss Hoar whacked compacted crumbs out of the bottom of the toaster. Miss Plover hurried for dustpan and brush.

"Might as well leave it until I've finished, Mildred," said Miss Hoar. "There'll only be more. Why it's so difficult to remember to empty out the crumbs *before* they all get stuck on the bottom and start fires, I don't know."

Miss Plover subsided, her throat mottling, still holding the dustpan. Isobel mounted a diversionary tactic.

"Do you have plans for the weekend?" she asked. "We're going down to Christchurch to visit a former colleague. You'll have the house to yourself."

I said I would probably be a tourist and go and see the sights.

"Well, as long as you'll be here, would you mind feeding Mao and Orlando for us? You don't have to worry about Fergus—Evelyn'll see he's shut up in her room with plenty of food. Unless he escapes, of course," she added.

I promised I would cope.

I had two days to explore London, and it seemed like a penance. I made myself work out a program of activities; I would play tourist and wear myself out. In that I succeeded. The two days passed in a confusing, exhausting welter of images: mad-eyed pigeons blowing about like leaves in Trafalgar Square; a kaleidoscope of neon signs as I whirled round Piccadilly Circus on the top layer of a doubledecker bus; Elizabeth I gazing imperiously out of the sombre background of her portrait, a fan of ostrich feathers in her hand; the same face, sunken, the bony nose like a prow, on her tomb in the Abbey; an escape artist struggling free of chains and ropes just behind the Tower; roving bands of young men with pallid stubbly heads and bovver boots; the shabby tiled tunnels of the Underground, like a vast neglected public convenience, sucking me in, down, down the creeping escalators, blowing their foul warm breath in my face, the reek of old sweat and exhaustion, to Mind the Gap and fight the pull of the shining rail, then spitting me up and out again into the struggling light and the din of changing gears and the ceaseless countermarch of people, to continue my solitary way with all the others.

It was a relief to trundle back to Wimbledon and let myself into the silent house. The cats insinuated themselves into my room, and we curled up on the windowseat, found a concert on the radio that was to include Elgar's Cello Concerto, and listened to the wind keeping the night on the move outside while we shared a chicken tikka masala from the Indian takeout down the road. There was nothing more to be done. There was nobody I could see or talk to, nowhere I could explore, nothing I could search out. The hours before Monday morning stretched elastically into the dark, but a little sleep would gather them in, make them nothing. I had never felt so peaceful, so entirely let off, so free of every claim on me. Canada, Neil, you—even Daniel— seemed impossibly remote. It was as if I did not exist at all except in that ring of purring light filled with the first achingly beautiful notes of the cello.

Monday saw me up early. A phone call to Miss Warner at the Lodge assured me that Mrs. Blacklock was having one of her good days, "so far, at least," and I set off with the director's directions in my hand, brimming with confidence.

Southwark Lodge was a handsome brick building pinched between a diocesan office and a funeral home. A line of discouraged trees wilted along the property line between the Lodge and the undertaker's, but it formed an inadequate screen; a sign that read CHAPEL OF REST flickered above the thin branches, clearly visible.

The front door of Southwark Lodge opened onto a pleasant lobby with a reception desk at the back. A huge split-leaf philodendron stood in a vast tub by the entrance. Its leaves, like big green hands with spatulate fingers, groped up the wall and dangled, loose-wristed, from strong, fleshy stalks. New leaves, waiting to unfurl, pointed stiff as gun dogs. A tiny old lady with wispy grey hair skewered into an untidy bun held a green hand in her own as if she were about to kiss it, dusting its leathery surface with a grubby handkerchief. She caught me watching her.

"They have to breathe, you know," she said. "I dust them all every day."

"It obviously appreciates it," I said.

The old lady leaned closer, still holding the leaf tenderly.

"I talk to them too," she whispered.

"I've heard they respond to that."

She nodded vigorously and patted the monstrous vine as if it were a prize pig.

"Proof of the pudding," she said conspiratorially.

"Mrs. Lambert giving you some gardening tips, is she?"

The face from the newspaper photograph had materialized at my side.

"Hilda Warner," it said, extending a hand that lay cold and limp in mine. "And you must be Mrs. Alvarsson. Won't you come this way?"

The director turned and led the way down a wide hallway with a gleaming floor. We passed either side of an aged man shuffling with infinitesimal steps after his walker down the centre of the corridor, and my guide shouted cheerily as we surged by.

"Taking your morning walk, Mr. Simmonds? Good for you!"

Mr. Simmonds seemed unable to cope simultaneously with the bow wave of our passing and conversation. He stooped and slowly raised his face from its rapt observation of the ground.

"What's that?" he asked in a frail thread of a voice. But the director, like the express trains I had seen rocketing through Wimbledon Station, was already in another place, urging a cleaner to hurry up and get her bucket and mop out of the way. The old man mumbled to himself and almost imperceptibly got under way again. I felt obscenely large and healthy.

I caught up to the director as she stood in the doorway of a large room at the end of the hall. A sign on the wall read SUNROOM, and it was indeed filled with light, if not sun. Plants crowded the space, some the size of small trees, fingering the skylights as if yearning for a way out. There were clearings in the greenery filled with bentwood chairs and couches, occasional baize-covered card tables, wheelchairs and discarded walkers, and populated by residents reading, chatting, playing cards, doing crossword puzzles, talking to themselves or sitting, chins on their chests, puffing gently as they slept. Just like the day room in any hospital ward. You can see it, can't you, Stephen? Lord knows, you've seen enough of them.

Miss Warner led me through the jungle to the far side of the room where the windows gave on to more green, for the Lodge had a small garden at the back, a little oasis in a desert of brick and concrete. This was obviously the prime position in the room, and there, supported by cushions in a gleaming electric wheelchair, was Mrs. Blacklock.

"Here we are," the director boomed. "Here's the visitor I told you about, Mrs. Blacklock. Remember I told you someone was coming?"

Jessie Blacklock was tiny and bent, as if she had leached away over the years and folded in upon herself, weightless as a leaf. Her hands were skeletal, the fingers restlessly playing with the satin edge of the blanket over her knees, the knobbly joints too large, poking at the dry skin covering them. A thin gold band slid up and down the third finger of her left hand, stopped only by the first knuckle from falling off altogether. She was bundled in a padded pink nylon dressing gown, as insulated and cocooned as a baby in a bunting bag.

Her face, though, immediately challenged this impression. The flesh covering her skull had dwindled to nothing, and the skin, left with little to cover, had collapsed into folds and seams, little dewlaps and pouches, trenches and troughs, the mouth a puckered scar, the whole surface crazed with a network of fine spidery lines, just like a dried-out lakebed in a long drought. Her white hair was fine as a baby's and very sparse. The pink scalp was clearly visible through it. She peered at me through gold-rimmed spectacles. Her eyes were dull and rheumy.

"I don't know her," she said suspiciously. Her voice quavered.

"No," said the director, "remember I told you you wouldn't know her, but you might have known somebody she wants to find, somebody who lived on your street."

"I don't know you," the old woman repeated.

"No, you don't," I said. "We've never met. Can I explain?"

Mrs. Blacklock grasped my hand and leaned forward.

"I'm one hundred years old. Fancy that!"

"Congratulations," I said, "that's wonderful. And it's partly the reason I've come to see you."

"You've missed the birthday cake. We ate it all."

"It's probably just as well. I eat too much as it is."

"Hundred candles there were, all lit up. Did you see my picture in the paper?"

"I did."

"First time I ever got my name in the paper. I told that young man. First time I ever got my name in the paper. I said to him,

I said, will I have to wait another hundred years before I get my name in the paper again? And he said, well if you're planning to live that long, I guarantee they'll send someone round to take your photo. Made me laugh, he did."

The director coughed.

"Mrs. Alvarsson wanted to ask you about a woman who lived on Morocco Street during the war."

"Which war would that be?" asked the old woman. "I've seen more than one in my time, you know."

"It was the Second World War," I said, "in 1941, during the Blitz."

"I remember the Blitz. Terrible, that was. Lived from day to day. Never knew if you'd make it through the night. One of them incendiaries fell on the house next door to me, lucky I was down the Underground that night or I'd've been a goner too. Made a terrible mess of my house that did."

"Can you remember a woman called Sarah Murphy at all? She lived at Number 14."

The old woman mumbled, the end of her nose edging closer to the point of her chin as she did. She looked more and more like a diminutive, wrinkled Punch.

"I went to school with Sarah Porter," she said finally, "silly girl, married a fishmonger. I don't know how she could put up with the smell, but then she always was daft."

"Sarah *Murphy*?" I prompted.

"There was a Murphy down the Cut before the war, but he disappeared. Never knew what happened to him."

"But you can't remember a Sarah Murphy on Morocco Street?"

"Well, dear. I didn't live on Morocco Street myself. I lived round the corner on Leather Court. We kept to ourselves on the Court. You can't expect me to know everyone, can you?"

Her reedy voice sounded aggrieved, and the fingers fidgeted restlessly.

"No, no, of course not. It's remarkable you remember as much as you do."

She was mollified.

"They say I'm a wonder. I'm a hundred years old, you know. You wouldn't think it, would you? I had a cake with a hundred candles on it. I don't look it, do I?"

Oh yes, you do, I thought, *you look as old as time. You look as if you've just left Shangri-La, and the years are catching up with you, like they did with What's Her Name, at the end of the film. I'd believe you if you told me you helped build the Pyramids, but you don't remember Sarah Murphy and that's all I care about right now.*

"What a shame," said the director over the sparse hairs.

"Well, it was a long shot. Back to the drawing board."

A gentle snore punctuated the silence. Jessie Blacklock was fast asleep, drooling a little from the corner of her purse string mouth.

"I'll get her back to her room," said Miss Warner. "Can you find your own way out?"

For a moment I stood staring into the garden where a light rain was falling, exciting a flock of starlings who were striding about, stiff-legged, prodding and poking at the grass.

"Penny for them?" said a voice.

Another woman, using the support of a cane, had made her way quietly to my side. I smiled at her.

"Not worth that much," I said.

"Come and sit down over there a minute," she said. "I may be able to help you. I couldn't help overhearing. There's no such thing as a private conversation when you have to talk to oldies deaf as posts!"

I followed her to a table close by screened by a large ficus. She plumped heavily into a basket chair and waved me to its mate opposite her.

"Now," she said, breathing heavily, "did I hear you say you wanted to know about a Sarah Murphy? From Morocco Street?"

"That's right."

"Well, you asked the wrong one there. Thinks she's the bee's knees just because she's a hundred. Thinks she's the world authority on everything! Well, I'm ninety-seven and I can still get upstairs if I don't have to hurry, and what I can't remember isn't worth knowing. And besides, I lived on Morocco Street during the war, at Number 39, and I remember Sarah Murphy very well!"

Her round face beamed with triumph at my astonishment.

"This is incredible!"

"Didn't expect that, did you? Yes, she was just a young thing, in her twenties then, with a little girl, I seem to remember. Married to an Irishman, drove a lorry for Carter Paterson's, something like that, but a bit of a wide boy, if you take my meaning, always got his finger in some pie or other, not too particular about keeping the right side of the law. She was a sweet little thing, though, too good for the likes of him, but there, that's the way of the world, isn't it? Is she a relative of yours, then?"

I admitted I didn't know.

"I think she may have been someone my mother knew, maybe someone she was planning to stay with in London. She was killed before she got there, I think. But if I could find this Sarah Murphy, perhaps she could tell me something about my mother, where she came from, what her name was, stuff like that. I've got very little else to go on."

"I can't tell you much. Sarah was a nice little thing, always said good morning if you saw her in the street, you know. Now there's a thing—funny how it comes back to you—she didn't come from round here, she wasn't a Londoner, I'd swear an oath on it. She had an accent, one of those nice country ones, like they have on *The Archers*, you know."

I didn't, but I could imagine a sort of generic Mummerset. Was there some place they actually spoke like that? But there were more urgent questions.

"Do you know what became of her? There's no house at Number 14 now."

"Wouldn't be, would there? I think they knocked down all the old buildings after the war. I had to move into a flat in a big block in Bermondsey, more room, mind you, but thin walls, you could hear a nit cough in them places. I missed my little house, even if it didn't have an inside loo and hot water tap, I can tell you.

"But there I go, you don't care about that, do you, love? What happened to Sarah? I have an idea she moved down to the seaside somewhere. Littlehampton perhaps? Hastings? Tell you how I know, she was friends with a woman I knew did the odd bit of dressmaking, and I was talking to her one day about all the changes round about, and she says to me, 'Talking of changes, did I tell you I heard from Sarah?' and she fishes out this postcard with a picture of this fancy place on the front, and on the back she'd written, 'Like my new house? Ha, ha, just joking!' and on the bottom there was something about a pavilion, and I said, 'That's a funny sort of place to keep sports stuff in, isn't it? They must be a funny lot there.' She laughed and laughed, did Beryl."

"You don't happen to know why she went there, or what she or her husband were going to do there, to earn a living?"

"I couldn't say. Chances are with that Murphy fellow it wouldn't be on the up and up. I did hear he'd lined his pockets on the black market. But what would you do at the seaside? Run a boarding house? That would suit Murphy, having his wife do all the work so he could sit back and rake in all the profits!"

So. There I was, cast down one minute, encouraged the next. Admittedly, it was a very tenuous lead. I looked at the old lady opposite me. Her face was flushed, but her eyes were bright and knowing.

"Still here?"

Once again the director had materialized unheard. I wondered how often she startled the residents the same way.

"This lady—I'm sorry," I said, "I don't even know your name."

"Enid."

"Enid *did* remember Sarah Murphy. She was telling me about her. Wasn't it lucky we met?"

The director smiled indulgently.

"Enid's been telling you some of her stories, has she?"

Was it my imagination, or did the director lean ever so gently on the word? Enid scowled.

"They're not *all* stories," she insisted. "She didn't want stories."

"Time for lunch, now," said Miss Warner, shaking her head at me ruefully as the old woman levered herself out of the chair. "I'm sorry we couldn't be more help."

I watched them slowly making their way between two potted palms. Miss Warner was diverted by an altercation at a card table, and Enid stopped and swivelled awkwardly.

"Not a story," she said. "Why would I tell you a story about that?"

Without waiting for an answer she shuffled away.

She had a point, don't you think, Stephen? Why *would* she tell me a story?

I struggled with her question through the dreary outskirts of London. Was Enid a liar? Had she simply been amusing herself? Was the whole tale a product of aged malice? But she hadn't struck me as senile. Old, certainly, but fully aware and competent. Maybe just the kind of person who *would* fabricate to make a boring life more interesting? Apparently, she had a reputation for invention; if you found yourself with all your faculties intact among contemporaries who were mostly gaga, bossed about by well-meaning but insufferable youngsters, wouldn't you keep your brain sharp by making up plausible stories and seeing what you could get away with?

"But then," I explained later to the three ladies round the Aga, "there were some details that were so convincing, like Sarah's accent, for instance. How would she have known I might want to hear Sarah was a country girl? And the postcard thing. Why bother with all that? I'd have accepted any place she suggested."

Isobel had already explained that Enid's funny place to keep sports stuff was likely to be the Brighton Pavilion, George IV's eccentric seaside palace.

"Well," said Miss Plover, "it's my experience that really accomplished liars would do something exactly like that. You're prepared to believe her simply because she was more involved than strictly necessary—so she obliged you with a complicated story, 'remembering' what was on the back of the card even, and making fun of her own ignorance. It does sound very convincing, but it might just be the mark of a very talented actress."

"But she was so put out when the director hinted that she might be spinning me a line. She was *annoyed*. *Offended*. Not embarrassed, or rueful, or laughing it off as you'd expect if she'd been caught doing something naughty." I warmed to Enid's defence as I remembered something else. "And she said, 'about that.' Why would she tell me a story *about that*. Almost as if she's admitting she does make things up but not about important things."

"So she was annoyed because her habit of storytelling got in the way this time of being believed?" Miss Hoar said thoughtfully. "That rings true, I must say."

As usual, Isobel put her well-manicured finger on the point.

"It's all you've got, isn't it? You *have* to follow it up. What other choice is there?"

149

Even Miss Plover agreed with that observation. She had another question, though.

"Am I missing something? Why do you think your mother might have come from the country somewhere?"

For answer I went upstairs to fetch the gas mask case and spread the shabby contents across the kitchen table. They looked forlorn lying there on the wide, well-scrubbed wooden surface. Hopelessly inadequate. I explained the possible significance of the seed packet, and realized again how thin the connections seemed. Isobel exclaimed over the Mickey Mouse gas mask.

"Good Lord, it's a museum piece!"

I showed the ladies the name written on the strap.

"And you think that may be your real name?" asked Miss Hoar.

I shrugged. "It's possible. It was with me, and there was no other child around."

With a pang I remembered Olivia, that other lost child, and with that memory Daniel suddenly filled my mind. It was painful to tear my attention back.

"It's a pity you have no idea as yet where your mother may have come from. Without that you couldn't hope to get any information out of Somerset House, though it's not Somerset House any more, it's gone to Wales or something."

I must have looked blank. Miss Plover came to the rescue.

"The Registry of Births, Marriages, and Deaths," she said succinctly. "They'd be able to tell you if such a birth had been registered around 1940, but a name without a place of birth or a parent's name would be a needle in a haystack."

"So I need to investigate Brighton."

Isobel was peering at the seed packet through the glasses she always kept folded and dangling round her neck on a beaded chain.

"I can't make this out," she said. "I can see what might be 'Park,' but the first part is too faint."

"Let me see," said Miss Plover, taking the packet and dragging Isobel's glasses closer to her own eyes.

"Wascot?" she said after a long pause during which she angled the tiny envelope into a better light, towing Isobel with her. "Nescot?"

Miss Hoar stiffened.

"That rings a bell somehow. Why is that name familiar?"

The other two looked blank, shaking their heads.

"Never mind," said Miss Hoar, "it'll come to me."

"It will too," whispered Miss Plover as she returned the envelope to me. "Evelyn's got a splendid memory!"

But you know, I was beginning to have reservations about memory. How many of our recollections are myths of our own making? In the elaborate, unconscious filing system we carry about with us, how much is real, and how much wishful thinking or embroidery, theft or suffocation, excuse or justification? Even the big things must suffer erosion eventually, a gentle blurring of outline and feature, not enough to disguise the original completely, just to soften and blunt the harsh angularities into Sphinx faces the Pharaohs would barely recognize.

Daniel's disappearance remains as stark in memory as the day it happened, but what about Daniel himself? I know his face and the colour of his eyes and the tender hollow at the nape of his neck, but could I swear to the way his hair swirls on the crown of his head? The exact shape of his earlobes? The design of his navel? And if this much has blurred in eleven years, what could my family possibly remember of me and my biological mother after all this time—or even *want* to remember—that would be of the slightest use to me?

SEVENTEEN

Stephen, you would have approved of the practical approach I took to Brighton. Directory Enquiries were no help on a Murphy without an address, but they gave me the phone numbers for tourist information and the local council offices. A woman at the council office, sounding adenoidal and put upon, reluctantly told me there were several S. Murphys on the electoral roll but declined to reveal their addresses. She sounded quite pleased to be able to refuse.

"Oh no," she said firmly, "that would be quite against regulations. More than my job's worth. So sorry." I didn't point out that the local phonebook would give me their addresses if I could get my hands on it. I didn't want to give her a second opportunity to say no.

The Tourist Information Office was more outgoing, or less righteous, but not much more helpful. The girl who answered the phone soon realized that she was too recent an addition to the staff to have the answers I was seeking and chirpily summoned up an older colleague. I waited, listening to the rustles and background noises, and then the barely audible voice of the girl making a rapid explanation to someone else and the noise of the handset being transferred. A quiet voice sounded in my ear.

"How may I help you?"

I explained.

"There's no Sarah Murphy on our lists at the moment running any sort of hotel or boarding house or B&B, but you know, there used to be. She had a boarding house somewhere near the station if I remember correctly. There was something about it that's nagging at me, something odd, but I can't . . . Anyway, she retired, I suppose, some years ago. I've no idea whether she's still in the same house or moved elsewhere. I couldn't even tell you what street the boarding house was on, and I don't have any of the old lists to refer to. I'm sorry I can't be more helpful."

"But you've helped a lot. At least I know there was once a Sarah Murphy there. You don't know if she came from London, do you?"

"That would have been before my time, I'm afraid."

"Never mind. It was a long shot."

"Cats!"

"What?"

"Cats! I've just remembered what was odd about the house. She kept cats too, dozens of them. Anyone who stayed there had to be able to put up with the cats. Caused a little bit of a stir with the health inspectors, I seem to remember. And the neighbours. May even have been why she gave up taking in PGs."

I caught the train at Clapham Junction. I was armed with a very old AA map of the Brighton Hove area, donated by Miss Hoar, and from Isobel, a bag of crusty ham rolls, a slice of Dundee cake, two apples, and a quarter-pound of sherbert lemons in case I got peckish on the journey. Maybe she was remembering the expeditions to the seaside of her youth or some outmoded form of transport so leisurely that iron rations were a must if one were not to faint for lack of nourishment.

"You never know with public transport," she said darkly, "and even if you don't actually *need* it, the sherbert lemons will be nice and refreshing. Trains are always so stuffy, don't you think?"

Her precautions lay like a stone in my bag along with the gas mask case. The train bucked and skittered its way to the right line across the maze of tracks at Clapham Junction and then gradually picked up speed through the suburbs until the stations became illegible stammers as we rocketed past. The countryside opened out, the farther south we went, into green hedged fields, cows and sheep grazing, the land gradually undulating to rounded hills. These were the Downs, covered with the short turf and thin pale soil of chalk uplands, forming a barrier between the city and the sea.

We stopped at East Croydon and Redhill, skirted Gatwick airport, and rattled finally into the terminus at Brighton. After the serenity of the hills and the open skies, Brighton was disappointingly ordinary, at least round the railway station, lines of identical houses that could have come from any suburb, faceless streets with names like Trafalgar Terrace and Kensington Gardens and Cheapside, as if they yearned to be somewhere more cosmopolitan but had settled instead for imitation as a more realistic substitute. The sea might have been a hundred miles away.

But a salty, iodine, seaweedy smell was in the air, and I followed my nose to find its source. The Channel was heaving up and down, grey and white, as far as the eye could see. The old West Pier, like an Edwardian conservatory on stilts, sat in the water to my right. The other pier, much longer, edged out into deep water on my left. There was a stiff breeze coming off the sea, and soon my face felt sticky and I could taste the salt on my lips.

A sudden vision of my house on the water at Davis Bay overwhelmed me, and I felt a clutching pang of homesickness. What was I doing in this strange town on the southern edge of England when I could be walking with Neil along our beach, idly looking for shells and driftwood, watching for eagles and osprey, laughing at the sandpipers running as if on wheels in and out of the final reaches of the waves? What did I hope to find here that could be any more important to me than that?

What *was* I doing? Wasting time, obviously.

In the Lanes I found a pub that had once been a chapel, ordered a half of bitter, and borrowed a phonebook. The Murphys took up a column. I could see no quick or sure way of eliminating any of them, so I jotted down all the numbers, putting all the S. Murphys at the top of the list. I hefted the rolls of ten-pence coins I'd provided myself with for a marathon session at a public phone. Time for some dogged detective work.

I stared through the grimy windows of the phonebox, listening to the double rings at the other end of the line. I'd exhausted the S. Murphys and was into the Ds. Hope was flagging. I watched a man, hunched against the wind, tugging a reluctant Jack Russell down the street. Both looked miserable. The handset pressed to my ear smelled bad. I visualized the thousands of mouths opening and closing, the invisible spray of saliva hitting the black plastic, the ears in clammy intimacy with mine, the hands building up a thickening film of sweat. I was about to put the phone down, retrieve my money, and tumble out into the air when the ringing abruptly stopped and a female voice spoke, amazingly close, as if her head were alongside mine, whispering into my ear.

"Hello."

I told her my name and went through the explanation for my call. I had refined this over the last dozen failures, learning that a full explanation was a waste of time and would only have to be repeated.

"I'm trying to trace a woman who used to live in Morocco Street, Bermondsey. In London. During the war. I was told she moved to this area and maybe ran a boarding house. Her name is Sarah Murphy. Do you know of her at all?"

There was a profound silence. For a moment I thought we had been cut off, but it wasn't the sort of deadness on the line that tells you immediately that all the electronic connections have been severed. It was more the silence of those disturbing phone calls late at night where the caller never speaks, and after bellowing, "Hello? Hello? Who's there?" you listen in your turn, controlling your noisy breathing to catch the slightest sound, and there you both are, at either end of the line, waiting for the betrayal of a single sigh or rustle, waiting for the tiny click or the furtive slide of the handset back onto its rest so that you can leave your own phone off the hook and prevent your persecutor from making any more calls for the time being.

"Hello?" I said at last. "Hello? Are you still there?"

"Why do you want her?" The voice was thin now and strained.

"She may be able to tell me something about my mother. I think my mother may have been on the way to see her when she was killed. I've only just discovered this."

It sounded lamer to me every time I said it. But the voice came again, flat.

"My mother's called Sarah. We used to live in London. But she can't tell you anything."

"I'd really like to talk to her if I could. She might be able to remember something, just a little thing maybe. I've come this far on very small clues."

The voice was stronger now.

"Wouldn't make any difference. She died yesterday in the hospital. Cancer."

It was my turn to fall silent. With dismay, in my case. As I tried to collect my thoughts, another sound came over the wire, distant but unmistakable. Cats yowling.

"I am so sorry. I'd never have bothered you if . . ."

"You weren't to know."

She sounded almost brisk now. I took the plunge.

"Look, I know it's the worst possible time, and I'll just go away if you want me to, but do you think I could come and talk to you instead some time? Not now, obviously, but in the next few weeks, when you're not so overwhelmed?"

"Overwhelmed? What makes you say that?"

"Well, all the arrangements to make, the shock, you know."

"The funeral's all in hand. Made her own arrangements ages ago. Nothing for me to do, really. It's not as if it wasn't expected. Where are you?"

"Down near the Pavilion, at a public phone."

"If you want, you could come now. Might as well. I've got nothing better to do with myself."

She wasn't exactly welcoming, but I couldn't pass up the chance. She gave me directions to her house on Tidy Street. As an afterthought, I asked her name.

"Deirdre," she said, "Deirdre Murphy."

So she wasn't married. And the phone was in her name.

"See you in a bit," I said. Another cat mewed, but Deirdre made no reply.

The house on Tidy Street was tall and thin, crowded on both sides by newer homes of pallid brick, semi-detached clones differentiated only by the colours of their front doors and the efforts their owners had made at individuality: brass carriage lamps, wrought iron gates, window boxes, and a startling array of front yards, cultivated, hidden by hedges, lawned, concreted, asphalted, gravelled, crazy paved, most with at least one car parked on the road or crouched by the front windows if the garden had been abandoned to vehicles. The Murphy house by contrast was an older, darker brick, and it stuck up like a rude finger among the others. All the drapes had been drawn, and the house looked blind. There was no car, but a bicycle leaned against the railing of the front porch, manacled to it by a padlock and chain. There was a privet hedge along the wall by the road, but no other sign of horticulture.

I crunched across the gravel to the front door and rang the bell. It was one of those bells that give no sound, so you have no idea if it is functioning or not. A brass plate by the door read SEAVIEW HOUSE in curly copperplate, but the metal had acquired a dull patina in the salt air. Nobody had polished it in a long time. I was just about to try the bell again, or give the dolphin knocker a thump, when I heard shuffling steps on the other side of the door and faint mewing. The door opened.

"Come in," said a voice. "Mind the cats."

The house reeked. I'd experienced the smell in that concentration only once, when I visited a dotty old woman in Halfmoon Bay who bred Siamese cats and allowed them the run of the house. Holding my breath and hoping I'd get acclimatized soon and not notice it so much, I edged in and followed Deirdre down the dark hallway. I half expected the whole house to be shrouded and plunged in gloom, but Deirdre flung open a door at the back of the house, and I was blinded for a moment.

We were in a sunroom. But obviously lived in. There was a dining room table on one side, and the rest of the space was filled with shabby armchairs, the worn patches covered with crocheted squares, protruding springs buffered by lumpy cushions, old ottomans and stools, small tables littered with newspapers and magazines, rolled-up knitting and half-empty chocolate boxes. Sharing all these surfaces were cats of every size, shape, and colour. Their collective unblinking gaze was unnerving.

"How many are there?" I asked.

Deirdre looked about her.

"I'm not absolutely sure," she said doubtfully, as if it had never dawned on her to count. "Twenty-five, maybe?"

She was about my age, a few more years on her perhaps, but immeasurably older in some deepseated way. If an artist were to draw her, all the lines and pencil strokes would tend downward. Her limp, ear-length hair, a faded greyish blond, emphasized the smallness and narrowness of her head. The outer corners of her eyes, which were a muddy brown, tilted down, and the line was echoed by the pouches under her eyes and the deep runnels that gouged trenches from her nose to the corners of her mouth, where they formed little curved hooks in imitation of the contours of her lips.

She was short and stocky, barrel-like, an impression accentuated by a shapeless brown garment that belled out from her narrow shoulders and hinted at padded hips and a massive belly. Its droopy hem sagged around mid-calf, and peeping out from below it were two tiny feet, lumpy with swollen veins and bunions, in black cloth shoes with ankle straps. She reminded me of a candle that had burned to extinction, its wax melted in rivulets, puddled and heaped at its base.

She motioned me awkwardly to a chair, inhabited already by a round-faced tabby with a fierce yellow glare who seemed disinclined to move. I squeezed in beside him, and Deirdre lowered herself with a thump into a sagging basket chair that squeaked in protest. There was a silence. Obviously she felt no compulsion to play hostess, but I decided her ungraciousness was the result of lack of practice, not indifference or malice. I floundered ahead.

"I was right, then? Your mother came here from London?"

"Yes."

"And she lived on Morocco Street? Number 14?"

She shrugged.

"Couldn't tell you the number, but that was the name of the street, I think. I don't remember much about that."

I pulled the gas mask out of my bag and showed her the torn fragment from the address book. She fingered it absently while I explained how I had come by it, and my theory for its presence in the case. She listened, but her attention was caught by the mask.

She picked the grotesque little thing up and smiled, running her finger over the snout-like filter.

"I had one just like this," she said. "Never used it, but we had to carry them about all the time."

She turned it over to investigate the inside, lifting it to her face to inhale its rubbery smell. I saw her freeze, a moment of utter stillness in which I swear she did not breathe. I was suspended in the same tension, waiting. Then her breath gushed out, and she looked at me, an awed expression on her face.

"Goodman," she said slowly. "That was my mother's maiden name."

We stared at each other. In her eyes I saw a reflection of my own wild surmise dawning. Could it be . . . ? Are we . . . ? I hardly dared to ask another question, in case the fragile thought should crumble under the weight of one more fact.

"Tell me," I said at last, "did your mother have any sisters?"

"She had a younger sister. I never met her."

"Is she still alive?"

"She died, that's all I know for sure. I can remember asking Mum about her, round about the time Dad scarpered. I don't know why I would have. Mum kept a picture of her on the mantelpiece."

Her voice trailed off. I had no difficulty imagining why a child would want to know about other members of the family when her father disappeared from her life, and I felt a pang for the bewildered little girl who had grown into this plain, stunted woman.

"Maybe you just wanted to populate your world," I suggested, and she looked startled, and then speculative. I tugged her back.

"Do you know *how* your aunt died?"

Deirdre thought for a moment.

"Not really," she said. "I asked Mum how come her sister died if she was younger, and Mum said that sort of thing happened in the war. You never knew, she said, who was going to cop it in the night. She never said outright, but you know how kids pick things up. I always assumed she was killed in an air raid."

"I was found sitting beside the body of a young woman during an air raid, not more than a few blocks from your home. This stuff was with me."

"My God," she breathed, "it's like one of those mysteries on the tele. Are you going to tell me we're *cousins*?"

"It looks that way, doesn't it?"

"Wow," she said, "the long-lost cousin returns! It's like a fairy story!"

It was the first sign of emotion she had displayed and it transformed her. The planes of her face tilted upward as her mouth stretched into a wide grin, pushing up her cheeks and crinkling the corners of her eyes. I felt myself grinning hugely too.

"Well, *coz*," I said, "tell me more. Are you the only one?"

"Oh," she replied, suddenly serious, "I'm a one and only, and Uncle Magnus never married . . ."

"There's an *uncle*?"

"Oh, yes, I've only met him a few times myself, when he came down here. We never went there, of course."

More mystery?

"Why 'of course'?"

Deirdre shifted in her seat. The basketwork creaked and two cats abruptly lifted their heads from their paws, alert for trouble.

"There was a falling-out, long ago. It's funny, you asking. I only found out about it a few days ago. I think it was on Mum's mind, just before she . . . you know."

A tear sneaked out of Deirdre's right eye and she smeared it away quickly with the heel of her hand.

"Anyway," she continued, "apparently she ran away from home, to marry Dad. Her parents were so angry, at least her mother was. They said they washed their hands of her, told her they had no daughter called Sarah any more. She said she wrote, but she never got a reply. She never went back. Never spoke to them again."

"But why? Why were they so angry? She got married, after all."

"Yes, but Dad was Catholic, wasn't he? And Irish."

I was appalled at this evidence of intolerance, but something else had struck me.

"So did you ever see your—our—grandparents, then?"

"Never. I don't think they even know about me. Uncle Magnus used to come on the sly, I think. He wouldn't have said anything. And Mum told me she'd never take me there. 'I'm not letting you get anywhere near the old witch,' she used to say. 'She's not going to poison you with her nastiness.'"

This was intriguing enough, but my ear had caught another nuance.

"'Know'?" I asked. "They're still alive?"

"What? Oh no, leastways the old man's dead, died years ago now, early 1960s, something like that. Mum always had a soft spot for her dad, said he was a nice old thing. I found her in the garden crying her heart out not long after Uncle Magnus rang up to tell her the news. They found him lying outside in the rain. Had a stroke, poor old love. He hung on for a few days, but . . . And Grandma wouldn't let Mum go and see him, told the hospital they weren't to let her in if she went there, spiteful old cow. Mum was that upset. It was his funeral that day, when I found her crying."

"But that's awful! Wicked!"

My mouth formed this trite response with no help from my

brain, which was churning. I *was* appalled; even though I had never known my aunt, I still felt an automatic outrage at the treatment she'd received, indignation that this sad-sack cousin of mine had had to witness her mother's grief and exclusion and adopt it as her own.

At the same time, I own up to a tingle of anticipation, excitement even. There was something fascinating about a being capable of such enduring, implacable enmity, something monstrous in its wholehearted rigidity, turning every cherished notion about motherhood on its head, trampling remorselessly on ideals of unconditional love and forgiveness, deaf to appeals and argument, *and able to make it stick.*

My grandmother loomed in my imagination. She was more than all the wicked stepmothers, all the mad, bad women of myth and history, more like a grotesque female Cronus, gobbling up children to preserve power and keep things the way they had always been. I couldn't wait to meet her.

Almost as if she'd heard my thoughts, Deirdre spoke.

"She's a holy terror, that's what Mum called her. Hateful old bitch, mad as a hatter, if you ask me."

"Have you ever tried to make contact, tried to see her or anything, on your own?"

Deirdre frowned and looked puzzled.

"Why would I want to do that? Why would I want to see someone who doesn't even admit I exist? Why should I talk to somebody who'd hate me automatically?"

They were good questions. Why did I? Did I have some dumb idea that I was going to drop into her life and change the attitudes of a lifetime? Devastate her with my charm so that she saw the error of her ways and folded me into her arms, weeping for the lost years? Not likely.

But I might be able to force her to acknowledge me. Even a vituperative rejection would be a victory of sorts because you don't reject with such animosity things that don't matter to you, that have no significance. And I don't mind admitting to you, Stephen, that there was a competitive element, a sense of pitting myself against a powerful opponent, which carried with it all the strings of choosing such a confrontation. Whatever happened, I would have a new yardstick for measuring myself; whatever happened, there would be knowledge and finality in the outcome.

But you have to know where someone is to meet them.

"I suppose we can safely say she won't be at your mother's funeral?"

"Fat chance of that!"

"How about Uncle Magnus?"

It felt strange to say the name, but then it would have felt awkward to say "your uncle" too. There were hidden traps in these new relationships, if such they really were.

"I've invited him. Maybe he'll come, if She doesn't get her claws on the announcement first. I don't know."

Her voice trailed off, and she fiddled with a crumpled tissue. Her face drooped even further. I knew what was coming.

"You couldn't come, could you?" she asked, resignation at my refusal already in her voice. "No, 'course not, silly of me."

Refusal was no longer an option. Where do you most often encounter family members you rarely, if ever, see? Weddings and funerals, of course.

"Yes, I'll come. When and where?"

Deirdre brightened.

"You don't have to, really, but if you do, it's on Wednesday at 2:00 PM. Just a memorial service, she told me she didn't want any big thing. Actually, she always said I should roll her up in a rug and put her out on the kerb for the dustmen when she fell off her perch. Here"—and she handed me a card from a funeral home—"this is where it'll be."

"How far would Uncle Magnus have to travel if he came?"

"He probably won't," she said, "it's a bit of a hassle for him. I think he'd have to go into London from Reading or Oxford and then come back out again to get here. And he'd have to get a bus from the village to the train."

Not much help. The direct approach always works better.

"Where does he live?"

"Oh, of course, you wouldn't know, would you? Well, I've never been there myself, come to that. He lives in Berkshire, or is it Oxfordshire? A village called Sharrington, anyway."

"And what does he do? Or has he retired?"

"Oh no, I don't think so. He's the head gardener at some big estate there, what's its name? Grandad did the same, and his dad before him, I think. I'll remember it in a minute."

I was longing to suggest a name, but I didn't want to influence her recollection.

"Have you got your mother's birth certificate? Maybe it'll be on there. Don't they usually have the place where the parents live on them?"

Deirdre braced her hands on the protesting arms of her chair and heaved.

"You're right," she said, "and I know just where to lay my hands on that. I've been sorting through a bit."

She shuffled away, followed by several cats who roused themselves, jumped from their perches, and stretched langorously as soon as she moved. The tabby at my side yawned, giving me a closeup of his entire mouth and a blast of fish breath.

"Here it is!"

Deirdre was waving a sheet of paper in her hand.

"There," her finger pointed. "It's all there."

I looked down at the rectangle of pink paper. It was worn and the ink had faded to a soft grey. The paper was velvety and disintegrating along the folds, but the careful copperplate of the clerk was still perfectly clear. It told me that a female child had been born to Adam Goodman and his wife, Esther, on the seventeenth day of March 1919 in the parish of St. Luke, Sharrington, Berkshire. Adam Goodman's occupation was listed as Gardener, Hescot Park, Berks.

Confirmation punched the breath from my body in a noisy whoosh. Slowly, I reached for the tiny seed packet from the gas mask on the table in front of me and pointed to the faint pencil marks.

"'Hescot' was one of my guesses," I said. "Is it a big place, do you know?"

"I always got that impression from Mum. She used to tell me about the big house, and the kitchen garden with high walls and a fish pond, and the hothouse where they grew grapes and stuff like that. One of these big country mansions, you know. They lived on the estate, in a cottage. Still there, as far as I know."

She peered inside the envelope.

"What's this? Seeds?"

I explained.

"Oh," she said, "they'd have been able to grow something like that. I wonder why your mum was bringing them with her? My mum was always keen on her garden, but she never had a greenhouse. They wouldn't have been any use to her, would they?"

"You'll watch for anything that mentions her sister, won't you?"

And with that, and sundry pleasantries and renewed promises to come back for the funeral, I waded through the cats who were now milling about, hoping for food, and left.

EIGHTEEN

The air outside struck cold and curiously tasteless despite its overlay of salt and seaweed, homogenized after the concentrated cat fug in the house, but it matched my rarified mood of elation. I turned into a brisk southwesterly and made my way to the station, full of certainty. Buses and trucks lumbered past in a pall of diesel, carving their way among miniature cars, much like dogs swimming in the company of frightened mice. People hurried by, preoccupied and glum, or dawdled past shop windows, taking up three times their share of space with the overstuffed plastic bags or small children dangling from their hands. Empty chip packets and styrofoam cups bowled along the gutters, and a dog lifted its leg against a streetlamp.

I sped along the street as if I were invisible, hugging my discoveries to myself, pitying these dreary-looking people for their ordinariness. I could have done anything at that moment; leaping tall buildings at a single bound would have been a breeze. I looked forward to astonishing the Wimbledon ladies with my cleverness, and while I waited for the train, I calculated the time difference with Canada and rehearsed how to tell Neil my news. Spontaneous as ever, you see.

But there's nothing like a long train journey alone for introspection. As soon as I stopped buzzing from the adrenalin, the doubts crept back like ferrets down a rabbit hole. You've had enough ups and downs in your life, Stephen, to know exactly how you swing helplessly from hope to despair. Suppose I'd got it all wrong? Stumbled, quite by chance, on some people who *seemed* to fit the bill and simply swallowed everything whole because it suited me to believe? I am quite capable of it. Look at the time I fought with Neil over the car keys.

I *knew* I'd given them to him after I'd been shopping. I recalled, in angry and vivid detail, how I'd gone down to the studio to hand them over so that he could catch the five o'clock ferry, and he'd just got to a ticklish bit in the painting and needed both hands, so he'd gestured at the table with his chin and told me to put them down there, which I'd done, feeling irritated because I had to move two mugs and their disgusting scummy contents, as well as an apple core, a plate with half a dried sandwich curling on it, and an unruly pile of pages from a dismembered *Vancouver Sun* before I could find a space to lay down the keyring without having it drop instantly out of sight.

I defended myself with conviction when he asked me about them at about four o'clock. I can see it now, I told him: a bare, clean tabletop with the keyring lying in the very centre of its shining surface. I felt no guilt whatsoever as he turned the studio fruitlessly upside down, then scrambled to find the spare key, last used months before and buried almost without trace in his sock drawer. I was so convinced I was right that my mind had completely erased the part where I'd put the key in my pocket to handle the garbage, and walked away with it, leaving behind a clean table and fulminating silently about the slovenliness of men.

When I felt it digging into my leg as I sat down to a coffee long after Neil had left, I gaped in disbelief, then laughed. But now, remembering the tricks my mind could play over such a little thing was sobering. What might it get up to with really serious things at stake?

Like searching for long-lost relatives, for example. Hadn't

everything come much too easily? Why was I prepared to trust all the people I'd talked to so far? How could I think they would all have my interests at heart? Take Deirdre. A lonely, recently bereaved, half-dotty spinster surrounded by cats. And I parachute into her strange life with my romantic tale. Would she say what I wanted to hear just to keep me around? I only had her word for her mother's maiden name being the same as the one in the gas mask. Oh, there was the birth certificate, but I'd been fooled by one of those before. Why did she seem so determined to put me off contacting my grandmother? If she'd never seen her, as she said, how would she know what she was really like? Perhaps Sarah had been the dotty one, filling her mind with nonsense about big houses and gardens. Perhaps Uncle Magnus was a fabrication, no more part of a dynasty of gardeners than I was, simply invented to fill the gap in the life of a child whose father disappeared one day and never returned.

By the time I reached Wimbledon I had convinced myself I should be a lot more cautious. I was even considering cancelling my trip back to Brighton for the funeral, but the possibility of meeting a Magnus made me waver. Anyway, I was very subdued as I opened the front door and let myself in.

A glimmering shape greeted me with a soft meow. I bent to stroke Mao as he twined round my legs, then made for the stairs, intending to take myself quietly upstairs to my round room and go to bed. But the kitchen door flung open, and I heard Isobel's voice.

"I told you I heard the door!" she crowed. "Come in here a minute, dear, and see what we've got!"

The last thing I wanted was a post-mortem session with the three of them, but there was no refusing Isobel. She was urging me into the room, standing in the doorway beckoning urgently, and making little mews of excitement. As soon as I got near enough, she clutched my sleeve and pulled.

"Just look what Evelyn's found! We said she'd remember, didn't we?"

Miss Hoar was laying a large book on the kitchen table. With a flourish, like a magician whipping the covering off the magically empty box, she opened it. The paper was glossy, and the picture invisible in the glare from the light. I stepped forward to see better.

I was looking at a double-page photograph of an elegant house with an elaborate white dovecote on the lawn in front of it. Fantail pigeons, white and ruffled as folded napkins in a superior restaurant, strutted on the grass. I bent over the small print of the caption. "The Queen Anne mansion at Hescot Park, Berkshire," it read. I turned over the book so that I could see the title. It was *The National Trust*.

"I knew that name rang a bell," said Miss Hoar. "I just couldn't remember the context. Then Mildred mentioned the National Trust and I remembered this book. We always drop in at their properties if we're near one."

"Yes," said Miss Plover wistfully, "such gracious houses. We do our little bit to keep them alive."

"Not that we've ever been to this one," said Miss Hoar. "Like to, though. Pretty, isn't it?"

It was. I stared at the picture, willing it to give up its secrets. The building fitted my idea of eighteenth-century houses, graceful and well proportioned, sitting comfortably in its manicured surroundings, but I couldn't say it was familiar. Where had the feeling come from then, so insistent, that I would recognize what was offstage, so to speak? That if I could see behind the house or off to the left beyond the dovecote, or walk away from the house across the lawn into the foreground, I might know where I was?

"That's amazing," I said. "I was talking to someone today who told me about this place. She said it's where her uncle works and where her mother lived as a child. It looks as if I really may have found some of my family."

Their pleased cries drowned out my remaining skepticism, and my confidence returned as I related what had happened. They didn't seem to have any doubts at all.

"Obviously the next step is to contact the uncle," said Miss Hoar. "If the grandmother is still alive, she'll be very old, and there seems to be something odd there. I'd say the uncle would be the best bet. If he's a gardener, he's bound to be all right."

Her logic eluded me, but there was a force to everything Miss Hoar said, probably a hangover from her days as a teacher in that golden time when parents and students looked on teachers as superior beings, like doctors, almost godlike in their knowledge. Personally, I've never experienced this reverence, but I've heard of it. Even little Miss Penfold sometimes hints at a different world, hidden now in the mists of time, when she wasn't harassed by lumpen boys and tittering girls, and her teeth were her own and never a source of humiliation and ridicule.

Whatever the source of Miss Hoar's authority, it had its effect on me. I felt encouraged by her discovery and judgement. Neil caught it too, when I called him later.

"You sound very chipper," he commented when I had brought him up to date. "I guess the uncle's next?"

You'd think I'd feel peculiar sitting here talking to you like this, Stephen, but believe me, I felt a lot stranger talking to Neil. We had shared so much, and he had encouraged me to start my search, yet his interest in the outcome was inevitably an outsider's. Over there I was literally another person; I had seen things, been to places, met people he had no knowledge of beyond my descriptions. They were *my* experience, quite disconnected from the Livvy he knew, and his only way into them was through my narrative, which could be as closed or revealing as I chose. There was a tiny, shameful delight in that.

I tried to make up for it by pressing him for details about home. He told me about his work; he'd just been reading Bruce Chatwin, so his latest country was something like Patagonia. And there was another project under way, but he was tightlipped and awkward about that, hedging and taking refuge in artistic uncertainty, or so he claimed. "I'll tell you more when it's clear in my mind," he said, "or when it's finished, if I ever get that far." A few minutes of that and we were like two acquaintances trying to prolong a conversation out of politeness.

"How's Maisie?" I asked desperately.

"She's fine. Missing you, of course."

Of course? Did that mean he missed me too?

"She's taken to haunting the studio, but I'm a poor second best." There was a pause. "She'll be glad to see you again." Another pause. "We all will."

It was as close as Neil would come to saying he was lonely. I knew what he wanted to hear, but a mulish voice in my head muttered, *Not yet, not yet.*

"I know," I said, "but I've got to see this through now, haven't I?"

I could almost feel him giving himself a shake, injecting enthusiasm into his voice.

"Of course! Everyone's dying to know how it all turns out. Stephen was asking me just the other day if there was any news."

Another pang of guilt. When had I last thought of you? It was a shock to find that my other self could let you drift away to the edges as well. Hastily, I asked how you were getting on.

"Not too bad. He's back at work, says he's feeling better, says the thing's in remission. Just have to wait and see now. Maybe he'll be lucky."

"He's due for some of that."

"We both know luck has nothing to do with what you deserve, Liv."

Daniel's presence hummed on the line.

"True. I've been telling myself that these last few weeks. It's all fallen together so easily, I know it can't last, I'll hit a roadblock and that'll be that. I'll be a jigsaw with missing pieces forever."

Neil's snort of derision exploded in my ear, the first unstudied thing in our conversation.

"That just makes you more of a challenge, not impossible!"

I know when I'm over the top. I tried to match his mood.

"Okay, you can put me in my box and stuff me in the attic when my mystery wears thin. You go and paint a masterpiece—I've got a past to dig up. Give my love to everyone. Maybe I'll have an uncle next time I call!"

NINETEEN

I went to the funeral. For the occasion, I dragged out my black leather jacket, shabby from overuse, a black skirt creased from being crushed in the wardrobe, black tights, and a black turtle-neck sweater that had pilled under the arms and definitely seen better days. The number of shades of black was a revelation. The overall effect was sombre enough but amazingly scruffy. I looked like a cross between a Dickensian mute and a shabby Goth. Common sense reasserted itself, and abandoning deep mourning and its attendant feelings of hypocrisy, I set out for Brighton again in comfortable beige pants and a blue sweater, with the black jacket on top because it was windproof.

A taxi deposited me at the funeral chapel. There were no vehicles in the parking lot except for a hearse. Obviously Deirdre had been right; there were few mourners for her mother.

I was still hopeful there would be an elderly man among the few; Deirdre had seemed to expect her uncle to come by train if he came at all. Inside, though, I found Deirdre sitting on her own in a front pew. Three old ladies whispering with their heads together occupied a pew several rows back. An invisible organ was funnelling *Ave Maria* into the chapel much as Barry Manilow tunes flood into elevators.

Deirdre brightened as she looked up at me.

"Oh you came," she said. "That's nice. You didn't have to, really, but I'm glad." Her voice dropped as she looked over her shoulder. "Not much of a turnout, is it? Those three used to play bridge with Mum down at the Golden Agers. They seemed more annoyed than anything. I suppose they'll have to find another partner now Mum's gone."

"Uncle Magnus not here?"

"He phoned and said he couldn't make it. Said the old lady's poorly and can't be left. Probably threw a fit just so's he couldn't come, miserable old cow."

"Did you tell him anything about me?"

The organ had segued into "Amazing Grace" without a pause. Despite the sound the silence was oppressive and Deirdre mumbled self-consciously from behind her chapped hand as if to shield the occupant of the coffin, sitting spare and unadorned save for a single sheaf of white carnations just in front of us, from the evidence of our continuing vitality.

"Well, yes. I told him you'd been to see me and that. Was that all right? I didn't mess up, did I?"

Before I could answer, the organ ground out the finale of the hymn and extinguished itself abruptly. At the same time a lanky man in a black gown materialized at Deirdre's side and touched her elbow, making her jump and clutch at her bosom reproachfully.

"If you're ready, we'll begin," said the man, then inclining his head graciously to her stammering, glided to the front of the chapel and took his place beside the coffin.

"We are gathered together," he intoned mellifluously, "to remember our sister in Christ, Sarah Faith Murphy . . ."

He'd had a lot of practice. His voice was consciously beautiful, like John Gielgud playing Hamlet, and soporific. Sarah Faith Murphy meant nothing to him, and there was not the least suggestion of emotion or involvement, simply a dispassionate recitation of the appropriate words, to everything there is a season, sparks flying upwards from the dried grass, dust, and ashes, resurrection and life eternal. We were enjoined to sing a hymn, and the old ladies behind us perked up and launched their quavery sopranos into "Abide with Me" with little regard for its lugubrious tempo, racing the minister and the organ to each line, and embarking on the rallentando of the last three notes well before the rest of us, so that our finale came as a kind of echo and was unexpectedly moving.

I felt a pricking at my eyes and hoped my nose wouldn't turn bright red as it usually does when I cry. Emotion was short-lived, though, as the undertaker slid forward to remove the carnations and press some hidden switch. With a slight jolt, the coffin rolled forward rather like a large suitcase on an airport carousel and nosed its way through a discreet opening. Deirdre squeezed her hands together and gave a muffled squeak. The curtains flapped together behind the coffin and that was that. I wanted to yell, "Stop! Let's do it all again, properly!" but the minister was advancing on Deirdre, and the undertaker was whisking away the flowers. I had the strangest feeling that they would have looked quite blank if I'd mentioned Sarah's name.

"Well, that was very nice, dear," said one of the old ladies, holding Deirdre's limp hand in both of hers. "It was a lovely send-off. I do like the old hymns."

"We'll miss her down the centre," said another, whose black felt hat was skewered to her head with a large silver pin.

"Yes," agreed the third, "I don't know where we'll find a fourth to replace her, I'm sure."

"Deirdre isn't interested in our little problem, Mabel," reproved the first lady. "What are you going to do now, dear?"

"I'm just going home," said Deirdre. "There's the cats to feed."

"Oh yes, the cats. Sarah was so fond of them, wasn't she? I'm allergic myself. Not having refreshments, then? Well, it's probably better for you just to go home and be quiet. I always think having everyone back after a funeral is horrible."

She looked disappointed, though, and it gave Deirdre another reason to feel inadequate.

"I should have invited them, shouldn't I? But I don't have anything in the house. I don't think I've even got a loaf of bread. Tins of cat food, plenty of that, but that's not much use, is it? And what would I give them to drink? Aren't you supposed to have sherry and stuff like that?"

I stemmed her agonizing and led her to a café up the road. I couldn't just wring out the information I wanted and leave her to trail drearily away to the cats. Nor was another immersion in that special feline smell inviting. Isn't there a planet with an atmosphere of ammonia? Venus? Imagine being a creature that could only exist in air that reeked of cats or untended public lavatories.

Over tea and scones I steered Deirdre back to her conversation with her uncle.

"So what did Uncle Magnus say when you told him about me?"

Deirdre looked thoughtful.

"Well, he didn't say much really," she ventured at last. "I said we thought we might be cousins and he said, 'How d'you reckon that, then?' so I told him about the things you had with you, and how you were found and that, but he still said no, couldn't be, there had to be some mistake."

"Did he say why he thought it was impossible?"

Deirdre licked her finger and foraged about her plate for crumbs. There was a smear of jam at the corner of her mouth.

"He just said there's a grave and that's an end of it. 'Tombstones don't lie,' he said. I don't know what he was talking about there."

"But that's like saying cameras never lie," I retorted. "We all know they can. Just because we hardly ever want to check doesn't mean that every grave actually contains what it says on the headstone."

"Oh yes," she breathed, "I saw a film like that on the tele. They dug up this grave, and the coffin was full of bricks. The person who was supposed to be in it had faked his own death to get away with all the money after a bank robbery, but the others had their suspicions, and so did . . ."

"Yes, well, that's a story, but it's possible, isn't it?"

Deirdre nodded her head but continued to look puzzled.

"What I don't get is if he's talking about your mother's tombstone, how does that make it impossible for *you* to exist?"

It was my turn to look uncomfortable. If, as I suspected, the headstone mentioned both my mother and me, I could understand Uncle Magnus's conviction very well. And how did I explain the presence of a child in the grave without revealing Mum and Dad's peculiar role? It dawned on me that I was reluctant to expose that element of the story, and my hesitation had nothing to do with the difficulties I would face trying to tell such a wildly improbable tale. I felt the need to protect the two people who had brought me up; after all, they must have committed more than one crime, and I had no idea how vindictive my new family might feel. I might see some mitigation, but would they? In the meantime, there was Deirdre's awkward question, left hanging in the air between us, to answer. I had to think fast.

"Sometimes gravestones are used as memorials," I said. "The child disappeared and they had to assume she was dead too. Maybe they just included her on the stone when they buried her mother. You've seen those family graves that say, 'Here lies so-and-so, and his beloved wife such-and-such, and what's his name, dearly beloved son of so-and-so, lost at sea in the sinking of the *Lusitania*, blah, blah, blah.'"

Deirdre brightened.

"Right," she said, "you *are* clever. Why didn't I think of that? That's what it'll be. You'll have to tell him that. He won't be quite so sure, then."

Maybe, I thought. And maybe Uncle Magnus will be a tougher nut to crack than Deirdre. And what about the Holy Terror, implacable in her rejection of everything? If it had been easy so far, I sensed the tide was now running against me. There were, after all, two sides to this situation and no guarantee that the people I claimed as my family would have any desire to take up that role.

To defend myself against thought while on the train, I bought a copy of *The Times* at the station. At least the crossword would distract me, I hoped. I was partly right. The crossword drove me to distraction, and I abandoned it angrily for the Letters to the Editor. There I discovered that the readers of *The Times*, those strange superior people who could actually solve the crossword, were concerned about public money wasted on the education of morons and thugs whose only ambition was to destroy everything that decent people hold dear, about unrestricted parking, busking in the Underground, gazumping and squats, the negative effects of the Common Market on the English sausage industry, the proliferation of regional accents on the BBC, and the tricky qualities of Margaret Thatcher's face, which could be seen in all its deceptive femininity smiling reproachfully at a deputation of union spokesmen on the front page.

There was also a cuckoo letter, claiming to have heard the first call of the year, so triumphant and excitable I thought it had to be an endangered creature and resolved to find out more about it. Perhaps, I thought idly, there was a Cuckoo Trust, dedicated to preserving its habitat, along the lines of the group that struggled on behalf of hedgehogs and persuaded local authorities to build escape ramps for them underneath cattle grids, or the snake and toad supporters who agitated for tunnels under major roads to save the migrating reptiles and amphibians from being squashed flat in their headlong dash to reproduction.

First, though, I had to tackle Hescot Park and the Holy Terror.

That night, I slipped away in the stillness of my round room as the darker bulk of the beech tree nodded outside, tapping a message in code on the windowpane, and floated again, for the first time in ages, to the white house without walls. There I waited while cloud shadows raced across the surface of the lake at time lapse speed, scanning the water for a sign, any sign, eyes wide and unblinking, muscles clenched with the intensity of my yearning. When I woke, I was exhausted, and tears were crawling down my face.

TWENTY

My landladies got me to Berkshire in the end. Inquiries into train and bus services convinced me that any approach to Sharrington by public transport would be complicated and tedious.

"Never been the same since Beeching closed down all the branch lines," said Miss Hoar when I lamented the difficulties of dovetailing timetables. "Used to be able to get anywhere by train. Idiots said it wasn't profitable."

Miss Plover recognized a hobbyhorse and came to my rescue.

"We were wondering," she began delicately, "if we could drive you there? It really isn't far away. It would make a nice trip, and the country's lovely."

It was the solution, but I didn't want them to be left hanging about, waiting for me.

"I don't know what kind of reception I'm going to get," I replied. "I wouldn't want you to be inconvenienced."

"Oh nonsense," said Isobel. "There's a fourteenth-century church in the village with a spectacular rood screen and some wonderful brasses. We'll have lots to do—you'll probably end up waiting for us while we poke about. We're terrible when we get our teeth into a bit of history!"

I could believe it when I saw the rolls of paper, the bag full of soft brushes and balls of what looked like black wax for the brass rubbing, and the cameras and lenses and rolls of film that went into the trunk with the sandwiches and thermoses, apples, oranges, Penguin biscuits, and the inevitable sherbert lemons.

Miss Plover drove a venerable Rover with characteristic dignity. She sat bolt upright, her large hands clutching the wheel in the approved position, and cautiously steered the car out of the driveway. The Rover was old, but its motor whispered along, and the interior was luxurious in a way none of the cars I've ever driven could boast. The seats were dark brown leather, and the dashboard was a polished wood, walnut, at a guess. There was plenty of leg room in the back and convenient pockets for maps and guidebooks and sherbert lemons in the doors. This solid comfort was all of a piece with our majestic progress through the suburbs, through the Green Belt, and into countryside I thought existed only on calendars: rolling fields bounded by thick hedges, windswept downland with huddles of sheep in the dips and hollows, and stone cottages in villages where the church tower or steeple poked out of a tangle of branches and rooks and yew trees stood among the graves.

Sharrington was just such a place. Isobel squealed in approval as she caught sight of the lych gate and the churchyard, crowded with weathered headstones, and Miss Hoar craned her neck to see the top of the cross erected in the middle of what looked like a market square, colonnaded and cobbled. Houses and shops huddled round this central point but soon petered out as we followed the main road through the village to be replaced by a long wall that parallelled the highway for what seemed like miles.

The stones of the wall were golden with lichen and looked as if they would be warm to the touch, but they were an efficient barrier. Inside the girdle of stone, ancient trees stood in pools of shadow, and there were tantalizing glimpses of rooftops and driveways, grazing animals and open fields through the wrought iron gates that punctured the wall at intervals. One set of gates was particularly ornate and had twin cottages attached on either side. This, I presumed, was the main gate of the estate, and the lodgekeeper used to live there, handy for his task of opening the gates for carriages. Perhaps he still did, for cars, but the cottages had a still, sad air of disuse. As we passed, I just caught a glimpse of the signboard outside the gate: HESCOT PARK, it read. NATIONAL TRUST.

Following the wall even farther brought us to another gate, of the five-barred farm variety this time. A driveway curved out of sight between two fields. A large herd of Friesians grazed in one, and the other lay fallow, the heavy clods of earth hardened just as the plow had turned them in the fall. Another sign announced PUBLIC PARKING, JUNE 1–30, and an arrow pointed mutely to the drive.

"This is probably the way in," said Miss Plover, parking neatly on the grass verge. "Shall we try?"

Suddenly I wanted them gone. I had become very fond of them, and I was grateful, but this was something I had to tackle on my own, not accompanied by a gaggle of elderly ladies as if I needed support but had few resources to choose from. I urged them to go and visit the church since the park obviously opened to visitors only one month in the year, so they wouldn't be able to wander around while they waited for me.

"Didn't you plan to do brass rubbings?" I asked. "You'd better get started; don't they take a long time?"

"Are you quite sure you'll be all right?" Miss Plover looked anxious.

"Stop twittering, Mildred, she's perfectly capable of looking after herself. Got a brain and a tongue in her head, hasn't she? Leave her to get on with it; she doesn't want us around for this. It's private. Besides, she'll tell us all about it later."

I could have hugged Miss Hoar for her bluntness and acuity.

Miss Plover subsided, and we made arrangements for them to pick me up at the gate later in the afternoon. I watched them pack themselves into the car and smiled at the three faces turned my way.

"Good luck!" Isobel mouthed as the car bumped slowly off the grass and three hands waved simultaneously as if conferring a blessing. I turned quickly without giving myself time to reconsider, climbed the gate, and set off up the driveway.

Canada is a land that puts its inhabitants in their place where scale is concerned. I'm used to insignificance against vast skies and forests and seas that might cover the face of the earth for all you can see an end to them. Yet I've never felt so vulnerable as I did toiling along that narrow road in the midst of a pretty, domesticated landscape straight out of one of the Gainsboroughs I'd seen in the National Gallery. I half expected to find a complacent young gentleman, dressed in silks and lace, his dogs at his side, leaning nonchalantly against a noble oak, his outstretched hand directing my eyes to the expansive woods and fields picked out in loving detail behind him, his knowing smile saying, "Mine, all mine. See how important, how successful I am?"

I was quite alone, in fact. The cows near the fence watched me pass with the heavy attention of their kind that makes you think their blood must be like molasses, sliding slowly through their veins. I could hear their breathing and soft snorts as their wet rubber noses tilted and dilated at me, and one or two, bolder than the rest, took ponderous steps closer to the wire to inspect the alien.

The road wound around a stand of trees, rising gently. Open fields lay to my right as far as I could see. In the distance, a tractor no bigger than a toy crept along a track, but I saw no other evidence of people. The road I was on plunged into a wood, full of new leaf, and my footfalls were deadened by the mast lying on the ground. There were tracks through the trees, too narrow to have been made by men, and where one of these opened into a shallow ditch I met a hare. We both stopped dead, he rigidly upright, trembling with tension, one black eye watching intently as he held his Roman nose in profile. Then he was gone, back the way he had come, and in the still moment before I started walking again, I heard a sound.

It was a bird, but not one I had ever heard before. The two-note call came again, distant but quite distinct, ahead of me. I knew what it was because it told me. "Cuckoo," it said, "cuckoo," the second note a third lower than the first, exactly like someone calling, "Cooee!" but the tone full and liquid, not shrill and high. I stood listening, looking about, hoping for a movement or the flash of a wing, but there was no sign of the bird, and when it called again, it had moved farther off. I felt absurdly pleased to have heard it and went on, smiling.

Soon I came upon signs of occupation, if not life. The road emerged from the trees, and I found myself walking beside a grassy expanse bordering an artificial waterway. The grass had been tended, but the low stone walls and steps that guided the water down the slope were covered in moss and there were long curtains of algae in the pools. I followed the watercourse, thinking that the house must be somewhere close by, but all I found was an old tennis court by the stream, cracked wooden posts at each side with the remains of a net trailing from them.

A man was bending over one of the posts. He straightened up as I approached and looked at me expectantly.

"You haven't come about the tiles, have you?" he asked obscurely.

"I'm afraid not."

"Pity," said the man, then added hastily, "not that it isn't a pleasure to see a lady, of course."

"Of course. But tiles are uppermost in your mind today."

"Well, yes, though I'm trying to make up my mind about this too. Should I turn it into a swimming pool, d'you think?"

I thought of the algae and wondered who would look after a swimming pool.

"Awful lot of upkeep," I said, "chlorination and such."

"Yes," he said doubtfully, "there is that. Weather's usually bloody awful too. Have to think about it."

He was about my age, with a thin brown face and hazel eyes with remarkable eyelashes. He was very tall, attenuated as a Masai, and dressed in filthy jeans, mudspattered Wellington boots, and an ancient sweater with a large hole at the right elbow and fraying cuffs.

"Can I help you with something?" he asked. "We're not actually open to the public this time of year, I'm afraid."

"I'm hoping to see Mr. Goodman, Magnus Goodman. If you could tell me where I'd find him."

"Oh," said the man, "come to see the boss, have you? Just follow the road around. You'll come to the stables, well, they used to be stables, more storage for equipment now. You'll probably find him around there."

He was pointing the way with his left hand. I couldn't help noticing that his watch was a Rolex.

I left him tugging at the frayed rope on the post and returned to the road. As he had promised, it soon brought me to a sprawl of buildings, dark inside, still smelling faintly of horse but inhabited mostly by sacks and boxes and farm machinery. I wandered through a gateway in a high wall of rosy brick and found a row of greenhouses surrounded by bins of soil, stacks of seedling trays and punnets, barrels and pots, wheelbarrows and carts. A man emerged from a shed carrying a garden fork. He looked much too young to be Magnus Goodman. He stared at me curiously but would have passed with a mumbled greeting if I hadn't asked him where I could find the head gardener.

"He'll be in his office, I reckon," he said, "down the end there, last one."

Office was an overstatement unless you understand it simply as a place of work. The greenhouse was the way they used to be: brick base, wooden frame, and real glass. Some of the glass had been whitewashed to cut down on the glare, and the greenhouse had an enclosed, separate feel to it like a cave. The benches on each side were covered with trays, many sprouting seedlings, and underneath huddled tanks of water and longnecked watering cans.

There was a space at the far end of the greenhouse. An old wooden table had been shoved into a corner and was littered with papers, many smeared with earth, and skewered on spikes, balls of twine, plant labels, and small tools like secateurs and knives. A large cabinet of tiny drawers with brass handles and nameplates stood in the other corner, and in between was a bench with a number of sticks lying on it, arranged in a neat row. Sitting in a sagging chair with his back to me was a large man.

"Mr. Goodman?" I ventured.

The massive shoulders twisted and his face peered round. "Yes?"

Now that I had come to the moment I'd been anticipating for weeks, I was mute. How was I going to introduce this topic? "I have reason to believe" sounded far too much like the police to make a good impression. "You are my uncle," too challenging by far. Launching myself at him with glad cries of "I'm your long-lost niece!" just asking for rejection. In the end, I made use of Deirdre again.

"I think Deirdre has already mentioned me to you."

"Is that so?"

"Yes, I'm the one who thinks . . . no, that is, I'm pretty sure I'm related to her. I know it sounds impossible, but I think I'm your niece. You did once have two, didn't you?"

He swivelled the chair around so he could see me better. His bulk filled the chair, and he looked immovable as he sat with his feet in their heavy boots planted firmly wide apart and thrust his large head at me, bracing the weight of his upper body with his hands on his knees.

"Not only sounds impossible but *is*," he said, "and I'll tell you for why so's we don't get ourselves in a bother for nothing."

I said nothing and let him take his time. I could tell already he would be impossible to hurry; even his speech, with its lovely broad vowels and lilting cadence, was leisurely, although there was a force to it, and he wanted no argument.

"My younger sister was killed in an air raid in London in 1941," he began. "She shouldn't have been there, but there you are, those things happen. She had a little girl, one year old or so, maybe less. The child died too. They were found together and identified eventually, and my dad brought them back home to be buried, lying together in the same coffin. I don't think he ever got over that; he were a sad old man the rest of his days. And I saw them laid in the earth. I stood beside my dad, and we saw them home together, and I cried, I don't mind saying. And there's the headstone on the grave, plain as a pikestaff for all to see, with the two names. My old dad put his foot down about that, insisted, he did, and got his way for once, poor old chap. So you see, it doesn't add up, does it? I'm sorry if it's a disappointment, but it'd be best to forget the notion and lay it to rest."

"But you haven't heard my story yet."

"That I haven't, but there's no getting round those two bodies in that grave, is there? My dad saw them both. He knew."

"I'm sure there are two bodies in the grave. In fact, I *know* there are. It's just that the baby wasn't your sister's child."

"What are you saying?" he asked, then went on to tell me, "You're saying that some baby was buried by mistake with my sister? How am I to believe that? You expect me to believe there just happened to be *another* baby on that street? And what happened to my niece, then? Got up and walked away, did she? Come on now, you'll have to do better than that! My dad had to identify them. And he did. Said he just had to take one look at my sister even though . . . and the baby's red curls. D'you suppose he'd say they were his kin if they weren't?"

"I don't suppose that for a minute. But think a bit. It's not always easy to identify people, especially when they've died from head injuries, especially when some time has elapsed before you see the body. I don't suppose they were knocking on your door with the news right after it happened, were they? Maybe your father recognized your sister some way and more or less assumed the baby was hers. Babies look alike. It would be a reasonable assumption."

He was looking at me strangely.

"How did you know that?" he asked slowly. "How did you know she died of head injuries?"

I was caught. The detail had slipped out heedlessly. The small fact had seized his attention; I could tell he was no longer disposed to usher me out without listening. But I wouldn't be able to capitalize on his curiosity without telling him about Mum and Dad's strange role.

"It's a long story," I said. "Would you like to hear it?"

"I'm listening," he said grimly and settled back with his arms folded, as imperturbable and incorruptible as a cricket umpire.

For a while there, I became Scheherazade, fighting to keep a reluctant Sultan hooked. Not that I was trying to entertain; it was much more a question of the hard sell to a cynical customer. But we had one thing in common, that inventive strategist and I: a desperate wish to keep ourselves alive, she literally, and I, well, wasn't it literal for me too? Wasn't I struggling to inhabit a life that had been waiting for me all those years? And if I failed to convince this monolithic slab of a man that I was his niece, what would remain but a retreat into what I could only think of as an alias? I would be like a permanent ward of the Witness Protection Program.

I told him everything. At first he listened sternly, witholding any hint of involvement. There was no more give in him than there is in a glass slipper. When I explained how I had stumbled on the fact I was not related to the people I had always called my family, a shadow crossed his face, and his arms, which up to then had been tightly folded as if to keep himself intact, relaxed. By the time I reached Mum and Dad's flight with a dead child through the air raid, he was reaching into his pocket for a pipe and an oiled silk pouch, banging the dottle from the pipe on the corner of the bench, and filling it one handed with tobacco that smelled as sweet as any flower. His hands froze, holding a lighted match, when I told of their discovery in the doorway in Fenning Street, and his exclamation and violent start as the flame burned his fingers punctuated with impeccable timing my account of Mum laying down her dead child and picking me up.

I pointed out my similarity to the dead child that enabled Mum and Dad to maintain the fiction I was their daughter. I explained their lack of contact with any sharp-eyed relatives or neighbours who might have noticed a difference, the way their real daughter's ration book, identity card, and birth certificate gave an unarguable foundation to my identity and prevented any problems that might have arisen, and how my own youth made me the perfect accomplice and war the perfect setting.

Finally, I laid the gas mask and its case, the scrap of paper, and the tiny envelope on the bench by his elbow and told him that these had been found with me and were the only clues to my identity. He settled a pair of half-glasses on his nose and picked the items up one by one. He grunted, an involuntary bark of surprise, when he found the name written on the strap, but he flashed a look over the spectacles at me and shook his head.

"R for Ruth," he said almost to himself, then looked at me. "'Twasn't the child's name, you know," but then, as if he couldn't help himself, "but 'twas her name for the little maid, right enough."

I was longing to ask what the name should have been, and why my mother hadn't used it, but I didn't want to interrupt his inspection. My caution paid off. He picked up the scrap of paper with Sarah's address on it and stiffened.

"My oath," he breathed and laid his pipe, which had gone out, on the bench. Still holding the paper, he reached for the envelope and peered at the faint writing. A strange little noise escaped him and his hand went to his mouth. I was stunned to see a tear trickling down his cheek, but still I kept silent.

"I thought you were just having me on," he said finally, "though why you'd bother, I can't rightly say. But I believe you now, and I'll tell you, it's not your clever story as did it, it's these here"—gesturing at the paper and envelope—"I know where this bit of paper come from. I should. I tore it out my very own self, stole it from Mother's book to give to my poor sister. And this here"—fingering the packet of seeds—"I'd know that hand anywhere. Don't I see it every day of my life? Look here."

He pointed to the cabinet full of drawers.

"That's my dad's writing on all those labels, see?"

I bent closer to look at the elegant copperplate, written with a fine pen, the downstrokes broad and the upstrokes mere threads of ink. Magnus held the envelope close to one of the drawers.

"Now," he said, "see here."

The label on the drawer read STEPHANOTIS. The name on the envelope was like an echo, faint but unmistakably the same. He slid open the drawer and inside lay the same downy seeds I had found in the packet. It wasn't proof of anything, yet it felt like a smoking gun. I looked at Magnus. He looked at me.

"Well," he said slowly, "it's a facer, but I seem to have found a niece, and I never thought to say that."

"Uncle Magnus," I asked, the words odd in my mouth, "what is my real name?"

His face fell serious again.

"Ah now, there's a thing," he said evasively. "What have they called you all these years?"

"Livvy, short for Olivia."

"Well, you might want to stick with that. That's a pretty name. I don't reckon you'll much fancy the name you were given here."

"But what *was* it?"

"My old dad, he were right against it. 'You can't call the little maid that,' he said, ''twill be a millstone round the child's neck.' But she would have it; made the old man go and register the birth, not a second would she wait."

"Who wouldn't? My mother?"

"Lord bless you, no! *My* mother, that were. Your mother would have given you some dainty name out of her poetry books, but she never got the chance."

"You're driving me mad, you know! What's my name? Something awful like Bertha or Gladys?"

Uncle Magnus looked flushed and embarrassed.

"That wouldn't be so bad," he said. I wondered what on earth it could be if that wasn't so bad. Blodwen? Hagar? My uncle took the plunge.

"The name on your birth certificate—and none of us wanted it, remember, except Mother—is . . . Rue. Rue Tribulation," he finished in a rush.

"Rue? As in the herb?"

"Well, more like 'you'll rue the day.'"

"Oh, I see. And Tribulation too. Can I take it my grandmother wasn't too smitten?"

The sound Uncle Magnus made wasn't really a word, but it was eloquent. It was part sigh, part groan, a sad, resigned acceptance of the way things were, a melancholy commentary on the nastiness of some, on the waste of lives, on his own ineffectual contribution, a wry shrugging of the shoulders as if to say, "What's the good, when all's said and done?"

"Why? What was wrong with me? You've got a story to tell as well, haven't you?"

Uncle Magnus heaved himself out of his chair.

"Let's take a walk," he said.

TWENTY-ONE

I hope you're taking this in, Stephen, wherever you are. We're coming to the part of the story that smacks of dream worlds, of lurid Gothic emotion, the stylized excess and lunacy that hangs about the subconscious and peeks out in nightmare.

All the more dramatic for me, recounted as it was in my uncle's slow countryman's voice while we ambled through the Eden that is his kingdom. We started off by entering another walled garden—and isn't that what the source of the word *Paradise* means?—and strolled the outer circular path past the fruit trees heavy with buds, the currant and gooseberry bushes, the espaliered fruit clutching the brick, and the glass house on the south side that sheltered the white peaches.

The order and abundance formed the backdrop to Magnus's account of his youth. He told me about his father, Adam Goodman, who was also the head gardener like his father before him, and about his mother, Esther, as we sat on the parapet of a large pond at the centre of the garden and dangled our hands in the water. Big goldfish, used to being fed, rose lazily to the surface and sucked on our fingertips while Magnus told of his mother's autocratic rule and her fearsome religion that branded everyone a sinner and admitted very few to salvation.

"Primitive Baptist she is," he said. "I don't hold with all that miserable nonsense, not after what happened, but I had to wait till I was grown to get away from it. Hale us all to chapel, she would, two, three times a week sometimes, so we could hear just how wicked we were. No hope for sinners like us, I can tell you! And Sundays! What a misery. No going out, no games, no hobbies, no books even, except for the Bible. We used to sneak out when we could and play in the woods, but then we were even more damned and got sent to bed without our supper to pray for forgiveness. Worth it, though, just to get away from the house, and Dad used to creep upstairs with apples and bits of bread when he could. He didn't like it, but those days raising children was the woman's job—he was too busy putting food on the table to interfere, and he got the sharp edge of her tongue when he did, anyway. He were a quiet soul, my dad. I expect he reckoned she were a good woman and couldn't do no harm. Besides, he were fond of her for all her waspish ways. It were just easier to leave things be.

"My two sisters had the worst of it. None of us had friends, couldn't really, when we weren't allowed out, never went anywhere. None of us ever thought about bringing anyone home from school for tea or anything like that. And all this for a playground! Wicked, that was. But I used to go with Dad sometimes, fishing, shooting pigeons, out to the market, just working. She allowed that because I was a boy, and that's what the men did. But the girls! They might as well have been nuns for all they saw of the world.

"And that was part of the trouble, of course. She thought she was keeping them safe, I don't doubt, but when you've no experience, that makes you an easy target for all the things she was so busy keeping them from. Trusting, they were, both Susanna and Sarah, could recite the Bible, chapter and verse, but knew as much about the world as babes in arms. Murphy come to the door one day, selling brushes. Sarah took one look at him, curly hair and enough sweet talk to rot your teeth, and that was that. I don't know how she arranged it, but she went off to Bible study with Susanna one evening and only the one came back. Next we know, she was writing to say she was wed and living in London. I don't know if Sarah ever really got married, or whether she were just saying that to make it look better when the baby arrived. Murphy didn't stick around for long anyway; he run off after the war, and we never heard another word."

We had wandered past a rose garden and herbaceous borders, the plants neatly pruned and mulched, the ground raked smooth and absolutely weed-free, and were now approaching a lawn. I let out a muffled "Oh!" for at the far side appeared the house and the dovecote from Miss Hoar's book. As if on cue, a cloud of white birds circled and landed in front of us. They were fantail pigeons, and as we watched, some of the males puffed out their breasts like spinnakers, spread their tails fully, and ran to and fro in front of the females as if they were on wheels. They reminded me irresistibly of overweight Italian tenors, throbbing with unrequited love and high Cs.

"We'll go this way," said my uncle. "Lordy's home."

"Who?"

"His Lordship. Lord Sharrington. He lives here."

I had a sudden thought.

"Is he a very tall thin man with a brown face, looks as if he spends a lot of time outside? Shabby clothes and hazel eyes?"

"That's him."

"We met," I said. "I thought he was a gardener. He called you the boss."

"Likes his little joke, does Lordy. Though mind you, he's here so seldom, maybe it's no more than the truth."

"It explains the Rolex."

We came out of some trees to find ourselves back on the slope where the artificial stream carried the water down in a long series of pools and steps and followed it right down to a large lake surrounded by trees. A small island floated a short distance from the shore, covered with tall trees whose tops were full of untidy bundles.

"That's the heronry," said Magnus, and even as he spoke a large grey bird, neck coiled like a teapot spout and long legs trailing as gracefully as a ballerina's, flew across our line of sight and made an awkward landing on one of the bundles, thrashing its wings until it secured a firm foothold on the nest. I heard a familiar noise too and round the corner of the island came a flotilla of Canada geese, honking sociably to one another.

"Some fellow countrymen," said Uncle Magnus. "Used to come just for the winter when I were a lad, but they stay year-round now."

We found a place to sit by the water.

"Susanna loved this place," he said. "This and the summer house were her boltholes."

He stared out across the water, unseeing. I watched a fresh-water clam trudging through the mud in the shallows, leaving a wandering trough behind.

"Go on," I said. I wanted to know how Susanna met my father, if her life was so circumscribed. Who was he? Another travelling salesman? But I didn't dare prod too hard. My uncle was obviously finding it hard to speak of his dead sister; I was tearing open old wounds. Press too hard and he might retreat as effectively as the clam, which had half buried itself in the mud and would soon disappear altogether.

Uncle Magnus sighed as if he were weary and got to his feet again.

"We'll go this way," he said. "I'll show you the hothouses."

He set off round the shore, and soon we crossed a small bridge where the stream entered the lake and made our way up a slope to a large building with columns and tall windows all round. A white peacock stood on the steps, and as we approached, it swelled and shivered its tail into a fan.

"This is the orangery," said my uncle. "The peacocks roost here sometimes. We shut them in when we can't stand the noise."

As if to demonstrate, the peacock opened its beak and uttered a piercing cry. It repeated this several times, and from a distance we heard another one answering.

"Mating season," said my uncle. "No holding them."

We left the orangery behind, but the thought seemed to linger with Magnus as we crossed another lawn and returned to the rose garden, skirting an elaborate sundial and passing under a long pergola draped with the canes of ancient ramblers.

"Full of romantic ideas she was, your mother. Chit of a girl, her head full of daft stories, well, I thought they was daft, being a boy, all about love and getting married and such. I used to tease her something fearful, I'd say, 'Who's going to marry you then? Old Ted down the village?' Old Ted, he were the local daftie, no harm in him, just simple. And she'd say, 'You wait, he'll come one day, and then I'll be off, you see if I don't, and I'll live happy ever after.' Poor girl."

"What happened?"

Magnus scowled.

"Pastor Lewis Selby happened, is what. Worst day ever dawned on this family when he arrived."

"How come?"

We had come full circle back to the yard with all the greenhouses. Magnus opened the end door of one and urged me to enter quickly. The atmosphere inside was thick and steamy, cloyingly earthy and wet. The place had an unruly, faintly menacing quality, as if it caged young delinquents bursting with vitality or hungry predators on the prowl. The plants were not confined to the benches or pots. There were woody vines thick as anacondas that climbed posts and crawled across the skylights, waxen gardenias, orchids thriving on rotting logs, and in one corner a banana tree with bright green leaves like the banners Japanese armies used to carry in the time of the Shogun. I saw petals thick and matte as suede; large fleshy leaves polished to a high gloss so that beads of moisture skittered over their surface like ball bearings; stems and branches writhing to the light, clinging grimly with invisible claws. Everything was excessive: too tall, too vigorous, too gaudy, too strange.

"Here, I wanted you to see this," said Magnus. He pointed to a creeper covered in small trumpet-shaped flowers, waxy as the gardenias and giving off an intoxicating smell.

"Your ma, she were very fond of this one. That's stephanotis. The seeds you got must have come from this plant. My old dad planted it. She always said she'd put the flowers in her hair when she got wed."

"And did she?" I prompted, knowing the answer even as I asked the question.

"Never got the chance, poor lass. Pastor Selby put paid to that."

"How?"

"Got her in the family way, didn't he? Not as he'd ever admit it, but it stands to reason. There she was, all the time at the chapel for Bible classes, and helping the pastor with this and that, and him telling Mother that Susanna was one of the Saints, buttering her up, making her believe our Susie was something holy, just so she'd be allowed to spend all her time with him, no questions asked. But then even I noticed Susie went quiet and pale as a dish of milk, and then of course she got big and the fat was in the fire and no mistake."

We were silent for a while. I thought about my young mother, artless and afraid, carrying her secret about with her for the months before the inevitable discovery. She lived at a time when an illegitimate baby was a hideous shame, when people would whisper and point fingers and label her as a trollop, no

199

better than she ought to be. Did she go on hoping the man would come to her aid? She would have no other resources, no friends, a sister who had escaped in similarly improper circumstances, and a mother obsessed with sin.

"How did your parents take the news?"

"Lord love you, I've never seen the like! Dad and me, having our tea quiet as you please, then Mother bursts in, dragging Susanna by the arm fit to tear it off, and Susie crying, begging her to stop and saying she was sorry over and over. We sat there with our mouths agape I shouldn't wonder, then Mother shouts at Dad over all the din, 'Here's your whore of a daughter! Ask her what she has to say for herself!' and Dad just manages, 'Now, Mother,' before she cuts him off again with her harlots and Jezebels.

"My poor sister can't speak for sobbing, so it's Mother tells the sorry tale, and there's no pity, I can tell you. You'd think my sister were the Antichrist, to hear her. And Dad's face got longer and longer, and he looked as stern as I'd ever seen him, worse than when he caught the Macken twins boring holes in the beeches and filling them with copper. It scared me. God knows how Susanna felt."

"But didn't she say who was responsible? Surely they'd have been angry with him then, rather than her?"

"She did in the end. But it made things worse, if anything. Mother wouldn't hear a word against the pastor. She would have it that a man of God would never do such a thing. She said it just showed how steeped in wickedness Susanna were that she'd dare to make such an accusation. And Dad turned to Susie and said, 'You disappoint me, girl,' and she wept as if her heart had snapped in two."

"I'm not surprised. What a betrayal! Everyone she trusted turned against her."

Magnus's face was heavy with remembered emotion.

"She were on her own, right enough. She had to stay in her room, out of sight, only allowed to go out for a walk at dusk, so nobody would see her. I had to take her meals and set them outside her door, and I'd whisper to her and tell her things and smuggle up the odd pencil or book or piece of paper. Those were Mother's rules; 'If there's sin in my house,' she would say, 'I don't have to let it run free to spread its poison.' I think Dad would have come round, especially when the baby arrived, but Mother—you might as well have set a stone in water to soften, she were that rigid."

"Didn't anyone say anything to the pastor? Ask him?"

"Didn't have to. He knew. Came to the house even, 'ministering to his flock,' he called it, 'bringing succour to those in need'—I can hear him saying that even now, standing in our kitchen with his back to the window so his face was all in shadow but his hair lit up from behind so it stood up all round his head like flames, and I said to myself, I know what the Devil looks like now, never mind the cloven hooves and horns in all the pictures. And he didn't say a word to Susanna, just prayed over her, begged the Lord to forgive her great sins."

"He had red hair?"

"Indeed he did," said Uncle Magnus. "Bright red." He looked at me consideringly and grinned. "Very like your own, I'd say."

"Wasn't that a giveaway, when my hair grew?"

"Like enough. Even I noticed, though Dad shut me up when I made some remark about it. But Mother! She didn't have quite so much to say about our holy Mr. Selby, and she let Susanna out and about a bit more, but she'd never admit she'd been wrong, not in a million years, and if you want to know, I think it made her take against you all the more. Rubbing her nose in it, you were, with every curl on your head. And she couldn't take it out on the real culprit anyway because at about the same time as you were born, he vanished."

"So you don't know what happened to him?"

"Enlisted, so they say, and killed in the war. Far as we were concerned, he just disappeared."

"Do you know where he came from?"

Magnus paused, his hand on the doorknob.

"He were a bit of a mystery. Our old pastor fell ill, and this young rip come to take his place. One minute there was the old man, same as always, and the next, there he was, causing a right flutter, I can tell you, just swooped in and caught us all up in his hellfires and damnations. He were a rare preacher, give him that. Mother thought he were the Second Coming, I reckon, but you asking—it just dawned on me we never heard a thing about his past. 'Tweren't something you'd ask, somehow; it'd be like asking the wind where it came from, what it'd been doing. If you'd asked him, he'd probably have said it didn't matter, what mattered was that he was here, now, and he'd fix his gaze on you and clasp your arm, as if you were the only other person in the world. There was something about him, some force, no denying it. It made me squirm, and my dad didn't take to him, but there were plenty as did. Some of those women would've laid themselves down in the mud to save his boots getting mucky, I reckon."

My father a Manson? A Jim Jones? A Maharishi? Or just a hypocritical little con man, forced to exercise his talents within the straitjacket of a Calvinist sect? I suppose I shall never know which is closer to the mark, but I can't help a sneaking preference for the former. If I can get no closer than fantasy, a colourful monster who could have been a cult leader has more to offer than a latter-day Uriah Heep.

Magnus ushered me out of the hothouse, and we trudged back across the muddy yard, past cold frames and compost heaps being excavated by busy starlings. The young man I had met before came toward us, his arms pulled long by a laden wheelbarrow, and nodded as he passed.

"Just put a cuppa in the office, guv," he said. "There's one for the lady too."

Magnus grunted. *He's not best pleased I've got a reason to stay*, I thought. *He's not sure what comes next. Or perhaps he is, and wants to put it off, pretend it's not going to happen, can't happen, because it's too alarming, too unpredictable, and he's too used to being in charge of his little world to welcome something so far out of his control.*

I crunched over the gravel beside him, trying to visualize his life: the comfortable round of the year, measured in change, endless cycles of seedtime, nurture, and harvest, unswerving as the course of the planets. Day after day, he juggled the powers of earth, wind, and rain, and the kindly fire of the sun, and out of this elemental play came beauty and order. *If He exists at all*, I thought, *God has to be a gardener, and people like Magnus, His lieutenants.*

But a gardener with a taste for practical jokes and an Olympian disregard for their consequences. To the ordinary mortal kind of gardener, like Magnus, I was the infestation of beetles, the killing frost in May, the Dutch elm disease, the anomaly that can never be planned for or guarded against that can wreck everything.

I knew what he didn't want to hear. I waited until we were back in his office and he was passing me a mug of tea and carefully unwrapping a half-eaten McVitie's Jamaican Ginger Cake he took out of a drawer marked ESCHOLTZIA in the cabinet. As he extended a moist dark slab toward me, skewered on the end of his penknife, I asked the question.

"Can I see my grandmother?"

He was still for a second, then carefully wiped the blade and folded it up. His answer, when it came, was oblique.

"She's very old. No hurrying her."

Not you either, I thought. He moistened a rough forefinger and chased down the last crumbs of cake.

"Got to come at it gradual," he said, "roundabout like. No good just blurting it out. I'll have to feel my way, introduce it casually, and then maybe she won't throw a fit and say no. But I'll need a little time."

The thought of Magnus doing a Polonius, using indirection to arrive at his end with the Holy Terror, probably in more ways than one, amused me. My smile must have suggested I was skeptical about his motives.

"Don't you worry yourself now," he hastened to reassure me, "I believe you, and you should see your folks. But she's difficult, you know. I can't promise she'll agree to meet you. She's a pigheaded old besom when she gets an idea in her head, I'll tell you. But if I can fix it, I will. You'd better give me your address or phone number, and I'll be in touch one way or another."

I can recognize a dismissal. I gave him the information and started to repack the gas mask case.

"Hang on a minute," Magnus said as we left the greenhouse. "Wait here. I'll be right back."

He crunched away across the gravel and disappeared through an archway in the wall. The sun was low, and there was little warmth in it, but the old bricks glowed in its last rays, and the air was quiet and soft. Into that stillness dropped a now familiar sound, the two liquid notes falling, one after the other, clear but not close, somewhere over the water trickling downhill in its mossy course, or over the tall trees of the heronry, or deep in the thickets behind the cow pastures.

"Listen," I said as Magnus crunched back. "A cuckoo."

"Ah," he said, "they've been around a while."

"Why do people get all excited about hearing one? Are they rare?"

"Not round here, they're not. Not that you ever *see* them, really. You just know they're around, and then they're gone."

"Sounds like my father."

204

Magnus looked at me sharply and rubbed his chin, a gesture I had come to realize meant he was weighing something up.

"'Out of the mouths of babes,'" he said. "You know what cuckoos do, don't you?"

I didn't, but I was distracted by the small book he was holding.

"What's that?"

"It's what made me a believer," he replied. "Look."

He opened the book and I saw immediately it was an address book. He turned the last page of the Ls and held it so I could see. The letter M was missing, torn out with the last entry on the page. I rummaged in the gas mask case and brought out the scrap of paper with Sarah's address and laid it on the book. It fitted perfectly.

"Soon as I saw that, I knew," said Magnus. "I ripped that out because Susanna needed it. She'd decided to take you and run off to London to stay with Sarah, but Mother would have stopped her. She would never have got hold of that book on her own."

"So you were her accomplice!"

"Her executioner, more like," said Magnus grimly. "She'd be alive still if I hadn't helped. I gave her all the money I had too. 'Tweren't much, just from odd jobs, but it must have bought her a ticket. And then look what it took her to. Out of the frying pan, into the fire, all right."

What can you say to that kind of guilt? Useless to make the usual disclaimers—you can't blame yourself, it was an accident, you couldn't have known, you were little more than a child yourself. They were true, but not true. My uncle may have acted out of affection for his sister, but he would never be able to see that as mitigation. Magnus had carried the weight of responsibility for his sister's death all his life, just as I carried the guilt of turning my attention from Daniel for those critical minutes, and I knew that no rationalization could lighten the burden for him, any more than it could for me. With a sigh, Magnus put the past on one side.

"You wait until you hear from me. I will call, don't you fret. Now I'll just set you on your road and say goodbye."

And with that, he guided me back past the greenhouses and through the kitchen garden, round the stable block and down a path through some trees that brought us, like the hare, to the edge of the road through the fields.

I looked back after a few steps and the solid figure raised an arm. His voice floated toward me.

"You wanted to see a cuckoo," it called. "There she goes now," and I realized he wasn't waving but pointing over my head. I just caught a glimpse of an undistinguished brown bird as it rocketed past, making for a stand of trees that marked the edge of the pasture. Another instant and its diminishing form vanished against the camouflage of leaves and branches, so completely gone that it was almost as if Magnus had conjured it up only to dazzle me with his sleight of hand. I turned for one last goodbye, but he had disappeared too.

The three ladies were relieved to see me sitting on the gate when they drove up. I expected them to be full of questions, but they simmered and bubbled, ready to burst, like children with a secret.

"We've got something to show you," Miss Plover said, and Isobel squeaked in excited agreement.

We drove back to the church. They led me under the lych gate, then left the path and steered across the grass to a corner of the churchyard out of sight behind the squatting mass of the building. The grass was longer here and the graves less tended. The angel bending over one had lost her nose, and another had once held flowers in an empty jam tin, rusted now and lying on its side. We stopped beside the last grave in the angle of the wall, no more than a grassy mound with a headstone canted to one side.

"There," said Miss Plover with quiet satisfaction.

The stone was unadorned, plain grey granite. The names glared out, softened only a little by time and a dusting of grey-green lichen.

SUSANNA CHARITY GOODMAN
1925–1941
AND
RUE TRIBULATION GOODMAN
1940–1941

I was aware of Isobel twittering about the injustice of burdening a child with such an appalling name, but I didn't even spare a thought for the hapless baby pinned down forever under it. I was doing the math.

My mother had been no more than sixteen years old when she died in the doorway of the warehouse trying to shield me with her body as the bombs fell around us and the world went up in flames.

TWENTY-TWO

Have you ever read Boswell's account of Dr. Johnson on horse-back? It has always filled me with sympathy, that image of the great man at the mercy of the horse's inclinations, quite unable to compel it to go in the right direction or at the right speed. Waiting for Uncle Magnus to phone induced a similar feeling of helplessness, as if everything that mattered had been taken from my hands.

I didn't have the heart for much more research. I tried to find out something of my father's fate by contacting the Ministry of Defence and the War Museum, but you know how frustrating officialdom can be.

Finally, I did manage to talk to a real person who turned up three Lewis or Louis Selbys or Selbies or Selbeys. All were dead; obviously not a name that brought any luck. The most likely, since he enlisted in Reading in 1941 and put down his occupation as minister, was recorded as Missing in Action; Presumed Dead following the battle of El Alamein, and there were no more details to be harvested, apart from a birth date in 1915 in the village of Terrington St. John in Norfolk. I trudged out to the village and the local church, just to say I'd been, really, but I found no trace of any Selbys at all.

Truth is, I didn't even *want* to hunt him, or his family, down. Do you think that's strange? Somehow I knew it would be a waste of time. My father had come out of nowhere, despoiled my mother, and vanished. I couldn't imagine him with a father and mother, couldn't see him playing and fighting with siblings, going to school, looking for jobs. I couldn't even imagine him in the army, although if I'd got the right one I knew he'd been in a tank regiment. He was a solitary, unattached in any way, and he would have left no tracks. Even his death fitted the pattern; he'd gone missing and his body had never been found. Maybe he'd turned to ash in the flaming hulk of his tank, or maybe his bones still lie in the desert. Bleached white in the sand. But there'll always be the sliver of doubt, the tiny shred of possibility that he managed to disappear yet again into thin air and still shares the world with me somewhere, invisible against all the strangers. And I don't think I want to know him any better than that.

I found out about cuckoos. *The Shorter Oxford* was terse. "A migratory Eurasian grey or brown speckled bird, *Cuculus canorus*, which leaves its eggs in the nests of other birds and has a distinctive cry, the hearing of which is regarded as a harbinger of spring."

Which explained both Uncle Magnus's comment and the triumphant letter in *The Times* but left me dissatisfied.

Miss Hoar looked up from a large botanical text with lavish coloured illustrations as I knocked on her door.

"I knew it!" she cried. "It was a bee orchid. I saw it under some trees in the churchyard the other day. I haven't seen one since I was a child!"

She slid the book toward me, and I looked obediently at the small flower under her finger, brown and yellow, distinctly reminiscent of a bee.

"Left it there, of course. They're very rare now. Sorely tempted, though."

"Yes," I said, "can you tell me about cuckoos?"

Miss Hoar's conversational style was so economical she saw nothing odd in this abrupt request.

"Opportunistic little beggars," she replied. "You know about the eggs, I presume?"

"That's *all* I know."

"It's the main thing, really. They lay their eggs and have nothing further to do with raising their young. The foster parents hatch the eggs and do all the work of feeding, and it *is* work, because the cuckoo usually chooses the nest of a smaller bird, so the parents are faced with an enormous chick with a voracious appetite."

"Don't they notice the egg is different?"

"They don't appear to, nor do they reject the chick when it dwarfs them. Their instinct is to stuff food down that gaping beak, and that they do until the fledgling is ready to fly. Unfortunately, their efforts come at a price."

"What's that?"

"The baby cuckoo gets so large, it fills the nest, literally, and it's so demanding that the foster parents' own chicks never get their share. They weaken, and it's an easy matter then for the cuckoo to push them out of the nest. I've got pictures somewhere."

She surveyed a shelf of books above her bench, and her hovering finger darted at a thick tome devoted to birds. Soon she handed it to me open at a page with a series of pictures. They showed an outrageously fat baby bird, beak wide, vestigial wings flapping, in a tiny nest. A small bird had landed nearby with a beakful of food and seemed to be working out how to reach into the baby's mouth. Subsequent shots revealed another small beak wavering up at the edge of the twigs as if it had been trampled underfoot and just managed to squeeze between the cuckoo and the lining of the nest. Later shots revealed the cuckoo filling the time between parental visits by edging its wing under the other baby. Persistence brought the hapless infant onto its back and it was then an easy matter to tip it out to fall to its death.

"Parenthood without tears," I said, "but a bit hard on the foster birds."

"Biologically," Miss Hoar replied crisply, "cuckoos are very successful at reproducing themselves, which is, after all, their whole reason for existence. And ethical or moral standards are irrelevant in the case of a totally amoral creature, are they not?"

I murmured neutral agreement. She couldn't know my interest was figurative. And I was struggling at the same time to understand how *cuckoo* had also, according to the dictionary, become a term for a silly person. Self-serving, maybe, exploitative and opportunistic, certainly, but daft? Never! And I should know.

I was the cuckoo's child.

Neil was much taken with my metaphor. I phoned him frequently during this time, trying to make up for the way I'd let him, and everything else at home, slide to the corners of my mind. He would call me when it was midnight in Sechelt and tell me what it was like in the house, what Maisie was doing, the noises the wind and waves were making, how Sheila and Ella had asked about me, such calm and happy images that I wondered why I didn't pack and leave immediately, why I clung to my round room in the treetops, why I had such a need to face my grandmother.

I asked about you. Not bad, said Neil. They still hadn't found a suitable donor; Dad was disqualified because of a bout of jaundice he'd had a few years ago. They were wondering about Jason, but he was very young. Perhaps if the remission lasted a while, that wouldn't be such an issue, but it was all up in the air, nothing definite, nothing guaranteed. I promised myself I'd find something really great to send you, something you'd love and never search out yourself, something you couldn't even find over there, maybe. Then I caught myself up, thinking, *What is this? A compensation prize because I feel guilty? A reminder that I'm still there and need attention, like a dog worming its way to your side and standing on your foot?* I was blushing as Neil rambled on about Ella plying him with dinner invitations because she assumed he was slowly starving on his own.

Boredom and impatience led me to walk miles. I could have got a job as a tour guide or passed the taxi driver exam by the time I'd finished hunting down ever-more obscure museums and art galleries. I pored over manuscripts and fossils, played in the Science Museum alongside schoolchildren on field trips. I browsed all seven floors at Foyles, investigated Harrods and Fortnum and Mason. I became quite nonchalant about the Underground; if you want to know how to get to Wealdstone or Walthamstow from Richmond, I can tell you.

I even spent some time with Deirdre. My new cousin was a bit of a disappointment to me, to be frank, but she's the only one I have and I thought she might become more interesting on closer acquaintance. I went down to Brighton to lend a hand when she sorted through her mother's belongings, looking for things to discard. Deirdre thought I might be helpfully ruthless, although her protests sounded terrified when I suggested she could well start with the cats, and I didn't have much hope she would bring herself to throw anything away.

She surprised me, though. Sentimentality was not apparently part of her makeup. She had arranged for the council to deposit a skip outside the house, and we started at the top floor and worked down. We set aside the clothes to be bundled onto the bike for several runs to the thrift shops, and the same was true of some household items Deirdre said she hated or had no use for. The rest we checked quickly and dumped with mounting glee in the skip, for Aunt Sarah had been a packrat of the worst kind, and it was soon obvious there was little of any value in the rubbish she had stowed away into every cupboard and drawer, piled in ancient cardboard boxes that leaned in towers against wardrobes, stacked under beds, behind chests and chairs, lining the hallways and spilling over onto the treads of the stairs.

It was mostly paper, and largely newsprint, although there

were boxes of household bills and receipts and several huge caches of silver paper.

"War effort," said Deirdre when I raised my eyebrows.

Hundreds of clippings about royal weddings, train crashes, murders, state visits, elections, film stars, exhibitions, and the opening of supermarkets and bingo halls. It was a sociologist's dream, but Deirdre waded into the dusty, yellowed remains with all the zeal of a Puritan removing the taint of Popery from the local church. None of my fictitious ruthlessness was required; in fact, I was the one who would vainly cry out as some gem flashed past on its way to Deirdre's rejection pile.

Maybe she was cleverer than I thought. She'd lured me to Brighton by representing herself as unequal to this task, and I'd fallen for the implied compliment. Perhaps what she really wanted was a witness to her scouring, someone who would know that Deirdre was, from that moment, someone to be reckoned with, an individual in her own right who stood alone with no reference to anyone else. And then again, perhaps she just wanted help with a filthy job.

When I left her in her strangely echoing house, the dust motes swirling visibly with the cat hair in the sunlight, she pressed a little packet in my hand.

"This'll mean more to you than it does to me," she said. "It's the picture of your mother Mum always kept on the mantelpiece. I left it in the frame for you. Let me know how you get on with the Holy Terror, won't you?"

I unwrapped it in the train. It was a typical snapshot, black and white, not quite in focus. A slender girl with dark hair in a long plait stood in front of a flowerbed and laughed at the camera, holding a kitten up to her face and pointing, as if encouraging it to pose too. She wore a simple cotton dress with a white collar, ankle socks, and sandals. Her face was guileless, consumed by the happiness of the moment. I could see little of myself in her, although I recognized the shape of her mouth and the way her eyes narrowed and curved downward as she smiled. Nothing bad could ever happen to her in her sunny garden. She looked about fifteen.

I was just setting the photograph in its frame beside the gas mask case in my room that evening when Isobel called up the stairs.

"Telephone!"

It was Uncle Magnus. He made none of the customary preambles.

"I've had a rare old time," he said, "but I've got her to agree to see you at least. Now don't you go thinking you're all set," he added quickly before I could respond, "she's not putting out the welcome mat, and I don't know what she'll say—it would be just like her to say nothing. I told you, she's wonderful stubborn."

"When should I come?"

"Sooner the better, if you ask me, before she has a chance to change her mind. Can you make it tomorrow?"

I said I could and would.

"I'll be seeing you then," said Magnus. "Just don't expect too much."

The three ladies were eagerly waiting to hear what had happened. Once again they launched immediately into plans to convey me to Hescot Park.

Late that night I phoned Neil.

"Oho," he said, "going to beard the Minotaur, are you? Make sure you take a ball of string!"

Before I went to bed, I slipped the photograph into my purse. And although I was keyed up and my head whirred with speculation, I fell instantly into a sleep so profound I was aware of nothing until the starlings woke me next morning, shouting to one another in the top of the tree.

TWENTY-THREE

Once again, the stately journey in the old car, floating through a landscape blushing green and greener as leaves clotted the skeletal arms of trees and solidified the walls of hedges. Once again, the ladies deposited me at the side of the road and waved as they drove off, and I stood and felt the stillness wash back as the car sailed round the corner.

I was on my own this time. The cows had moved to another pasture, and there was no sign of life in the far fields, not even a cry from a hidden cuckoo. The rotting net still drooped from its post, and the water lay dark in the pools, trickling sluggishly over the steps, but I was in no mood for elegiac reflection and hurried through the wood and the stable block, anxious to meet Magnus.

Black clouds were massing, marching up from the southwest, swelling importantly as they came. The louring sky darkened the interior of the greenhouse, giving it a green underwater cast. Magnus sat in his office waiting for me, a shadowy bulk in the dim light.

"Right on time then," he said. "Well, let's get this over with."

He led me through an archway to a grassy area bordered by a row of stone cottages. They were old and charming, sunsoaked stone, slate roofs neat as fish scales. Each cottage resembled a child's drawing of a house—symmetrical windows, front door in the middle—but there was a balance and grace of proportion that spoke of an earlier age with a thoroughly adult taste for elegance, even in the humblest things, such as dwellings for labourers.

We approached the middle cottage, which had a lattice porch wreathed in the canes of a climbing rose, already covered with tiny pink-edged leaves. In front of the house stood a fruit tree just coming into bloom. On one side the tree had pink flowers, while the other half was a delicate drift of white.

I stopped to admire it as Magnus fumbled his door key out of his waistcoat pocket.

"My old dad did that, back when he and Mother married. It were a wedding gift, I suppose."

"What are the two plants?"

"He grafted a flowering cherry onto a damson. Did a good job, didn't he? He were a dab hand at grafting, my old dad. I try my hand at it too, but you can never be sure it'll take, or last. The graft's always the weak spot, no matter how old it gets."

I clutched at the image of the pied tree as he held the door open. Can you see why? It was the first evidence I'd come across that anyone in this new family of mine indulged sentiment, and I wished I had known this grandfather who expressed his feelings in living symbols. What a beautiful declaration of love, of confidence in the union, that brought together two disparate entities, quite perfect in themselves, and out of them created an astonishing third. It was the perfect metaphor for the ideal of marriage. Had he been disappointed when the reality fell short, for I had no doubt it had from what Magnus told me? Did the tree then become a daily reminder of the frailty of humans, of the way ideals are eroded? The lovely innocence of my grandfather's act tugged at me; in it I thought I could feel a link between generations, passing from his tree and his craft to my mother's love of poetry and her flight, then on to the importance of images in my own life, my search for patterns in the natural world and my place in them. I can tell you, I needed the reassurance of connection at that moment. I feared what was coming.

I was in a dim cave. There were stone flags underfoot, and through a door that stood ajar, I could see into a pantry with black slate shelves. What light there was came in two shafts from the windows, which weakened as they penetrated farther so that although the walls were whitewashed, they reflected little, and the recesses of the room were shadowed and mysterious.

A large table, blond with years of scrubbing, stood in the centre of the floor, with ladder-backed chairs ranged about it. A tray holding a silver teapot, milk jug, and slop basin and three china cups and saucers stood ready. The cups were square, and I wondered briefly how one drank from them. Behind the table loomed a large oak sideboard and china cupboard, a range of blue-and-white plates, and two copper pots winking against the sombre wood.

On one end wall was a fireplace with a coal fire quietly glowing in the hearth. To one side of it crouched an old leather armchair, sagging in the seat and highly polished where heads and hands and backsides had rubbed against it. A small table stood alongside, and I deduced from the clutter of pipes, ashtrays, and a large box of Swan Vestas that this was my uncle's chair. At the other side of the fire, with its back to the window and a standard lamp behind it, was a large Windsor armchair, upholstered in nubbly brown tweed. The Holy Terror filled it.

Magnus urged me to sit down, and I pulled out one of the wooden chairs and perched on the edge of the seat, keeping a substantial piece of the table in front of me. While my uncle laboured through an introduction that produced no reaction, I stole a first glance at my grandmother.

I don't know what I was expecting. Well, I do. Movies and cartoons have equipped us well to imagine villains. I expected a monster, massive and overbearing, ugly and menacing, wearing her malevolence openly on her face. Jabba the Hutt in a dress, perhaps. What I saw was so ordinary, I was disarmed. Looking back, though, that unremarkable exterior was what made my grandmother doubly terrifying.

What I saw was an old woman who looked exactly what she was: a countrywoman at the end of a long life, white-haired, toil-worn, and plump. She sat very straight in the armchair, hands clasped loosely in her lap, thick legs mummified in elastic bandages beneath opaque stockings planted solidly on a small footstool. Her hair was looped off her face in graceful snowy curves like the wings of the fantail pigeons and skewered to her head with long silver pins. Her cheeks were pink from the network of tiny veins broken in a lifetime of exposure to the elements, but the skin was soft and faintly furred like a peach.

She wore a dark blue long-sleeved dress, the bodice tucked and buttoned up to the uncompromising square neckline. An old locket, also square and heavily chased, hung around her neck. Her torso was a tightly packed cylinder, rigid under the cloth, as if her flesh had solidified over the years into something dense but slightly yielding. Rubber, perhaps. I suspected old-fashioned corsetry, pink and laced and stiff with whalebone.

The hands lying still in her wide lap were large and ugly. They spoke of days plunging sheets and clothes into laundry tubs, baking the week's bread, scrubbing the stone floors, stripping the feathers and guts from chickens, sewing long seams, waging war on flies and ants and dirt, grubbing in the earth, and clambering up ladders into the trees to pick bushels of fruit, then enduring steam and spitting pulp and boiling syrup as she put it up in jars of preserves that glowed like jewels on the cool slate shelves of her still room. Even now they showed calluses and rough, cracked skin on the fingertips, but lumpy veins squirmed across their backs, and the joints were swollen and contorted, making useless claws of the once nimble fingers.

I was so swayed by these images that I said the first thing that came into my head as I met the old lady's eyes and Magnus ground to a halt. There was a silence. Magnus was mutely urging me to fill it.

"Grandmother," I said.

The effect was immediate. The pale eyes behind their wire-rimmed glasses were clouded and rheumy, but for a second they glistened like wet stones. A red tide swept up her throat to her face. Apprehension clutched my throat.

"What did she say? What did she call me? The sauce of it!"

Magnus weighed in hurriedly.

"Now, Mother, you know what I said. You *are* her grandmother. I'm quite sure of it. I told you all the things she has. How else could she have them, if she weren't Susanna's girl, eh? Come on now."

She steamrollered over the voice of reason.

"Don't you tell me to come on! You're a simpleton, Magnus, daft as a brush, taken in by a chit of a girl with a silly story. Anyone can make up a story about some old pieces of rubbish!"

I felt I had to interrupt.

"Why would I want to do that? It's not as if I'm laying claim to a fortune or anything."

"And short shrift you'd get if you were, miss," my grandmother snorted. "You'd have to get past me first, and I'm not so easy to fool."

"Mother," Magnus insisted, "this is silly. She has Sarah's address on a scrap of paper I tore out of your address book and gave to Susanna myself. It fits exactly. Want to see for yourself? How in the world would she have that if she hadn't been with my poor sister when she died? Why would anyone else in the entire world be interested in that address? And how did she come to have that seed packet with Dad's writing on it? And the gas mask with our name on it? Don't tell me she found the lot in some junk shop and just decided to make the whole thing up. What in God's name would she want to do that for?"

"Blasphemer!" shouted Grandmother, but I could tell her reply was automatic, a cover for rapid thought. "She's no grand-daughter of mine. How can she be? *You* don't have any children, do you? Never found a woman to take you on, as far as I know."

"But you had two daughters as well," I objected before Magnus could speak. But I had given her the opening she wanted.

"I have *no* daughters," she crowed.

"How can you say that? You had two: Sarah and Susanna."

"There were girls, oh yes, but they were no daughters of mine! Shameful hussies, the pair of them, sunk in their shameful wickedness. So how can there be grandchildren, tell me that, eh?"

"You can disown them all you want, but you can't erase them just because you didn't approve of them, and expect everybody to go along with you. They existed! Sarah died just a few weeks ago! I've talked to her daughter, Deirdre, your other granddaughter, by the way. Was I hallucinating? She looked pretty solid to me."

"Jezebels! Harlots!"

"I beg your pardon?"

"Born to sin and darkness, turning from the light in their wilful wickedness, the filthiness of their walk and conduct!"

The leather chair creaked as Magnus stirred uneasily.

"Mother," he warned, "you said you wouldn't upset yourself now."

The old woman ignored him. Her small mouth worked, radiating wrinkles as if it had been pulled tight by a drawstring. It reminded me of an anus.

220

"Look," I said hurriedly, pulling my mother's photograph from my bag, and holding it close to her so that she could see it clearly. "Does this look like a Jezebel? She was a *child*. She was *your child*, for heaven's sake. And I'm her daughter."

"Flesh-pleaser," my grandmother hissed at the picture and, snatching it from my hand, hurled it at the fire. The frame cracked smartly against the grate and shattered. Magnus leaned forward with a grunt and rescued the photograph, already curling in the heat of the coals.

"Flesh-pleaser?" I asked. "What . . ."

"The body of the saint is the temple of the Holy Ghost!"

"Well, that may be, but . . ."

"Polluted it, she did, with her filthiness. Wasn't that committing the sin of Zimri in the presence of the Holy Ghost?"

"Zimri?"

My grandmother's voice was taking on a rapt quality, as if she were hypnotizing herself with the borrowed rhetoric. Certainly she was launched on a well-worn path, and I was lost already. I could no longer tell where her own words ended and quotation began.

"She gave herself over," she intoned, "just like her sister, carnally minded. They that are in the flesh cannot please God. So they cast themselves out. If a man abide not in me, he is cast forth as a branch, and is withered; and men gather them and cast them into the fire and they are burned!"

Rage and a sort of fascinated horror had strangled me, but a brief pause as the old woman heaved in some air broke the spell and I managed one protest.

"She needed protection, and you turned against her because she was a sinner? What would you call yourself?"

It sounded impotent even to me. Grandmother continued as if I hadn't uttered a word. Her oratory moved up another notch beyond any kind of rational discourse. Her bun was slipping from its moorings, and wisps of white hair haloed her congested face, giving her an unsettling air of wildness. She'd become one of the more misanthropic Old Testament prophets, Jeremiah perhaps, in mid-rant, the seventeenth century pouring from her mouth as if she were helplessly speaking in tongues, yet all the time with an appalling vindictiveness. I could feel the hair standing up on my arms.

"In the latter times some shall depart from the faith, giving heed to seducing spirits and doctrines of devils. He who is joined unto the Lord is one spirit. Would I not cut away the contagion? If your limb is mortified, do you not sever it? Shall those who are in spirit with Christ be in body one flesh with the vilest of the vile? She put away her faith and made shipwreck."

My grandmother's mouth was flecked with spittle, and a fat purple vein stood out on her temple. *My God*, I thought, *she's foaming at the mouth, she's barking mad, I should stop this, she's an old woman, she'll never change.* But I couldn't let her retreat into a mumbo-jumbo of self-serving quotation and imagine she had won. Magnus was unhappy, but we both ignored his feeble attempts to break in and defuse the situation, she with the ease of long practice and I with the callousness that a duel to the death brings on.

"Having an illegitimate baby in that day and age was punishment enough. Why did you have to add to it?"

She was waiting for me.

"Many sorrows shall be to the wicked," she proclaimed.

I exploded.

"Being seduced by a hypocritical lecher is *not* wickedness! Wickedness is making a prisoner of your child and her infant, ostracizing her, and driving her away with your hatred and your cruelty and your loveless religion to struggle on her own in the middle of a war. What happened to 'suffer little children to come unto me'? Where was 'God is love'? At the very least you sentenced her to poverty and hardship; as it is, you sentenced her to death."

"Hold on now," protested Magnus, but his mother over-rode him.

"What is the wages of sin?" she asked the air and answered herself with a hideous glee. "The wages of sin is death!"

"But that's my point! There was no sin on her part. She didn't *deserve* her death."

"She made her choice and turned away from the light! I said to her, Walk ye in the light of your fire and in the sparks ye have kindled, you and your bastard, the child of a bond-woman. It's death to be carnally minded because the carnal mind is enmity against God."

Her voice was powerful and steadily rising, her face almost purple with intensity. I could feel myself recoiling instinctively from her otherness. She was terrifying.

"You walk in darkness, I said, because you hate the light, and the Father will not raise you up on the last day. For you have turned your back, and the Father will not draw you to Him, but cast you out to be consumed in the fire. Kindle your fire, I said, and compass yourself about with sparks and at last lie down in sorrow."

At this point she heaved herself onto her feet and pointed a shaking finger at me.

"Coming here, expecting me to welcome you in! Spawn of whores, work of darkness, swine's blood upon the altar, pollut-ing my house with your wicked godlessness! Defiling a man of God with your vile and baseless slurs! Cleanse your hearts, ye sinners; and purify your hearts, ye double-minded. But you have no faith and walk in wickedness; where will you be at the last day?"

Her voice had grown thick and rough, as if all the blood ves-sels in her throat were dilating and squeezing her larynx shut, and her last question came out as a hoarse wheeze. Magnus was on his feet, but she flailed at him with one impatient arm as she gathered herself for a final effort.

"God now laughs at his calamity," she croaked, "and mocks when his fear cometh."

At which she tottered sideways, caught her foot in the footstool, and crashed like a felled tree into the hearth with a fearful clatter of fire irons. One hand flopped into the coals and stayed there.

"Oh, my God, my God, Mother!"

My uncle's distress and my horror made us clumsy. We jostled each other, wasting valuable time treading on each other's feet, trying to step over my grandmother's inert bulk, both of us manoeuvring for the best position in the confines of the hearth to snatch the motionless hand from the fire. The hand was hissing and there was a dreadful smell that caught at some fear deep inside and turned my gut to water. With the strength of panic, I hauled my uncle aside as he slowly tried to bend, seized my grandmother's sleeve, which was just starting to smoulder, and wrenched her hand out of the coals.

I tried not to look at the blackened skin, split like a roast pepper, as we struggled to lift her out of the fireplace to lie more comfortably on the hearthrug. She was unconscious, her face grey and sweaty. Her glasses had broken in her fall, and a thin worm of blood wriggled from the edge of her right eyebrow into the hair above her ear. She was drooling, and her face looked oddly askew and uninhabited. I felt for a pulse and found a thready faltering beat at her throat.

"She needs an ambulance, quickly," I said. Magnus nodded and heaved himself up from his knees. "Where can I find blankets?" I asked. He gestured toward a door in the far corner of the room and lumbered to the telephone.

The door opened onto an old-fashioned enclosed staircase,

steep polished wood steps that rose like a mine shaft toward light from a small window at the top. Through it I could see more gardens, humble ones this time, and extensive woodland at the end of the plots. Something stirred in my head, but urgency crushed it down again, and I hurried to the first door along the landing, flung it open, and tore the quilt and pillows from the bed inside.

Magnus had finished with the phone by the time I returned, and together we swaddled the old woman in the quilt and tucked the pillows under her head and shoulders. I was concerned about her hand.

"We need some clean cloth to wrap that in," I said. Magnus looked at me helplessly. "A clean dishtowel, pillowcase, anything will do."

Magnus nodded and disappeared into the kitchen, returning a few moments later with a crisp linen tea towel covered with British songbirds. I noticed it had been ironed while still damp, perfectly smooth with a faint sheen, perfectly square at the corners, and folded with geometric precision. Very gently I wrapped it loosely round the burned flesh, laying the linen parcel carefully on top of the quilt. Magnus relaxed a little when we could no longer see the blackened hand.

"I'll have to go to the hospital with her," he said.

"Would you like me to come with you?"

"I don't think so, my dear. There's little enough to be done, I reckon."

"I'm sorry," I said. "I didn't mean to bring this on you."

Magnus looked sharply at me. The adrenalin was still making me shake.

"Don't you go shouldering this load," he said sternly. "'Tweren't your fault. You can't fill yourself up with hate and bitterness all your life and not have it poison you inside and out. She's my mother, but I can say it where I wouldn't let others take the liberty. She's a nasty soul, and she's choked on her own venom at last, see if she hasn't. There's a justice there, somewhere."

I was still digesting this when the ambulance swept up to the front door, lights flashing. The two ambulance attendants took over, loud and reassuring.

"Come on then, Ma, let's make you comfy, then. Soon have you right."

"What's this then?" said the other, unwrapping the hand. "Bloody hell," he exclaimed and covered it up again, hurriedly. "Put your skates on with this one, mate."

Within minutes, my grandmother was loaded like an unwieldy roll of carpet onto a stretcher, the back doors of the ambulance slammed shut, and it sped away. Magnus and I looked at each other. "I'll wait for my ride," I said. "I'll go for a walk out the back, perhaps. Is that all right? I'll phone you later tonight, okay?"

Magnus nodded.

"Have your walk," he said. "I'm off to the hospital."

I watched him lumber past the pied tree and disappear through the archway in the brick wall. Then I turned back into the house.

TWENTY-FOUR

I snooped, of course. After all, it could have been my one chance to wander round the house where my mother grew up. I just wanted to learn its shapes and patterns, breathe its smells, hear its noises. Share this one thing with the mother I had never really known.

So I wandered about the still, bare rooms, listening to the crack of the floorboards and laying my cheek against the chill plaster to savour its damp, gritty smell. In my grandmother's room there was a cumbersome mahogany bed with a fat feather mattress and a matching wardrobe and dressing table, but nothing stood on any of the surfaces, not a brush or an ornament of any kind, no photographs, no flowers, no pictures, no cushions, no rugs, no slippers waiting by the bed, nothing except for a Bible, bound in black calf and clamped shut with a brass clasp, waiting on the pillow.

Uncle Magnus's room was also spartan, but it had the well-worn simplicity of a soldier's quarters. The bed was narrow and trim, almost a cot; a small table beside it held an ancient alarm clock, the wind-up kind, and a small pile of books, the top one lying open. I picked it up to see what my uncle chose as bedtime reading; it was William Cobbett's *Rural Rides*. The only luxuriant thing in this ascetic room was a massive maidenhair fern that stood in the window and gushed all over its brass pot.

I tried to imagine my mother as a little girl straining to reach the taps in the bathroom sink or splashing about in the big white bath with the lion's feet. My hand learned what hers had known as I stroked the polished mahogany of the banister and unscrewed the knob on the brass bedstead. Did she, like me, lean dreamily out of the dormer windows in the tiny rooms at the back of the cottage, warmed by the slice of sunshine they offered as she watched the hens scratching below or the squirrels jerking head first down the tree trunks at the bottom of the garden?

Contemplating the garden like that reminded me of my intention to have a walk. Despite all my longing to find some lingering traces, there was really nothing of my mother in the house. Too much time had crept by, too much had been wilfully erased, and not even the faintest echo survived. Only the most indomitable spirit could ever have prevailed against my grandmother's implacable will.

Downstairs again, I gagged at the smell lingering on the air. Was that how Auschwitz smelled? If so, how could anyone pretend they didn't know what was being burned? I hurried into the small kitchen, flung open the back door, and stumbled outside. The air was cool and sweet, reviving, and the finest of rain gently misted my face and hair.

I followed a grassy path toward the trees. There were garden plots on either side. The left side seemed to be devoted mainly to flowers. I recognized the remains of sunflowers and hollyhocks by the fence, and little islands of hollow stalks, with new shoots already showing where delphiniums had stood the previous summer. I passed a line of stakes and netting that had supported vines of some kind, for the dried tendrils still corkscrewed through the string in places: sweet peas, at a guess. And there were wigwams of bamboo canes that must have been covered with scarlet runners or beans of some kind.

The right side was more regimented. Here the lines were straight. There were two rows of dry-looking strawberry plants, wisps of their straw mulch still in place. Next came rows of kale and cabbage like green cannonballs and the large red-veined leaves of old beets. The rest of the plot was bare, dug over; there were mounds of earth, furred with tiny weeds, and a long hump like a Stone Age barrow. The garden had no defined end; the tame simply gave way to the wild. There was a stretch given over to the behind-the-scenes stuff any garden involves: a patch of ash where bonfires had burned; compost bins; a heap of broken pots and a coiled length of hose; a rusted oil barrel. Beyond this, I was pushing through long grass and the tough flowerless stems of last year's buttercups, with the sly claws of brambles clutching at my legs.

And then, as if I had crossed a boundary into another country, I was in the wood. Even on that sunless day, there was a marked drop in temperature under the trees. The light was dim, although the leaves were still young and had not linked up in a canopy; there were still some bare black branches and holes for the sky.

It was very quiet. There was none of the secret scurrying, the furtive rustling of dead leaves that would suggest small bodies darting through the undergrowth, none of the subdued chatter of finches, none of the flicks and dashes and vibrating twigs that betray small birds on the move. Not even my own progress among the trees disturbed the peace; my footfalls smothered in the short turf and there was little debris on the path, almost as if it had been swept. No dead branches, no twigs to snap under my tread.

Weightless, I drifted between the green-grey columns of beech trees. The path tilted uphill but so gently there was no effort involved, just a rise that had more to do with levitation than climbing, although I had to keep my eyes on the ground

229

now, where the roots of the trees snaked along just under the skin of the earth, breaking through in some places to lay snares.

I had never trodden the path before, but it was utterly familiar, as if I had rehearsed this walk many times in some other life. So the cry, when it pierced the stillness, though heartstoppingly loud and close, was no surprise. I looked up, and there, where I knew it would be, a white peacock sat on the branch, its filigree tail cascading like a bride's train. It cocked its tiny crowned head to inspect me obliquely with one dark eye, then turned and called again.

Help! Help! Help!

I could see the breath curling out of its open beak. We both listened, and sure enough, a faint reply drifted to us, and the peacock shuffled his feathers and dropped without warning from his perch, gliding away to disappear in green shadows.

There was no doubt in my mind what I would find ahead. The way was steeper now, and the trees were thinning. There at the top of the hill it stood against the sky. A miniature Greek temple, white, a handful of columns supporting a roof with unadorned pediments, open to the winds and rain blowing through it. My mother's favourite summerhouse, I knew.

I climbed into it and gazed down at the far side of the hill. The column I touched struck cold under my hand, as I knew it would, and there were no surprises in the view either. The slope, covered in coarse grass and bracken, ran down to a sheet of dark water. The lake was fringed with reeds; small black water birds, coots or moorhens, darted in and out of its cover. The surface of the water was dimpled like pewter and restless, and light flickered over it, until it seemed as if the very shadows of the gunmetal clouds flying intermittently overhead were pushing the ceaseless flow of ripples from right to left.

I've no doubt it was a reservoir of some sort, with a humble purpose: supplying water for irrigation or livestock, for example.

It was a romantic stretch of water, though. Its darkness and isolation summoned words like *tarn* and *mere*, conjured up Grendel and his mother, or the Lady of the Lake and the tumbling, glinting flight of Excalibur through the air.

For the first time, as I sat on the step and submerged myself in that tiny piece of English landscape, I felt connected to my mother. If anywhere, her spirit lived in this wild place. I knew she had shared my thoughts, for didn't she love poetry and romance? Didn't she search, in her own way, for a better world? And more than that, I knew she had shared this place with me when I was very small, carrying me in the twilight through the garden and the wood, sitting in the little temple that represented her only liberty, plotting her deliverance as she watched the water and the dying light.

By the time I looked at my watch and raced back to the cottage, shutting the door firmly and hurrying back to the road to meet the three ladies, I had determined that whatever happened with my grandmother, whatever objections she might mount, whatever difficulties I might cause, I would return to that place where my mother lingered still.

There was no word from Magnus that night. I rang twice, once after reaching Wimbledon, once at ten o'clock in the evening. The phone rang and rang in the empty room. I imagined it vibrating on its little table in the dark cottage, stirring the molecules in the air, reviving the ghostly smell of charred flesh. No answer. Magnus had to be at the hospital still, or he would have phoned me. That was ominous.

At five minutes past midnight I was bundled in my housecoat on the bottom step of the stairs listening to the phone ringing thousands of miles away in my kitchen. I was rehearsing what I was going to say, how I'd tell the story of my encounter with my grandmother, what I'd found, how I wanted to stay longer and soak up the place where my mother had been a child, where I had been born. Caught up in this, I had just realized the phone had been ringing a long time when it suddenly ceased and Neil spoke in my ear.

"Liv? Where've you been? I've been trying to get hold of you for hours!"

"What's—" I began, but he cut me off.

"No, Liv, listen. You've got to come home."

"Home?" I echoed stupidly. "What's wr—?"

Again he cut me off. His urgency was palpable and I could feel the choking sensation that fear brings.

"Liv, are you sitting down?"

"My God, Neil, what's wrong? Tell me. It's Stephen, isn't it?"

"What? Oh, Liv, no, no, it's nothing wrong. Stephen's . . . no, nothing like that, nothing wrong, actually, it couldn't be righter . . ."

"Neil. Stop babbling and tell me."

"Yes," he said, "yes, sorry. It's hard. Well, it's not *hard* . . ."

"Neil!"

I heard him take a breath. Let it out. Carefully. When he spoke again, his voice trembled with control.

"Livvy, Daniel has come back."

TWENTY-FIVE

It's so peaceful in here. I know things are moving outside this room; gurneys and trolleys keep rolling past, and I can hear the chatter at the nurses' station down the hall, but it's all far away and hushed. I can sit here with my head against the wall, watching the green light tracing the peaks and valleys of your heartbeat on the monitor, listening to the slow whisper of your breathing as the lights in the parking lot flicker on one by one, and think. For the first time since Neil's phone call, I can scan the whole picture instead of poring over each detail.

That moment of hearing Daniel had reappeared was the most visceral jolt of my life, Stephen. I know what the victims of blast feel when the shock waves hit them, the great express train punch, everything silently exploding inside from the pressure, sucked empty in an instant by vacuum, compressed, flattened, before the smile can even start to fade from the unsuspecting face. You'd think it would be paralyzing, and it was, but only for a moment. In the next heartbeat, everything was clear, all hesitation and uncertainty swept away, my path absolutely plain.

It wasn't as simple as that, of course. There was endless talk, arrangements to be made in a fearful hurry, all sorts of loose ends to be tied up in some fashion before I bolted back across the world. And the story itself came in dribs and drabs: a first gush of stark facts from Neil, then more, some of it adding to what we knew already, some forcing us to revise what we believed was true, question what we thought was unquestionable, and all of it involving more and more people and lives, until the starting line of Daniel's disappearance receded almost to vanishing point.

Neil relayed the first facts in a strained breathy voice as if he were chasing after them and daren't let them out of his sight.

"Detective Mallory phoned," he said, "so I knew at once something was up. I was waiting for him to say they'd found some bones, then he said, 'Good news!' I swear he was crying, Liv. I bet they don't get to say that much, specially after so long."

I didn't want to hear about Mallory.

"Well, apparently a sixteen-year-old boy turned up out of the blue at a police station in Santa Barbara with a four-year-old in tow. He told the desk sergeant he'd found the kid crying on the beach alone and had brought him in because he didn't know what else to do. If the desk sergeant hadn't been on the ball, he might have let the teenager go at that point, but he recognized the child as the victim in an abduction that had taken place in Washington State five months earlier. Just the same sort of thing as Daniel: huge manhunt, no results."

I listened, mesmerized, to Neil's voice in my ear, stronger now, relishing the narrative. You can imagine detectives were skeptical, he went on, about how the teenager and the child came to be together. They questioned the older boy, who said his name was Jimmy, until they had wrung him dry. He was reluctant, but eventually he told another version altogether.

He lived with his uncle, he said. Mainly on a boat. But they moved about a lot.

While they had been moored at Astoria, several months before, his uncle had left him for a day and come back after dark with a large athletic bag. It contained the little boy, drowsy from the effect of some drug.

His uncle said this was Sam, and he would be living with

them now. The next day, they moved south, keeping well out to sea.

Sam, said Jimmy, cried a lot and would not be comforted. His uncle took to locking the child in the tiny forward cabin and warned Jimmy to leave him alone. But the child stopped eating and talking and, like an animal, took refuge in the darkest corners, sleeping curled up in fetal position. Jimmy couldn't bear the child's grief, waited until his uncle was forced to come into harbour for supplies, hurrying the process up by furtively tipping food overboard and sabotaging a bilge pump, then broke the lock with a screwdriver and ran with the child.

Asked why he had come to the police, he said, "Well, it wasn't right, was it? Stealing a kid?"

Asked the name of his uncle, he replied, "John Moore. But his real name's Jerry Murtry."

And Jimmy? He insisted that was his name and he had no other, so that's how the American detectives referred to him. But Jerry's name on a police bulletin had alerted one cop who dimly remembered following up some Canadian by that name, and he checked, eventually blowing the dust off the file concerning the disappearance of Daniel James Alvarsson.

That was what I got from that first phone call. The other things had to wait until later, after the initial shock had subsided and Neil had found out more. The reactions of the three ladies echoed all the questions that had gone so long unanswered.

"How did this Jerry person manage to get Daniel to accompany him?" asked Miss Hoar, and I asked Neil the same question.

"Apparently Jerry said he'd come to take him to Disneyland," Neil replied, and I could hear the conversation at Daniel's birthday party over again.

"Told Daniel we'd come for him after Disneyland, and then when we didn't, said that we'd decided he should stay with

Jerry. What could the kid do? He accepted it, of course. Wasn't happy, but it just became the way things were."

"What about school? Did he *go* to school?"

"Not on any routine basis, apparently. They were always on the move, slipping up and down the coast, and Jerry'd spend time ashore when the money got low, odd jobs, picking fruit, that kind of thing, and Daniel would get shunted off to some temporary school if there were social workers around to keep an eye on the migrant workers. He'd stay there until Jerry decided they had enough money for a while, or the school started agitating for birth certificates or transcripts, then he'd be whipped out and away. He can't remember how many schools he's been in, but the police have traced at least fourteen. They say he's not much of a reader, but he can tell you everything you want to know about boats and small engines."

All I could see was the small Daniel trustingly taking Jerry's hand to go to Disneyland, looking back, perhaps, to see me preoccupied with another child. Then the long wait after the promised excitement—if they ever actually got to Anaheim— the days and weeks that stretched interminably for the child with his limited understanding of time, hoping that Neil and I would appear one day to scoop him up and take him back to the familiar. How long had it taken for his hope to die? When did he finally decide that we had given him away, that his parents had abandoned him to this strange nest and were never coming back?

In my mind, I replayed Jerry's last phone call, his offer to return, his shock. His sympathy. The treachery. He had betrayed our trust, infiltrating our little family like a mole, angling, it seemed now, for that affection that would let Daniel take his outstretched hand, then using that same affection to head off any suspicions we might entertain with his phone call—for would the guilty draw such attention to himself?—finally using our son's belief in us as a weapon to destroy Daniel's hope of ever seeing us again as we failed, day after day, to live up to our promise to come for him. And for what? What was Jerry's motive?

"Was there sexual abuse?"

Neil paused, then plunged ahead.

"That's the first thing I asked. Daniel says no, but he's clammed up on the subject, he's not being much help about that." His voice dropped. "He *likes* Jerry, for heaven's sake. Getting evidence from him is like pulling teeth."

"He must be so confused," I said.

"Probably. I get the impression he's not easy. He'll need a lot of help."

I was silent because a hatred of such refined concentration had taken hold of me that I felt it as a physical pain, rather as if a stiletto of ice had slid between my ribs and was burning its way into vital organs. Daniel's explanation to the detective for bringing the second child to the police, so poignant at first, now took on other qualities. "Well, it wasn't right, was it? Stealing a kid?" What *had* he suffered? Could it possibly have been *jealousy* that gave him the strength to break the pattern?

"What made Jerry snatch another child after so many years, do they know?"

Neil's snort of laughter was humourless.

"Daniel got too big," he said grimly. "Time for him to go to work. Bastard wanted a new puppy."

I felt a surge of admiration for my son. Anger has its upside whatever the motive, I guess, and lucky for that other small victim that it does. But a little door slid shut in my mind as I contemplated the hell that living on that boat must have been, the dependencies and needs confined below deck like a cage full of alligators, hemmed all about by the indifferent sea. How do you recover from that? Or ever come to see it, after so many years, as the aberration, not the norm? Come to that, how normal would the replacement be? He might be our son, but it would be living with strangers again for Daniel, and trust had done nothing for him in life. The infant cuckoo never recognizes its parents, nor seeks them out to join its life to theirs.

I forgot about Magnus and my grandmother in the turmoil. So I was shamefaced when my uncle phoned, and his weary voice told me that the old lady had died. She had suffered a massive stroke, he said, the medical jargon awkward and unaccustomed in his mouth, and never regained consciousness. He had waited at the hospital until she died in the small hours of the morning. He apologized for not calling sooner.

"Had to get a bit of shuteye," he said, "and then there's the arrangements, of course."

Before he asked me to come to the funeral and I had to refuse, I hurriedly told him what had happened. He listened to the whole story without interruption. There was a weighty pause as I came to a halt. Then, "Life is powerful strange," he said slowly.

"Powerful," I replied, "and strange."

"One taken," he went on, "and one returned. There's a righteousness to that, wouldn't you say?"

"I would."

"You'll be off then, back to Canada soon as possible?"

He was making it easy for me.

"Yes. This will have to be goodbye. I'm leaving tomorrow morning."

"Well, don't forget us. There's a place for you here, you know . . ."

His voice trailed off, but I could have finished for him: especially now that my grandmother had gone.

"I know," I agreed quickly, "I'll be back. I want you to teach me how to graft trees. I'll bring Neil and Daniel next time. Maybe it would be good for Daniel—new and beautiful. Neutral ground."

"Ah. And there's another thing. When you can, I want you to send me the name, all the details, of that little mite who's buried with your mother. It's about time to put that right, and there's no better time than now. I'll have to be talking to old Walter about Mother's stone anyway, and he might as well do two as one."

"I think that would make Mum and Dad happy," I said, "and I won't be sorry to see the back of Rue Tribulation!"

The conversation ended as they always do. I felt sorry for Magnus, left alone after all the stalwart years of looking after his terrible mother, but at the same time I sensed the liberation he had to be feeling.

This was confirmed when I called Deirdre to say goodbye.

"Don't you go feeling sorry for him," she said firmly. "Best thing that ever happened to him, I reckon. I'm going up for the funeral. I'll get some flowers from the two of us, shall I? Put your name on the card? He'll like that. He's agreed to come and stay here a while after the ceremony. Says he hasn't had a holiday in years and the seaside'll do him good. So we'll be fine."

There was indeed a new briskness about Deirdre. She sounded competent and sure of herself, younger by far than the first time I'd met her. I asked after the cats.

"Well," she said, "they're fine. I keep them to the ground floor now, and it's much better. I'll hang on to them, but there'll be no replacements as they die off. They're a real tie. I'd like to travel a bit. Maybe I'll come and visit you some day. Now I've got new cousins, I can't let you all disappear again!"

She had been typically bowled over by the fairytale aspects of Daniel's reappearance, but the new Deirdre emerged in her final question.

"Know something about anger management, do you?"

"Not much," I admitted.

"Then you'd better find out," she said. "If I were Daniel, I'd be madder'n hell."

The three ladies were similarly sober. They were wonderful, of course, rallying to help me get a flight and pack and make my way to the airport. All three were overjoyed when they heard my news; Miss Plover's "Splendid!" kept erupting from her lips like buckshot. But when the euphoria passed, they, too, warned me that the way ahead might not be easy.

"So damaged," lamented Miss Plover. "You will need so much patience."

"Sixteen too," said Miss Hoar. "Rotten age, that. You'll have your work cut out."

And Isobel added wistfully, "You won't forget to let us know how you get on, will you? You're almost family to us now, you know."

So I left on one mission, and I returned to another, and my pattern-loving mind scrambled to find the connections. I was conscious of others on the move at the same time as me, all of us homing in on a single point, for a single purpose, the separate threads weaving together to make the cloth. Up there, with the North Shore Mountains clawing at us as we rocked over them through the thunderheads, and the whole city of Vancouver spreading itself out beneath us as far as the sea, gleaming like beaten gold in the distance, the notion did not seem fanciful.

I felt Neil waiting for me in the airport, tall, blond, dependable, and I remembered exactly how my son's hair swirls untidily from a double crown, just like his father's. I sensed Mum's and Dad's cautious progress along the Yellowhead to Prince George, where they would turn south toward Sechelt and the stranger they would call their grandson. I knew exactly how you and Holly were arranging your lives so that you could leave everything for a few days and come to us with Jason and Vanessa, both dying to meet the person Vanessa had begun to call "our long-lost cousin."

All of us converging on a single point that was not yet visible, but coming, coming.

TWENTY-SIX

None of it was like that at all. What was I thinking? That we'd all converge in slow motion, running through fields of wild flowers while the music swells, and fall into a loving group hug as the credits roll?

Neil was the only one there to meet me. We clutched and clung to each other, both talking at once, my "Where is he? Where is he?" warring with Neil's "No, no, not yet, not here."

I should have realized. The Americans weren't just going to ship Daniel back to us like lost baggage. He was a material witness in a kidnapping case, and one with a bizarre story they couldn't accept on face value without investigation, even if he was just sixteen and a victim of a similar crime himself.

Neil towed me to the gloomy coffee shop in the Arrivals area and told me all this, holding my hands on the tabletop between us as if to pin me down, stop me flying off on another wild search.

"We'll go down there," he said. "We'll see him soon. We'll get him home the minute they let us."

His pale eyes were so earnest, his voice so sure, I was soothed despite the disappointment. We made our way home, talking, but lapsing often into contemplation, breaking the companionable silence from time to time as one of us allowed a thought out and the other instantly picked it up, almost as if we were pursuing the same conversation inwardly all the time.

I pushed open the front door almost tentatively, but at once the familiar smell reached out to me and I went from room to room in a haze of delight, touching, fingering, straightening, stroking, gazing at the sea through the kitchen window as Maisie twined about my legs, purring thunderously.

"By the way," said Neil at some point, "how did the meeting with the Holy Terror go?"

For a moment I stared at him blankly. Already, that world had receded, and events that had filled my waking hours such a short time before, had dwindled.

"It was a lot more than I bargained for," I said.

There was a silence after I re-enacted that scene for him, and then he said, "Well, you don't get to choose your family, do you?"

"Some manage to!"

"You think that's what Jerry was doing?"

"Jerry? Of course not!"

But even as I denied it, I wasn't sure.

I'd been thinking of Mum and Dad lifting me out of the ruined doorway, and Neil's question shocked me. I could barely think of Jerry without loathing. When I spoke his name, the foulness of it flooded my mouth until I spat out the bitterness. Not for a minute had I considered his motives, just their result. And I didn't want to see Jerry now as a man without family stealing one for himself because that would make him pathetic and I wouldn't allow him that escape. What if it were true, though?

If I ever thought getting to see Daniel would be easy, I was soon disabused. At times it seemed as if a veritable army stood in our way: police, lawyers, social workers, immigration officials on both sides of the border, state functionaries of one kind or another demanding birth certificates and police reports, proofs of identity, medical histories, sheets and sheets of forms, affidavits, notarized this and that, and all with an insatiable need to hear our story over and over again.

Neil was good at patiently countering every demand. I was more inclined to shout and cry with frustration. That is, until the day we talked to the court-appointed social worker looking after Daniel, a weary-looking individual with a bloodhound's face, who urged us to call him Preston. He infuriated me by referring to Daniel as Jimmy even when I protested.

"That's what he calls himself, you know," he said reproachfully. "Just one of the little adjustments you'll have to make together."

I exploded.

"And how are we ever to do that if we never get a chance to meet? We want to see our son! Now!"

Preston gazed at me mournfully.

"I know," he said, "but we have to be sure Jimmy wants to meet you first."

It was a shock. Neil felt it too. I heard him gasp.

"Of course he will," I blustered. "Why wouldn't he?"

But I knew. He hadn't seen us for twelve years. We were strangers, and strangers he'd been convinced had turned their backs on him once at the time he needed them most, who had apparently broken their promise to come for him, who had abandoned him to the only alternative left. If he had survived, it was through his own resources, not through any guidance or assistance from us. Even if he no longer believed everything he had been told, we had been no part of his life for those critical years. What sort of weight should he give to these strangers who called themselves parents, whose values and personalities and experiences were unknowns, who might have nothing in common with him except shared chromosomes?

So I think we all approached our first meeting, on carefully chosen neutral ground, with trepidation. And it was awkward, at first. We were ushered into a small meeting room, the walls painted pale green and hung with soothing seascapes. We sat on chairs that contrived to look relaxed and institutional at the same time. After a while Preston came in and held the door for someone behind him, making encouraging noises as a lanky figure edged hesitantly into view. We both stood up.

"Daniel!" I said and instantly cursed myself. "Can I call you that? Do you mind?"

"I guess not," he mumbled. "They say it's my real name. But it's weird."

"We'll use whichever name you prefer," Neil said, "but we've thought of you every day for sixteen years as Daniel."

For the first time, he looked directly at us.

"You did?"

"Oh we did, every day, we missed you so!"

His face closed up and he stared off at a painting of sandpipers running at the edge of the waves.

"I don't remember you," he said. "I forgot you."

"Of course you did," said Neil. "I can't remember a thing from when I was four or five either. I just know the things my parents told me about that time."

I took my cue.

"We've brought our old photo album. Would you like to look at some photos of yourself when you were a little kid?"

Daniel edged slowly toward the table, where I was spreading the album, moving almost in spite of himself. Neil leaned over and started explaining the photographs, and I watched them both. Nobody could have any doubt that Daniel was Neil's son. I was sure that Neil at sixteen was exactly the same rail-thin six-footer with feet, nose, and shoulders he had yet to grow into. They had the same fine blond Nordic hair, though Daniel's was badly cut and unkempt, the same long head, delicate ear lobes, the same cool blue eyes. The same refined and elegant fingers—though again, Daniel's fingernails were chewed to the quick—pointed at the photos and turned the pages. I wanted to squeeze them both, but despite Daniel's growing animation and response to Neil, I sensed he wasn't ready for any smothering from me.

That first meeting paved the way for increased contact, for gradual acceptance. By the time Jerry's first hearing came around, we were constant companions and were able to sit with our son in court. It was the first time Daniel had seen Jerry since he'd left the boat; the first time we'd seen him in twelve years. I don't know who was the most apprehensive. I could feel Daniel thrumming like a taut wire beside me. His right knee kept up a frantic jigging that made the floorboards throb in sympathy. When I curled my hand round his, he didn't snatch it away.

Jerry's entrance was almost bathetic. Without any fanfare, two officers appeared on either side of a small figure in an orange jumpsuit. The years had not dealt kindly with Jerry. His face was lined and seamed, the skin a dark saltwater brown. The glossy black curly hair had greyed, and a pale spot like a tonsure showed where it had thinned at the crown. He had developed a little paunch. The jumpsuit he was wearing was too big; it bagged over his wrists and drooped at his heels. This, combined with the awkward shuffle imposed by the shackles he wore made him look shabby and impotent. He kept his eyes firmly on the ground.

"Jeez," breathed Daniel, "he's shrunk." And then, with a sort of wonderment and even pleading in his voice, "He was *nice* to me, sometimes, you know."

I think that was the moment Jerry finally lost his grip on my son. Certainly after that Daniel was more forthcoming, and with our assurances that he would appear when needed for the trial, he was free at last, and willing, to accompany us back to Canada. And it was the moment when I, too, was able to demote Jerry from monster status and relegate him to the rubbish heap of all those sad, wretched creatures whose own inadequacies and demons send them preying on the vulnerable and the trusting. Anger and vengeance still consumed me, but underneath there was now an immense sadness for the waste and ruin of it all.

Once home, Daniel reclaimed his old room with enthusiasm. I came upon him inspecting the battered Hot Wheels car he'd been playing with under the tree the day he disappeared, a puzzled look on his face.

"Is this important?"

I explained and his face cleared.

"Right," he said. "Maybe they'll let me have Tigger back too when all this is over."

He explained in his turn. "I must have taken it with me. It was still on the boat when Jerry brought the kid—you know. I found it in a locker when I was looking for something to make the kid stop crying. The cops kept it. Evidence, I suppose."

Yes, I thought to myself, *and maybe the first thing to start your doubts. Maybe it jogged your memory just enough to let them in.*

Daniel quickly made a place for himself in the house. He demonstrated amazing mechanical abilities: got our ailing lawnmower going in short order and corrected the timing on my car.

"Got plenty of practice on the boat," he muttered when Neil commented on his skill.

He seemed to like the flowers but ignored the vegetables in the garden, repotted my geraniums, and coaxed a struggling white lilac into putting out new leaves. He adored Maisie. He haunted Neil's studio, drawing on scraps of paper and experimenting with paint on leftover pieces of canvas and board.

He never sought out any companions, never wanted to go by himself to the movies or a dance, but he would lose himself in music, any kind, lying out on the lawn with his Walkman, eyes closed, foot twitching in time, and roam the beach for hours collecting shells and driftwood.

But he never picked up a book, or a magazine or a newspaper. At first he claimed there were never any on the boat so he just didn't think about them.

"I can find out what's going on from the radio," he said. "Why do I need a paper?"

The truth was, though, that he could barely read, something I discovered the day I asked him to read me the instructions in a recipe as I was cooking and had no spare hand to turn the page.

"Never cottoned on to it," he muttered. "Never stayed long enough in any school."

And there it was. We might have envisaged a son who would do well in school, who would be happy and well adjusted, popular with everyone, who would go to college and enter a profession or pursue a shining career in the arts. What we had was a solitary young man, friendless, in need not only of therapy but also of a basic education, an individual whose experience was totally alien and burdensome, who was miserly with his trust, always holding part of himself in reserve, reined in and undemonstrative, giving nothing away.

Neil made headway. From that very first moment he seemed to have the knack of the right word, the right gesture, while I couldn't find the way at all. Everything I did or said felt contrived somehow: too much or too little, like the pointer on an oversensitive scale, never on the mark. I felt hopelessly inept.

"I'm a failure," I said one night after a particularly disastrous attempt at a shopping expedition for clothes when Daniel had politely turned down every single thing we'd looked at. "He won't even let me buy him a shirt!"

"Give it time," Neil soothed, "he hasn't had much practice with mothers."

And I knew he was right, but that didn't stop me feeling envious—no, I'll call it by its proper name—jealous of the way he could get Daniel to smile and laugh, fool around, act goofy like any other sixteen-year-old. The way he could sometimes reach right into Daniel's heart.

Like the day he showed Daniel all the miniature paintings of the Boy. At first, Daniel glanced at each one, then studied them intently, the pages turning slower and slower, until he looked up and said, wonderingly, "That's me, isn't it, in all of them?" And when Neil nodded, his eyes filled and he swallowed hard. "You were keeping me alive, weren't you?" he said and smiled with such warmth at his father that I wept.

But Neil was right about time. I suppose I had been expecting Daniel to feel a sort of instant love for me just because I was his mother and that's what sons are supposed to feel. He couldn't, of course. I had failed him, after all. When I stopped expecting and started doing things without any motive beside their necessity, Daniel finally let me approach.

I taught him to read. On his own, he'd gone out and tried to find a job, but the manager at the very first place he tried had told him to come back with a resumé.

"What's a resumé?" he'd asked angrily when he came home. And when I told him, he shouted, "That's stupid! What do I have to have that for? Who wants the stupid job anyway?"

I pointed out that he apparently did, or he wouldn't have gone looking for one.

"Why don't we kill two birds with one stone?" I suggested. "I'll teach you to read and write properly, and then you'll be able to do your own resumé. And take courses, perhaps."

So that's what we did. At first it was babyish and frustrating, but Daniel was a quick study, and soon we were able to set aside the juvenile readers and make up our own material. I told him stories about living in Vanderhoof as a child, about school, about London; he avoided anything about himself but invented fantasies about the Boy in his perfect world. We wrote these down and read them out loud. Daniel shyly gave a copy of the Boy stories to Neil.

"I've never given anyone a present before," he said.

That night Neil showed me a page in one of the stories. Daniel must have written some on his own because I hadn't seen it before. It was set on an island, a tropical paradise. The Boy lived on fruit and fish; his companions were flocks of brilliant birds and monkeys. He seemed to have all he could wish for. I read on.

> The Boy had everything he needed. He could reach out and pick papayas and mangoes; he could spear fish in the lagoon. He had a hut made of driftwood with a palm leaf thatch. It was so warm all the time he didn't need any clothes. He could play with the monkeys when he felt like it, or just lie around and do nothing. But something was missing. He watched the monkeys in the trees over his head. The babies were clinging tightly to their mothers, and the teenagers were leaping about in the branches, very daring, showing off. Every so often though, they stopped playing and went back and chattered at their mothers, then sat still so that the females could groom them. The Boy envied them because they all had someone who would talk to them and look after them. He decided he needed a mother too.
>
> "I know just where to find one," he said to himself.

I wept again but with relief this time.

TWENTY-SEVEN

How I wish there was more time, Stephen! Not just for me, to finish what I have to say before the others come back, but more time for you to watch your children grow up, time to grow old with Holly, time to go on being part of our lives.

Meeting you again was the highlight of the family reunion for Daniel, you know. I'd been dreading the whole thing, worrying how Daniel would react to all those strangers laying claim to him. I'd warned him about Mum, told him to expect her to talk non-stop and treat him like a little boy, primed him with all the names and past history. Maybe I gave him too much. He was quiet on the way north, perked up only when Neil let him drive for a while on the straight stretches beyond Clinton.

"Perhaps this is all happening too soon," I whispered to Neil when we stopped for coffee at Williams Lake.

"For Daniel or for you?" Neil asked. "He'll be fine, see if he's not."

And he was. Maybe I'd been so conscious of having to face reality and not allow myself to indulge in happily-ever-after fantasies that I'd never entertained the possibility that some things might be as simple as could be. The psychologist warned us, after all, that abducted children become survivors first and foremost.

"They learn not to depend on adults," he said, "and they develop strategies to ensure their own survival no matter what,

251

and won't let anyone stand in their way. They can, in fact, develop sociopathic tendencies."

Covertly, I'd watched Daniel like a hawk after that, watching for the slightest evidence of sociopathic tendencies. I even quizzed him about how he felt when another kid landed the busboy job he'd applied for at the local café, but he just looked at me as if I were mad and asked why he should feel anything.

"It's a shitty job anyway," he said. "And Alex said I could start helping at the garage next week, so I guess you could say I feel relief, if anything."

He still keeps to himself, but he helps Neil in the garden all the time. I hear them laughing and chattering, two male voices in perfect accord, oblivious to me listening in. Daniel has an ongoing joke about Neil's ineptitude with the mower—he can never start it without practically dislocating his shoulder and flooding the motor—which he now extends to any kind of machine. I'll ask Neil to make a pot of coffee and Daniel will call out, "You'd better let me do it. It'll never work again if Dad gets his hands on it!"

Does he sound like a sociopath to you? Me neither. Of course, there are always concerns too, and I know you've thought of them. I saw the look that passed between you and Holly, that instinctive alarm, when Daniel and Jason were roughhousing with a soccer ball and Daniel caught Jason in a bearhug and lifted him off his feet to stop him kicking the ball. I've heard it all too, all the sad stories of abused boys turning into abusers when they grow up, and I know it happens. I know Daniel's still an unknown quantity, but I think Mum got it right, amazingly enough, although it was probably quite accidental. Remember what she said when Holly went to intervene?

"Let them have their fun," she said. "Daniel wouldn't harm Jason, would you, pet? Think how he looked after that other little boy, not that it was quite the same, but you know what I mean, he has a kind heart."

And that *is* a point, isn't it? I'm not just deluding myself?

Night's crept up on us. I can barely make out the cars and trees down below, just the impression of bulky forms, and the hospital wing opposite blazing with light, riding the dark like a great oceangoing vessel.

The others will be fast asleep at home now. They'll have eaten at White Spot and enjoyed one another's company in a slightly guilty fashion, embarrassed at being able to eat and laugh, even if it's only for a short time, while you lie here. Daniel's part of that. The family scooped him up the instant they saw him: Mum patting him and stroking, tears pouring down her face, Dad wringing his hand and pulling him close in a silent hug, Vanessa and Jason hauling him off to see the banner they'd strung across the living room—Welcome Home, Daniel—and then squabbling over who had had the biggest hand in its construction, Holly distracting them with chips and dip and bottles of pop as if she knew exactly what he'd like best. And you, gazing into the engine of your truck when we found you, flashing a smile and saying, "Hand me that wrench, will you, Daniel?" as if you were just picking up where you'd left off ten minutes before. I knew he was all right when you got him covered with grease under the hood.

All exactly what he needed. I could almost feel him relax and soften. How come you were all so unerring, when I couldn't put a foot right at first? But then, I've been a tangled mess for such a long time, I suppose I'd lost the knack of certainty. I'm hoping you haven't gone too far away to hear me now; I need you to know it's all right. I've got it all together at last.

The threads lie loosely in my grip, some short, some long and spun very fine. Many of them attach to my past, to my real identity, but I'm no longer concerned with who I am or where I came from. Heredity is an accident; environment, pure chance. With a turn of the dice, I could have been Olivia or Ruth or Rue Tribulation and no less myself, merely different.

For there is a sense in which we are all the cuckoo's children. Fate sets us down, little naked entities, and lets us struggle for survival. Many are lucky and find help, so abundant and self-less, perhaps, that they feel life is always so, that this is how we should expect life to be. Truth is, we are alone in a crowd, forever nudged this way and that by random forces, our forms dented and scraped by every person and event we bump into or rub up against. I am a composite. I am no more just Livvy than I am really Ruth, or my grandmother's Tribulation, but the sum of all my parts, just as Daniel is the little boy in the red shirt I last saw playing under the tree, and the victim, the angry stranger, the knight errant, and the prodigal son.

Thinking for hours without sleep produces a strange exal-tation. Here in this spartan room, I am Miss Penfold's hero returning from the quest exactly as Neil has painted me in his latest picture. He has me crouched on my battered vessel, heading for a distant harbour where two tiny figures stand, one a small splash of red, and says he waited to finish it until he knew what colour to paint the sails. White, I told him, white.

But returning heroes always bring back some sort of gift after their confrontation with the monsters. Could mine be knowing what it is to be a cuckoo's child? If I followed all the threads to their source, would I find a fragile chain of consequences all leading to this moment? From the grafting of the cherry on the damson tree and the blighting of Paradise with a Calvinist morality, down through birth and war and death, changelings and sickness, betrayal and love and rejection, to the old wom-an's hand in the fire and a son in exchange, I could trace the connections, see them pushing their way to this room, patiently lining up all the variables to produce exactly this result.

The future is mysterious. We will have to deal with concrete things: Jerry's trial and Daniel's testimony; seeing our son through therapy; repairing the holes in his education and getting him started in the world. Maybe my contribution will be to convince him that none of his life was a mistake or a waste, that he is who he is, a work-in-progress to be modified for the rest of his days. That he is alone, but not lonely, a cuckoo's child just like me and everybody else.

I am full of hope. It sounds almost heartless to say it now, but the future beckons. The weight of anger has dropped away. I can think of Mum and Dad without flinching at the names; they *are* my parents, and when Mum babbles and Dad strokes his moustache to cover his anxieties, I feel bound to them in a circle of loss, reinvented as an only child, the only one they will have left.

Horizons have moved for me, edging out to the remains of my other family, meshing Magnus's and Deirdre's lives into mine, into Neil's and Daniel's, even into our parents'. Soon Dad will write to Magnus, sending him all Olivia's details so that the gravestone can finally be put right.

"He's a good man," Dad said. "Forgiving. More of a Christian than his mother."

And he is. When the hurricane in England was all over the news, I called him to ask about the damage at Hescot. You could hear the grief in his voice.

"Tore up a lot of those old beeches," he said. "One came right through the roof of the orangery, glass everywhere. Not too bad in the garden because of the walls, but my dad's tree's gone—split right down the middle. The graft's always the weakest spot."

I was horrified, but he'd moved on.

"I've a mind to start another one," he said. "I've got the scions already. But that'll have to wait on some spare time; I've got a mort of work to do, clearing up the mess. I could do with that boy of yours; plenty for him to do here. And learn, I reckon."

And there it was. Another opening door, and one we'll walk through soon, I think. I have to show Neil where I was born, after all, and watch him and Daniel draw it into themselves too.

The others will be back soon, and the nurses are already here. They check their patient and their machines, and tell me quietly that you do not have much more time and we should get ready to make our goodbyes. I will not say it; there are no real endings, only revolution. You will not have gone while we remember. But I will take your hand in mine, so, and make myself believe that your fingers move against mine, an intimation from far, far away that you have listened and understand it all.

ACKNOWLEDGMENTS

I would like to thank all of the members of my writing group, past and present, especially Kathy, Helen, Gillian, Jennifer, Sara, Maureen, and Lynne, for their critical insight and many helpful suggestions over the years it took for this book to see the light of day. My thanks also to Leah Fowler, who proved to be a most enthusiastic and encouraging editor, and to Heather Sangster, for demonstrating the value of a sharp-eyed proofreader.

A note here about geography: The street names are all real, but those familiar with them may feel they are not portrayed exactly as they remember. I confess to taking some liberties with their topography, but this is fiction, after all.

MARGARET THOMPSON came to Canada from England in 1967, and taught English at secondary and post-secondary levels until her retirement in 1998. She is the author of seven books, including a BC 2000 Book Award–winning YA novel, short stories, and two collections of personal essays, and has contributed to five anthologies. She is a past president of the Federation of BC Writers and now lives in Victoria, BC, with a basset hound, a neurotic cat, and an itinerant peacock.